Talmud Night
Contents

Background

Talmud night is the book that people have been asking me to write for decades. It began with a conversation which eventually developed into a short story with my friend Amy Sales, senior research scientist Cohen Center for Modern Jewish Studies, Brandeis University. The more we thought about David, the more we drew upon our combined experiences working with congregational clergy, leadership and laity over several decades.

Talmud Night is a work of fiction wrapped in hidden truths. At the same time it reflects the challenges that confront community leadership on a regular basis. Those who know me, will hear my voice. I hope it brings you, the reader, laughter, joy coupled with a larger awareness of the concerns that most of our communities face.

―――――

All the names listed in the book bear no resemblance to people I might have known or know. On the contrary, they could be anyone.

The rabbi in spite of himself

Part One: The Secret Sauce

Study is the highest form of worship because study leads to practice.
Akiva, circa 120 B.C.E.

October 2017

"*This* is the last time I do this," Rachel hissed as she vehemently exhaled. "I've put up with this for six years and if it doesn't work this time," she said in an increasingly loud tone, "I'm taking Ari and moving back to Washington!"

"Rachel, I'm driving," David said through gritted teeth, "Why are you bringing this up now? It's only been less than three months. Can't this wait until we get home?"

"It's not my home, it's a shithole shack. It's ugly, small and looks like every other house in the shithole of a neighborhood. David, I tried. I am still trying but," she shook her head as tears formed in her eyes, "but, I can feel it. It's going to be just like it was in Atlanta. Mr. or Mrs. So-and-so, or Dr., no there aren't enough doctors who live here, they're all across the river, will get upset because of something you did or failed to do, and he or she will tell their friends and all of a sudden, we'll be….nowhere."

"It's a working-class neighborhood, maybe the people will be nicer than they were in Atlanta."

"I doubt it," she said. "I think the only difference between the people here and the people there is that this town is so middle class there isn't even a gardener. That's funny," she smirked. "Rabbi, you're gonna have to mow the lawn and till the soil."

"That's right," he said as he pulled the car off to the side of the road.

"Hey? What are you doing?" she asked

He took a deep breath looked at Rachel while shaking his head, "I didn't want to have a fight or an accident while we were arguing about our future. Let's make a deal. Right now, the way we used to when we were first going out. Okay?"

Rachel unbuckled her seatbelt and reached into her purse. She removed her lipstick, a mirror an eyebrow pencil and a brush. She shook her head allowing her shoulder length brown hair to move from side to side. She picked up the mirror and proceeded to apply lipstick.

"Rachel, what are you doing?" David asked.

"Looking my best," she said as she checked out her eyebrows in the mirror, "don't talk to me until I'm ready, I don't want to mess up my makeup."

"Rachel why are you doing this?"

"Because," she said as she unbuttoned the top button of her blouse. "Because you're a guy and capitulate much quicker when you're looking at me," she said with a smile.

David's mouth widened into a grin, "you can really be a bitch when you want something."

"Yep, "she said returning the smile. "Now what are you offering?"

David shook his head, smiled as he ran a hand through his thinning brown hair. "My body this evening?" he asked.

"Hmmn," she replied "A man in his late thirties about, she looked him up and down, "six feet one hundred and fifty pounds, a trifle too thin and bit too pale for me. He would be much more attractive if he spent more time outdoors instead of with all those old and musty books. Nope," she answered. "Not enough. What else can you offer?"

"How about this," he paused and responded in a thoughtful voice, "If I can't make it here." He shook his head, "if I can't make it here, I'll find a job as a translator. Lord knows, I'm still receiving offers."

She unbuttoned another button on her blouse and smiled, "Really? Do you promise? I know how much this means to you."

"I know you do," he said with a sigh. "You know just how to make me smile." He shook his head and raised a hand and pointed it at her chest. "Button up. I get the point. Perhaps, it was just a dream. Perhaps I'm not really suited for this type of life. You remember how different I was from my classmates.

"You certainly did stand out," she added. "the way you dressed, the questions you asked. You had so much to learn."

He smiled, "They were all rabbis' children," he nodded, "like you. And I had been raised casting the I Ching, smoking dope and hanging out with dancers and theater people. I was religiously uncomfortable with my classmates. My future colleagues. They were super conscious of keeping the dietary laws. They studied the laws to learn how to eat while I studied cookbooks. The prayed with intention while I studied the history of prayer hoping that by learning how prayer evolved I would learn to pray."

"I remember, when we were dating and," she hesitated, "I forgot his name but he tried to play that "I am more observant than you game" and you countered by having a pepperoni pizza delivered to his dorm room."

David laughed, "Rachel, this isn't easy for me. You know I decided to become a rabbi after hearing a lecture which challenged all of the stories and myths I had learned in religious school. People desire to learn about their heritage in an adult manner, and I thought," he paused. "I could build a vibrant caring community if I explained Jewish life in broader historical context." He sighed. "Unfortunately, while this method worked for my friends it wasn't overly successful in the congregation. Maybe your father was right. 'Maybe I'm not a sufficient scholar to be a successful pulpit rabbi. Perhaps, someone else can do it better."

She pointed a finger at him and waived it back and forth. "That means if we don't make it here, no more rabbi stuff."

"Yes," he replied glumly. "The family is more important. If I can't make it here, no more rabbi stuff."

"Start the car," she said. Let's go home. I need to pay the sitter and who knows after Ari goes to bed you just might get lucky."

Samuel Talbot – Ten Years Earlier

"It's been eight months since my wife died. Eight months. I doubt there is anything in the safety deposit box. She was so disorganized. But who knows?

Maybe she put something in the box before she died? No," he said to himself, "it's probably empty. Another empty reminder," he said as he entered the bank.

"I think it's time I made a major change. I might be sixty-eight but I'm slim, healthy, still have my hair. I could do anything, go anywhere. Just a few more items to take care of and then, then," he thought, "perhaps it's time to disappear. But first the bank."

Samuel Talbot tightened the knapsack hanging from his back and proceeded down a long corridor toward the windowed office with a sign on the door that read, Ms. Martinez, Bank Manager.

A woman in her mid- fifties saw him approaching and rose from her desk and stepped into the hall to meet him.

"Mr. Talbot?"

"Yes, that's me."

"Please step into my office, this will only take a moment and then we can go to the vault. The locksmith has already arrived. Do you have the death certificate and declaration from the estate which indicates you are the trustee?"

"Yes, I do," he said as he reached into the knapsack and removed an envelope. "I believe this is what you need."

She opened the envelope glanced at the papers and replied, "I need to make copies; could you wait here for a minute?"

She left the room, leaving him in an office completely devoid of character. He looked around as he sat in the arm chair in front of her desk. "Nothing of a person here, but it's quiet. I suppose that could be helpful. One could work with the absence of sound."

"I told you it would only take a moment", she said with a smile as she stood at the office's entrance. "Please come with me. The safety deposit boxes are downstairs. Have you been here before?"

He slowly stood up. "My wife died eight months ago, there's probably nothing in the box, I vaguely remember we had a safety deposit box, but I had completely forgotten about it. I never used it. It's only when I received the renewal notice that it came to my attention."

Her expression changed, and she began to walk forward and reached out to touch him. Unconsciously he stepped backward. She paused realizing he didn't desire her comfort, especially in that way. "I'm sorry for your loss, if you could follow me," she said turning and walking towards a staircase about fifty feet distant.

"I'm nervous, I'm babbling to a bank officer. It's probably empty, but if it's not, what could be in it? Could there be something, something I didn't know? Something I never suspected?" he shook his head, no. "I am listening to the unknown, not very becoming for Rabbi Talbot."

"Good morning, Mr. Rosser," she said to a man in his mid-thirties. "This is Mr. Talbot, he wasn't able to find the key to the safety deposit box. You'll need to break in."

"That's why I'm here," he said with a smile as he stood up and extracted a drill from the tool box at his feet. "Not a problem, this will only take a moment."

It was over in five minutes.

"It's all yours", she said as she handed him a long thin rectangular metal box. "There is a room over there, where you can sit down and open it."

He took the box, turned around and strolled toward the indicated door.

"Could someone open the door for me, my hands are more than occupied," he said grinning.

Ms. Martinez complied, and he entered and sat at the desk. "This could be the last time," he thought. "Could she have left a note, a living will, something, anything?"

It wasn't difficult to open the box. a slight catch on the side and it flipped open. The box was filled with jewelry. Some of it looked familiar. "We bought this in Paris," he said to himself as he lifted and admired a necklace. "Oh, this piece of ceramic was purchased in Spain on our honeymoon." Hmm, unfinished pieces of jewelry for future projects. He removed a series of objects from the box and placed them on the table.

"Aaah, what's this? What's hiding in this cloth bag?" He grasped it in one hand and untied the chords containing the objects and poured its contents into the other hand. A watch dropped out.

"Her father's watch" he said as he lifted the brown leather band and turned it around. "Her father's watch, the Ebel. Old, at least fifty years old," he reflected. "This watch was around before they made self-winding watches. It needs to be wound daily."

"I'll give the jewelry to the kids", he thought as he scooped up the contents of the box and placed them in his sack. "But the watch, the watch, he always meant well." He held the watch in front of him and began to wind it. He placed it on his wrist and fastened the band. "The second hand began to move. "Still works," he murmured. "Something this old still works." He smiled and thought. "I'm bringing you back from the dead. From death to life."

"Thank you very much Ms. Martinez. I appreciated your time."

"It's a pleasure to have been of service", she said as she escorted him out of the vault. He left the bank and began the ten-block walk back home.

"It's been eight months," he mused. "The phone calls and invitations have mostly stopped. I know they care but they have their own lives. If I want to see my old acquaintances, it's up to me to call them. And the others?" he thought, "the men with whom I have been working for and with for thirty-five years, they're hesitant to call. They don't want to disturb, "the rabbi". If I called and told them I wished to visit they would welcome me with open arms, but most of them, most of them don't want to intrude."

He stopped on the corner and stared at the watch. "My father-in-law's been dead for nearly twenty years and the watch still works and," he paused, "so do I. Almost forty years," he thought. Forty years in the same neighborhood."

He took a deep breath exhaling slowly. "I keep on thinking, I have a few close friends, a father and an adult child. I'm sixty-eight years old, healthy, moderately good looking. I've been maudlin for too long. I'm still capable of adventure. It's time I made some serious changes."

Arriving at his apartment building he nodded to the doorman and took the elevator to the eleventh floor. He entered the apartment and strolled into the living room, a room which overlooked the Hudson river. He pulled out his phone and pushed the button that read Sonos. The music of Rachmaninoff filled the room. He dropped into a comfortable easy chair and reached into a drawer from the end table adjoining the chair and extracted a joint. He lit it, inhaled, exhaled and smiled.

"This is a once in a lifetime opportunity," he said to himself. "It's time for a new place, somewhere else. It's time to build relationships with new people and occupy myself with new ideas. I never intended to be a couch potato." He inhaled again and exhaled smiling.

I remember Bilbo Baggins, in Tolkien's book, The Hobbit who found the ring. At some point he decided it was time to change his life. He needed," he paused, "'more.' And if I remember correctly on his one hundredth birthday he held a party for the entire Shire and at one point he stood on a platform, placed the ring on his finger and disappeared. The people in the Shire never heard from him again. It's time to get rid of Samuel and become, and become," he hesitated. "Sandy. After all," he said with a chuckle, "new name, new life. Today could be the first day of my new life."

November 2017

"Oh my gosh," Eddie said looking at his watch. "It's 5:20, I've got to leave."

"What are you talking about? Larry responded from a nearby desk as he stubbed a cigarette in an ashtray. "You've been working here almost ten years and you never leave before six,"

"You don't understand", Eddie said, as he pushed his chair away from his desk, stuffed a few papers in his briefcase, grabbed his jacket and started for the door. "It's Thursday night. I can't be late."

"Be late for what?" I know your schedule, you always…" Eddie, have you joined an earlier card game? You always take the 6:15 and play with Bobbie and the guys."

"No, I got them to switch to Wednesdays. Can't talk, can't play on Thursdays," he said reaching for the door.

"Can't explain," he said taking a deep breath, "I sit with them, I don't play. Not tonight, I've got plans."

"Don't run too fast, you might be losing weight, but you've still got those love handles. When you get to our age ya never know what will happen.

"Larry, I gotta go. No time for chattah."

"You're not from Boston and never will be, it's almost closing time, I don't think you'll sell another Prius in the next twenty minutes, so get outa here." Larry said with a smile and speak Queens".

"Tanks", Eddie said as he ran out the door. Running down the street, he was just another man in his mid-forties late for a train.

After a few blocks he slowed to a walk. It was a five-minute walk from the dealership to the uptown IRT followed by a quick shuttle to Grand Central. The Grand Central Station, Eddie thought. Not that anyone ever thinks about it that way these days, Eddie mused, they just say "Grand-central" as if it's one word, he thought as he hurried up the ramp to Gate 113.

The sign on the entrance read train to Peekskill departing at 5:45, stopping at Croton, Peekskill, Cold Spring and Poughkeepsie. As usual, the car was densely crowded. "Excuse me, excuse me, sorry lady but my game is about to start," he mumbled as he negotiated the aisle, sweating his way to the third car, fourth row where the guys were.

"Thought you weren't going to make it," Bobby said.

"Nah, he's always on time," Ronny responded,

"Deal the cards", grunted the third man in the group. His tie was loose, his shirt open, his belly hanging over his belt, his face pale, and his hair long, grey and straggly—all in all an image of exhaustion. He took a deep breath and said, "Eddie, you in?"

"Not tonight, Mikey. Just going to watch."

"What's so special about Thursdays? You used to play every day and now," he said shaking his head, "never on Thursday."

Bobby, a redheaded man also in his mid-forties chimed in. "Well at least will you drink with us?" He was a fit well-groomed man, more finely dressed than the two men sitting across from him.

"Not tonight Bobby", Eddie replied, "I need to be focused."

"Getting no satisfaction from Eddie," Mikey wheezed, "I don't believe it. Every night for the past ten years we take the same train, we sit in the same car in the same seats, and all of a sudden, you change the schedule. "Hey guys", you said, "do you think we can leave 30 minutes earlier on Thursdays?"

"Mikey," Bobby interrupted, "You really need to drop some weight and maybe see a doctah. You sound terrible."

"He's right," Ronnie responded as he shrugged off his jacket and began to loosen his tie.

"Don't change da subject," Mikey said as he reached into his pocket and produced a pack of playing cards.

"Eddie, what's goin' on?" Ronnie pressed.

Eddie stopped fiddling with his briefcase and settled next to his three best friends. He turned his head from left to right making eye contact with each of them. "Look," he said. "I've known youze guyz all of my life. We grew up together. We went to school together. We played ring-a-levio together and luckily, we stayed out of jail together. Trust me," he said, as he smoothed his dark but thinning hair, "I'll tell you when I can."

"Okay, we'll play with the three. Just like last week and the week before. I guess this is going to be our Thursday night game," Mikey added with a slight sigh or perhaps a controlled wheeze. "Ronnie baby, you deal."

Half hour later as the train rolled into the station, there were murmurings among the friends of:

"good game,"

"Yeah" Mikey said with a teasing smile, "considering we were without a fourth."

The train slowed to a halt. The four of them rose and walked toward the door, each of them similarly adjusting their ties and jackets to look more presentable.

"Eddie," Bobbie asked just prior to descending the stairs to the platform, "Are you in trouble?"

"Not really", Eddie answered evasively. "I'm just trying to make some things right and if I do, I promise I'll come clean. Hey, do I look like I'm in trouble?"

"No," Bobbie answered as he put the deck away. "You look like you're getting some."

Two WEEKS EARLIER

"Excuse me, Madame Le Presidente," a soft-spoken voice called out to Madeline Schwartz as she purposefully walked down the dimly lit corridor of the synagogue toward the sign that said, "Office."

She paused, glanced almost longingly at the sign, took a deep breath, and turned toward the voice. She looked like a synagogue president: mid-fifties, smartly dressed in a designer outfit with obviously expensive jewelry and stiletto heels. In her left hand she held a soft leather briefcase, in her right a matching clutch purse.

"I'm in a hurry Leonard and really don't have time for pleasantries," she said a bit abruptly but then she softened and let the exhaustion show. "I'm in the middle of a huge case, haven't slept well in days, my husband is just a memory, and now I'm snapping at you. Can this wait? The only reason I'm even here is to sign checks, which should have been messengered to my law office if this place ran like it should."

"Yes, no, I guess." Apparently, Leonard had also come straight from his office and had his own brand of stress. An athletic looking man in his early sixties, he was wearing a well-tailored blue striped suit, currently missing a tie.

"You look like you work on Wall Street," she said smiling. "And your hair is so long, I'm kind of jealous."

"I call it 'last blush' and, by the way, you look like you work on Madison and fifty-first, I'll tell you what, I'll walk you to the office and while you're signing the checks I'll complain."

"It's a deal," she replied as she reached into her purse and removed a set of keys. Let's get this over with" she said as she fumbled through the set, selected a key, inserted it into an old wooden door, turned the doorknob and pushed.

"This building drives me mad! It's so old and musty and run down. I can actually taste the dampness. It needs a new paint job, new carpeting a more attractive lobby. If we only had the money."

"I suppose," Leonard mused, "the two of us could somehow arrange to find two 'anonymous' donors who could cover the cost of painting the halls and refurbishing the office. What do you say to twenty-five k a piece? It would get rid of the smell. You could let the Board know next month."

"I'm writing checks so don't expect a response, but the check will arrive in your office by the end of next week Mr. Treasurer. Now for the third time please, ugh this chair is heavy" she grunted as she dragged it away from an old wooden desk, "don't say anything for the next ten minutes and if you're good you can tell me all about it as we leave the building".

She reached into a drawer, removed a checkbook, placed it on the desk, and began to sort and sift through the stack of letters that had been placed in the "To Be Paid" basket. She opened the checkbook, reached into her pocketbook and removed a pair of glasses which she carefully placed on the bridge of her nose, and said, "Well?"

"You told me to be quiet."

"I really didn't mean it."

"Too late, I can wait 'til we leave."

"It's that serious?"

"It could be."

Ten minutes later as they were leaving the building, she looked at him and said, "Okay, the suspense isn't killing me but I'm curious. What's the problem?"

"The rabbi, what else?"

She removed the keys from her purse and locked the front door. She took his arm and the two of them proceeded towards the parking lot. "Did he do something stupid?"

"No, it's not what he did. It's what he isn't doing."

"Lenny, I'm tired, very tired. This deal is taking too much of my time. I haven't been to a congregational meeting in two weeks, I really don't know what's going on. I told you I didn't wish to be president and… and…"

He stopped walking, turned towards her taking her hands into his. "Don't get frustrated, I know, I talked you into it. Who else could it have been? Look at this community. It was a great place to raise a family but it's very, very middle class. It's school teachers and small business people. It's car sales people and real estate agents. It's so middle class we don't even have landscapers and people to mow our lawns. Who else had the fiscal ability to run this place? Everyone who had money or who made money in the last decade has left. They're living in the city and commute to Boca like we should have done. But we didn't, and we are the only ones left! Who else but the two of us could rally the group to develop a vision to insure this place is here for the next generation?"

"I know, I know," she said. "So, tell me before I pass out. He received moderately good marks for the High Holidays, he's young enough to appeal to the young families, I know he makes hospital visits, he visited my aunt just last week. And I've been told he is teaching a class in Bible before services Shabbat morning. What hasn't he done or what isn't he doing?"

"Maddie", Leonard said with a sigh. He's not attracting new people or engaging some of the three-day-a-year members. You're correct, he's young enough. But I think he's too smart for this group. He's little too shy and passive. He's also somewhat awkward, a bit geeky and these people, our people… read USA Today if they read a newspaper at all and probably have never heard of CNN because they watch Fox news! I'm afraid he's not for us. We need a star! Someone with great speaking skills, a person with charisma, a draw."

She dropped his hands and walked toward her car. Shaking her head, she opened her car door and slid smartly into the seat. "I'm overworked, I need to get back to the gym and back to a life. Rabbi David was the best of the bunch, you know that as well as I. He was a fine assistant rabbi in Atlanta.

"He wasn't renewed."

"We need to give him some time."

"I know", he responded. "But how much time have we left?"

"Leonard, what do you want me to do?"

"Well," he said cautiously, "let's watch him, and perhaps we should bring a few people together from the committees and have a small discussion in a few weeks. It's almost November. Let's see where we are in January."

She started the ignition, rolled down the window and, with a heavy heart, said, "January it is."

Mid-September

It didn't look like it was going to be the kind of Sunday morning he had hoped it would be. A call from the Hebrew school teacher Thursday evening insisting that a parent bring young Martin to class fifteen minutes early for a meeting to determine if he could return to class, certainly did not enliven his prospects for a quiet, peaceful, stress free weekend.

Martin's explanation made too light of his behavior and with the bar mitzvah just a few months away, the synagogue had all the leverage.

"Jesus, Marty, I get one Sunday off a month and I have to spend the morning selling your teacher that you will toe the line, behave, not do it again, be a model student for the rest of the year! Do you know how angry I am with you?" The two of them were in the car, reluctantly heading toward the unwelcomed meeting at the synagogue.

"I'm sorry Dad, it just slipped out."

"Words like that just don't slip out, and you know it. I once was on the floor and one of my sales people let a word slip out and you know what I did? You know what I did?"

"What did you do?" the boy meekly replied.

"I said to myself, Eddie, the customer is always right. My salesperson lost a sale because he let a word slip out. A word he should never have used, and he was a Catholic. An Irish Catholic!"

The boy lowered his head and slumped further into the seat. He was keenly aware of the cruel irony of the bar mitzvah It's the day he's supposed to become a man, but here he was pre-pubescent, not even five feet tall, with residuals of baby fat, no signs of facial hair, a voice that squeaked into upper ranges uncontrollably, and early outcroppings of acne. Every night he secretly prayed that manhood would not pass him by.

"I docked him. I could have fired him, but I said to myself, Eddie, he's got a wife and kids, you shouldn't fire him, just dock him. Maybe he'll be more careful in the future. That's what I did. I docked him, and he never repeated that word on the floor again."

"I'm sorry, Dad", the boy tried again.

"Do you know how much this party; this bar mitzvah is going to cost? Do you know your mother and I haven't taken vacations, so we could save for your party?"

"But I didn't want…

"Your party," his father said almost shouting in the car as he interrupted his son. "Your party."

"I said I'm sorry, Dad. I really will try not to use that word again, in synagogue, school or anywhere," he mumbled as tears began to form.

Eddie turned to look at his son and softened. He parked the car in the synagogue parking lot and reached out and placed his arm around the boy's shoulder. "You're a good kid, Marty. I'm sorry I yelled. I've got a lot on my mind. A lot on my mind. Let's get this over with and maybe I can calm down enough to enjoy the game this afternoon all the way through. Now let's go meet your executioners."

As they got out of the car, Eddie noticed a tall thin man standing at the entrance of the school wing.

Eddie nudged his son and shifted his head in the direction of the door. "Is that the rabbi?"

"Yeah, that's him. He does that every day. He stands in the doorway and says hello to all the kids and schmoozes with the parents. He's kinda cool."

They walked across the parking lot towards the school entrance. "We're in step," Eddie thought noticing that Marty matched his stride and shifted his weight from side to side imitating his Dad's swagger. Eddie eyed the rabbi. He appeared to be in his late thirties or early forties. About five feet ten inches maybe 160 or 165 he thought, ten pounds or so overweight. Could have been athletic at one time, he mused. Still had his hair, not bad, not bad. A little dorky but a friendly happy face. I could sell him a lemon of a car and he wouldn't even know it, he thought.

They arrived at the door and the rabbi looked at them, no, he looked at him.

Why is the rabbi staring at me? Eddie thought. Did I do something wrong? Has the teacher told him about Marty? Was it that bad?

Eddie, cleared his throat stuck out his hand and said,

"Hi Rabbi, I'm…."

"Ed Friedman, Marty's dad", the rabbi said interrupting as he reached out and grabbed Eddie's hand and shook it firmly.

Not a limp fish handshake, Eddie thought. "That's new for a rabbi."

The rabbi continued, "I've been looking forward to meeting you, I'm, well you know who I am," he stammered. "You can call me David."

"David, you want me to call you David?" Eddie asked. "Should I call you Rabbi David?"

"No", the rabbi said as he turned slightly red, "then I'd be Rabbi Duvin. I just think first names are more appropriate. If you ever want to call me 'Rabbi', I promise I won't take offense."

This guy might be all right Eddie thought as he released the rabbi's hand. Might be all right.

The rabbi continued, "I heard you have a little meeting scheduled with Marty's teacher. Why don't you drop by my office after your meeting has concluded?"

"This is real bad", Eddie thought as he remembered the many calls from the school office to his parents regarding his class behavior as did a memory of the guys teasing him in class as he awkwardly attempted to learn how to read Hebrew. "Marty must have really let someone have it, he thought."

"Uhm, (I need some time). I'm kind of busy this morning, how about we do it another time?"

"Okay by me," the rabbi said with a grin. "How about Thursday night?"

"Well," he demurred, "I gotta check my calenda it's near the end of the month at work."

"Let's say 7:30," the rabbi continued as if Eddie hadn't spoken. "Does that work for you?"

He doesn't miss a thing, Eddie thought

"Sure thing. I'll be there. 7:30 Thursday. Shit."

One Month after Yom Kippur

Eddie opened his eyes placing his hands over them and attempted to extricate the grit that had accumulated over night. He slowly shifted onto his side as he turned toward the night stand by his bed to look at the clock. "Oh God," he groaned, "it's 6:15. I always set the alarm for 6:45 and always wake up at 6:15. I can't remember the last time I slept until 8 o'clock, or even 7 or even 6:45."

He turned his head and rotated his body to the other side in order to more clearly see the woman sleeping next to him. She was breathing quietly. Sleeping on her side with her back facing him.

"Maybe I should just move a little closer so that our legs touched. I could drape a hand around her hip and place it on her stomach and gently pull her a bit closer to me. Then if I could get close enough I could gently nibble her …."

"Nah," he said as he rolled onto his back.

"Maybe I could just reach out and stroke her hip?" He thought as he once again rolled onto his side and moving closer to her, "Almost touching", he thought. "And then I could lightly move my hand up and..."

"Oh shit, I'm getting hard. Time to walk the dog and see if I can work it out later in the shower."

One hour later

"Morning dear," Diane said, as she flipped a page of the USA report while flicking the ashes from her cigarette into an ashtray. She was a full-figured woman with blonde shoulder length hair with touches of gray dressed in a faded pink bathrobe. "Coffee's made, and I made you some lunch. There was a special sale at Walmart, so I bought some of that special cheese you like."

"Lunch? Well that's a pleasant surprise, Thanks."

"By the way, Eddie, how did you sleep?"

"The same," he responded with a shrug of his shoulders. "Not too good, not too bad. I had some dreams but can't remember them. And you?"

"I always take my pills and sleep like a rock. A bomb could go off and I wouldn't know it", she answered as she lifted her arm and inhaled deeply.

"Maybe you should take something to help you, you know a little pill, like the ones I have in the medicine cabinet. They might sweeten your dreams."

"Are you kidding me," he responded as he sat down and grabbed the sugar bowl and proceeded to dump several spoonful's into his mug. "It's the dreams that wake me up."

He dutifully drank his coffee and ate his breakfast. She absentmindedly continued reading the paper flicking her cigarette from time to time. She yawned and turned the page, shook her head, released the newspaper, stood up and began to leave the room. "Don't forget to put your dishes in the sink when you leave," she mumbled started shuffled toward the stairs, "I need a shower before I go to the gym. Remember don't forget."

"Diane!" he called out.

She stopped and turned, "what?"

"I'm gonna be home a little late tonight. Things are piling up at work and one of the guys at the office is having a hard time with…." He paused, "Well, it's personal. I promised him we would go out for a beer after work."

"Oh", she yawned, "Not to worry. I have my 5 o'clock Thursday coffee klatch with the girls and I missed some of my shows last week when we went to the movies and Marty will be eating at Charlie's house after practice. What time will you be home?"

"Sometime before nine I guess," And, I wish I knew how long this meeting is actually going to last, he muttered to himself as he gathered his things and rushed out the door to catch the train, leaving his dirty cup and dishes on the kitchen table.

THE FIRST MEETING – Early October

"A promise is a promise," Eddie said as he slammed the car door and reluctantly headed toward the synagogue entrance.

"Haven't been here since the High Holidays if you don't add dropping off the kid at Hebrew school, but a promise is a promise.," he repeated it as if to reassure himself he had no choice. I'm more tired than I should be," he thought. "My feet are dragging, I feel this terrible weight, the work, the bar mitzvah, the kid, the emptiness at home. I shouldn't be feeling this way. Everyone doesn't feel this way, do they? I see people on the train and in the street, laughing and smiling like they really mean it. While me, I'm just going through the motions. Maybe I should see a doctor? Or join the gym? Or maybe," he considered as he tucked his shirt into his pants and ran a hand over his head to smooth down his hair, "maybe, I have no idea what I'm doing."

The synagogue door was unlocked. He opened the door and raised his right hand reflexively kissing the mezuzah hanging on the door. "Imagine, me doing this" he thought. "Like a child."

The sanctuary was just across the lobby and a corridor separating the lobby from the sanctuary ran through the lobby. A sign was posted with an accompanying arrow indicating that classrooms and the youth lounge were on the left. A second arrow and sign indicating the direction of the offices was posted on the right side. He turned to the right and nervously shuffled in the direction of the rabbi's office.

"Copy room, Men and boys room, women and girls room, business office, and finally Rabbi's office. He read as he passed them by. "I wonder why his office is the furthest from the entrance? Maybe people shouldn't visit him?" he said to himself. "Maybe he doesn't want people to visit him?"

"Well, I'm here, just I like I said I would. A promise is a promise". Deep breath, everything smells so moldy, so tired. Well, not my problem. My problem, no, he said stopping himself, I'm a salesman, my situation is to get through the evening. I'm a salesman. I know how to behave in a room. He straightened his jacket, tucked his shirt into his pants and repeated in a firm voice. "I am not a child, I'm not a child."

Knock, knock.

"The door is open,"

"A promise is a promise", Eddie reminded himself as he opened the door. The office seemed smaller than his boss's, maybe because it was lined floor to ceiling with bookshelves jammed full of books of all shapes and sizes. He stood in the doorway, looking around. "like what a college professor's office must look like," he thought. Except for the drum set in the corner.

"You play the drums?" he asked incredulously.

The rabbi looked up from his desk with a warm smile on his face, waved Eddie into the office. "They're not just for show." "My wife doesn't like them in the house. Too much noise. I often practice late at night when the synagogue is empty. Playing them helps me think, I've also been known to replace the drummer at a bar mitzvah party or a wedding", he said with a chuckle. "I'm glad you came." He gestured to a chair in front of the desk. "Please, sit."

Eddie sat. He nervously began to rub a hand in front of his eyes as if to clear them, and then pushed an imaginary hair away from his forehead. "How bad could it be?" he thought. "He plays the drums and a promise is ..."

The rabbi reached into a drawer and removed a small box. He removed a pair of glasses that were resting on the bridge of his nose. He folded them and placed in the box and returned them to the drawer. He cleared his throat and then...

"Eddie, can I call you Eddie?"

"Yeah",

"And you can call me David, right?"

"Uhh, Right."

"Okay," he said as he stood up and pushed the chair away. "Is it cold outside?"

"Huh? Aaah, No. Why?"

"So, we won't need coats?"

"No", Eddie responded, "Why"?

"Let's take a walk," the rabbi replied. "I've been sitting at a desk all day. My legs get cramped, I get restless, and I read that too much sitting makes one's *tuchus* a bit too large. My wife prefers me small and tight."

"*Tuchus?*" Eddie said to himself. "The rabbi is talking about his wife and his *tuchus*? What kind of a rabbi is this?"

The two men walked outside together. It was a beautiful fall evening. The foliage had almost completely left the trees. The air was filled with the scent of Autumn. A gentle breeze was blowing.

"Let's walk towards the park, it's just a few blocks away and I enjoy being off the pavement. I like to walk at a fast pace, do you think you can keep up? If not", he said with a slight smile," just let me know and we can slow it down."

"I can walk as fast as anyone, Rabbi", Eddie answered responding competitively with a slight tone in his voice.

"Please, my name is David, and I was just joking. Can you imagine what it's like being called "Rabbi" all the time?" At parties, in the marketplace, I know some people, like doctors who insist upon it. I once knew a rabbi who listed the titles of his dead congregants in the yahrzeit list. Can you imagine? Bob Schwartz, Sarah Cohen, Dr. Sam Stein! I asked him why he did it and he said, "well they were doctors!" as if I was missing something. So, I asked him why not list everyone's profession in the list, Bob Schwartz, plumber, Mikky Cohen, gangster, Gloria Hyman, prostitute." Eddie smirked.

The rabbi continued, "It was a short friendship."

Eddie chuckled. This guy is funny, he's a real person.

"So, Eddie", David began as he gently slowed his pace, "I don't mean to pry, and you can tell me to mind my own business if you want, but when I saw you last week, you looked like you were carrying the weight of the world on your shoulders. Every step you took was a clump. You didn't walk, you clumped. And your shoulders drooped, and you looked so hassled. So, I thought, well, I don't know him, he doesn't know me, maybe if I stuck my neck out a little, I could be of some help. Sometimes getting it out, letting it go, is like taking a really good," he paused as if he was going to say something and changed his mind, "breath." He stopped and looked at him and asked in a slightly fragile way, "Eddie, am I out of line here?"

Eddie was silent. "let's continue walking" he said. They did. The two of them walked in silence for a few minutes.

"Didn't mean to offend you", the rabbi offered tentatively."

"Aah, you didn't." Eddie said, "It just ain't usual for someone to just cut to the chase so quickly. My friends and I don't really talk, we just… he hesitated, "shoot the bull, if you know what I mean, we just shoot the bull."

"You mean; I wasn't out of line?"

No Rabbi, er David, you just cut to the chase. I can't remember the last time someone asked me how I was really feeling. Maybe in summer camp and that was a longtime ago. Us guys just don't share on that level, if you know what I mean.

"Yes," the rabbi responded, "I know what you mean."

"Well," Eddie continued, "You're right. I'm clumping. It's," he stopped walking and placed his hand on the back of his neck. "It's just normal hassles, the bar mitzvah, the money, the pressures at work."

"Do you like your job?"

"I've been doing the same thing for about ten years. I'm good at it. It's not too hard, I don't take advantage of no one and…and it keeps me busy."

"Hobbies? "

"The usual, television, watching sports, I schlepp Marty around a lot. He's a good kid and smart too!"

"Do you and your wife have fun?"

"You really don't miss a beat", Eddie retorted stopping again, and turning aggressively towards him. "right for the jugular."

"Ah, sorry," David, said softly as he raised his hands in front of him and took a slight step backward. "Is he going to hit me?" he wondered? "Eddie, I'm sorry, I didn't mean to go so deep. Let's walk. This was supposed to be a 'getting to know you walk,' not psychotherapy. Let's change the subject. I only met her briefly at school orientation and the room was filled with a number of parents. Your wife's name's Diane, right?"

Eddie exhaled loudly, "You know, you're pretty good with names. I guess that's part of the job,"

"I looked it up before you arrived. Diane what?"

"Just Diane?" Eddie stopped walking and looked at him, "Look Rabbi, David, whatever I should call you, I don't' like feeling this way. I'm getting extremely uncomfortable. What do you want me to say!" He responded his voice beginning to rise. "That's her name."

"Got it. Got it," he paused, "Maybe we should get back to my office and call it a night but just a question, why did you push back when I asked if the two of you had fun? It was a harmless question. Don't you do things together? Whoops", he said, "there I go again, too pushy," he smiled.

"Sorry, you don't have to answer. This isn't an interview or an interrogation. I'm actually enjoying the company even though we don't seem to be hitting off. My wife and I take long walks just to be together sometimes. I was just being friendly."

Friendly? The rabbi is trying to be friendly? "Aaah, your wife, Rabbi, I mean David. What's her name?"

"Rachel."

David began to walk again, and Eddie matched his stride, "Yes, we're actually good friends. We work very hard trying to do things together, so we stay friends. It's hasn't always been easy with my job and all", David said, quietly. "And right now, our friendship is really being tested." He dropped his eyes as they walked. "It's not like I'm a superstar. This is my third congregation and I'm almost forty. Trust me this doesn't bode well. Sometimes, I wonder if I've made a big mistake being a rabbi."

"What are ya talking about," Eddie said, "I can't believe this," he said to himself. The rabbi is spilling his beans to me! "My kid likes you. You haven't offended the money people, or you would have already been gone, I remember not too long ago, we had a rabbi that didn't make it past Yom Kippah."

"Well, actually that might have been because of his wife," he continued. "The Rabbi was in his late thirties and she was very young and had just had a baby. I remember because she brought the baby to Yom Kippah services and in the middle of the Torah service, she took out her…" he hesitated, "well you know, and began to nurse. They were gone two days later. Didn't even make it to Sukkas."

"Thanks", David said warmly. "I suppose I needed to hear that. Besides Rachel, I don't have many people with whom I can share anything personal."

They take walks together, hmmm, might be a good idea. We could do that, he murmured. They continued walking for a few more minutes and then David said, "Let's turn back, it's getting late."

"I have no sex life," Eddie blurted out. "No intimacy. Nothing. It's like I'm living with a man. We get along all right but the last couple of years have just been boring. I don't think she finds me attractive. I don't know, maybe she just doesn't like it anymore. So, I watch a lot of sports and take a lot of showers. What about you, David? I noticed that you have a light step and a smile on your face. What's your secret Rabbi?"

David laughed, "Now you call me 'Rabbi?"

"Well", Eddie fumbled.

"I was joking" David replied as he lightly placed a hand on Eddie's arm. Eddie quickly stepped to the side removing David's hand from his arm. "But", he continued hesitantly, "if you're willing to take a risk, I'd be willing to share my secret with you. I call it 'the secret sauce.'

"What?" Eddie asked suddenly startled, "you are willing to help me improve my sex life?"

"No, I didn't actually say that," he hesitated, "well not exactly. But if you're willing take a risk and study with me, it might, no promises, make a difference."

"Wait a second, David, I mean Rabbi, I mean David," he mumbled, "You can't con a con."

"Not a con," he said, "a risk. Are you willing to take a risk and try studying with me on the chance that your relationship might improve, well, let's just say make you feel more satisfied with life?"

"mmmmm, what kinda commitment are you asking?"

"Four weeks, four sessions," the rabbi said thinking this through as fast as he could. "And if nothing happens, if you don't begin to feel better, we can stop."

"Four weeks? Four hours? Four sessions? How about three?"

"Uh, Uh, four it is or it's nothing."

"Rabbi/David," he mumbled, "I'm a very busy man."

"Four sessions, or nothing."

"Okay," Eddie agreed, (he would have made a good car salesman.)

"Shall we shake on it?"

"Na, I'm good for it."

I might have created the beginning of a friendship, the rabbi thought to himself.

I might get laid, Eddie considered with a smile.

SESSION ONE Mid-October

"We are going to study something called, Talmud," he said gesturing to a series of large burgundy leather covered looking books resting on one of his many many shelves. The books were huge, each volume was covered in a reddish-brown leather and stood at least eighteen inches high.

"And that's the secret?" Eddie asked. "That's why you smile, why you feel so energetic, why you and your wife, well, he paused as he lowered his voice and smiled, "you know what I mean."

"We shall see, we shall see", the Rabbi responded as he rose and walked over to a closet at the end of the room and opened the door.

Eddie noticed a long black robe hanging next to the rabbi's suit jacket and what appeared to be a winter hat perched on the shelf. But on the floor, was something else. It looked like, no it was a small wine rack filled with ten to twelve bottles. The Rabbi dropped to one knee and reached out and began rotating the bottles, so the labels could be read.

"Ah ha", he said smiling as he pulled one of the bottles out of the wine rack and held it in his hands. He reached behind the wine rack and wriggled his hand about until it emerged with a small clothe where the bottle has been. He began rubbing the cloth around the bottle wiping off the dust as he stood and returned to his desk. Still standing he reached down and pulled open a desk drawer and removed a corkscrew. He passed the corkscrew and bottle to Eddie, "Do me a favor Eddie, open the wine while I get the glasses"

Eddie shook his head in agreement and asked, "Do you always study Talmud this way?"

"Just open the bottle."

"Well, do you?"

The rabbi poured a bit of wine into each of their glasses, "we never did it this way at the Seminary, but everyone has their own methods. I know this might appear to some as a bit," he grinned, unorthodox? But you see, Eddie, it's often not what you study but how you study. Hold it! Let it breathe. It's an old bottle and it requires time before it opens up. I was actually saving this bottle for a special occasion," he said as he lowered his voice and said to himself, "I was saving this wine for a special occasion."

He paused briefly, Eddie looked at him, "Rabbi?"

David's head rose as he looked at Eddie and smiled, "Well, actually this is a special occasion. I am going to have the opportunity to share this twenty- year old bottle of wine with my first private student."

"Hey?" Eddie interrupted, "don't forget you're going to teach me the secret."

"I haven't forgotten," he responded as he raised the glass twirling it slightly into the light.

"For me studying can never be just for its own sake. Of course, one of the great sages disagreed. His name was Akiba and he was known to have said that 'Study leads to practice.' He meant that study, serious thinking, could lead to behavioral change. I agree with that but also think there are ways; kind of like short cuts, that one could employ. Most of the time when I study, I know I need some sort of dividend, immediate payback. It could be just a feeling, or a conversation, perhaps a little insight and more often than not, it comes from the wine or the conversation. In either case its the experience."

He looked around the room and frowned, "unfortunately this is not the best of venues, but these items, the wine, the glass and the company, heighten my experience. Now sit down and we will begin."

The Rabbi opened a book a very large book to a previously marked page and said, "I sincerely doubt you can read Aramaic let alone Hebrew."

"I can read Hebrew," Eddie interrupted.

"Sorry, didn't mean to be rude."

"It's okay." Eddie responded with a smile. "I'm kinda rusty."

The Rabbi paused, "this is how we are going to do this. I suggest", he said, pointing to a coat rack in the far corner of the room, "take off your jacket and hang it up over there. I want you to be relaxed."

Eddie rose and walked to the coat rack. He proceeded to hang up his jacket, "Rabbi, I mean David, this is not what I imagined was going to happen, but it looks like It might be fun" he said smiling weakly, as he returned to his seat.

The rabbi handed him a piece of paper. The title read, "Sanhedrin 71b"

"Now, I have to warn you, we are about to enter an ancient land." David said grinning.

All of a sudden it seemed to Eddie that David's voice took on a stronger cadence. His body appeared to grow. His posture changed. His voice grew in intensity. His eyes took on a look of seriousness.

"What am I seeing?" Eddie thought, "What's happening to him?"

The Rabbi continued. "Eddie, studying with me this evening isn't going to instantly fulfill your fantasies at home. That will most probably not happen. I'm a rabbi, not a magician, I um… well, he hesitated, "am not a magician."

"I know good salesmen when I see them", Eddie said smiling. "I promised four weeks and if I get what I need in four weeks, I'll be a very happy man. Let's get started."

David exhaled "this is how I like to begin. Take the glass in your hand and empty your lungs through a series of deep breathes, five or six of them and then lift the glass and place it in front of your nose and inhale, don't just smell the wine, inhale it. Don't let it touch your lips. Just look at the color, that deep color of red and try to breathe it in," he said in a hypnotic tone. "By the way," David said smiling, "it's very good wine. Do you like wine?"

"I'm mostly a beer drinker," he mumbled as he lifted the glass to his nose and jiggled his wrist like he'd seen in the movies. "Smells good."

"It's a Burgundy, probably worth about seventy-five dollars in a store, I've been keeping it for occasions like this."

"Like this? You expected someone like me to come to your office and drink wine?"

"Well actually, no, "David sheepishly replied. "I hadn't exactly been, been hoping to share this wine with someone who drank beer,' I'm kind of a show-off when it comes to wine."

"He's good," Eddie thought. "This just might be fun."

"Enough! It's time to begin. We are going to read a story, we call stories like the one we are about to read, 'Midrash' This is a story, a midrash, that takes place oh let's just say two thousand years ago, after the third revolt, the Bar Kokba rebellion during the time when Jerusalem, was called Aelia Capitalina "

"Huh?"

"Never mind", he said smiling as he placed his nose to the glass and inhaled, "just showing off. This is how we are going to do it. I want you to smell the wine and then jiggle it around and try to see if its smells a little different. Maybe it will just have more of a bouquet."

"Bouquet?"

"More of a smell."

"Then I want you to sip the wine. Roll what you have sipped around the back of your mouth and take in a little air like you're inhaling a cigarette. Swallow slowly and then begin to read. Don't worry if there are any words you can't pronounce. There will probably be some because the names and places are words we are not used to pronouncing. When that happens just pause and I will pronounce them for you. Smell, sip, breathe and read. Now please," he said, gesturing with a hand as he smelled, sipped and took a deep breath. "Begin."

"Okay, here goes, he replied. "If it doesn't get me laid, at least it got me high, he said to himself. "hmm smells good, hmmm tastes, tastes really good, my head feels like it is being emptied when I exhale, and filled when I inhale."

"There once was a yeshiva student who was very scrupulous in the mitzvah of tzitzit and who learned that in a far-off city across the river there was a house of ill repute of great renown and

"David, you've gotta be kidden, you're having me read you a story about a whore house?"

"Inhale, sip, taste, breathe and read, I'll do the interrupting. You're in a class, my class", was the strong reply.

"Okay", he thought wherever this goes, it can't be painful.

"The student was very serious," the rabbi continued, "about the mitzvah of tzitzit. Do you know what tzitzit are," he asked?

Eddie shrugged his shoulders and answered, "Scrolls, I guess".

"No, they are the fringes you have on your tallis. And some people, then and now, wore them under their clothes every day as a way of reminding them to love God. There are four of them, symbolizing the four corners of the earth and we take them in our hands when we recite the Shema prayer in the morning. The Shema reminds us to love God all the time, in the morning in the evening, at work all the time. Loving God is a way of helping us see beauty in everyone and in all of creation, take another sip and continue reading."

And in this house, was a woman, a woman who was reputed to be one of the most beautiful women in the world and one of the most skilled women in the world in her profession.

And the yeshiva student desired her. Now, in order for her to receive him he needed to do a number of things. He needed to send a courier to make an appointment and he needed to provide that courier with one thousand gold dinars. That was a lot of money then and I can't even think what would be equivocal to in today's market.

"I guess, it would be…"

"I don't need to know," the rabbi gasped. "Just inhale, sip, breathe and read, please!"

This is fun, Eddie thought, I can read this story and get a little rise out of the rabbi. hmm that wine fills my mouth…I guess porn was popular then just as it is today.

The Yeshiva student also had to shave his beard and change his student robes for a dark suit, so he wouldn't be recognized and bring shame to his teachers.

"Should I continue," he asked.

"Yes, of course but after you."

"You don't want to interrupt?"

"No I think you understand what it means to shave your beard, Now..."

"I know sip, taste breathe,"

"You're getting pretty good at this," he said.

And after some time, the yeshiva student, changed his dress, shaved his beard and journeyed to this far off city by the sea. He went to the proper street and eventually found the appropriate door. He knocked, and a small window in the door opened, a woman looked at him from inside the house.

"I have an appointment," the student said.

She closed the window and he heard her cry out, "Mistress the man who paid the one thousand dinars has arrived."

There was a moment's pause and the door opened. The servant was attractive and dressed in a manner that made the student blush. She grasped his hand and led him through the house to a door upon which was a special sign.

"Just knock and enter," she told him. "You are expected."

He opened the door and could not believe his eyes. Standing in front of him, filling the entire room was a gigantic three leveled bed with a stairway ascending between each level. The first bedframe and ladder leading up to the second level was framed in bronze, the second in silver and the third... the third, both frame and staircase was cast in gold embossed with gold and jewel ornaments that lead up to the object of his desire. The object which cost him one thousand dinars.

The student removed his shoes and leaped onto the first mattress firmly grasping the bronze ladder in his hands as he rapidly ascended to the second level. Upon reaching the second mattress he removed his jacket and lunged for the ladder that lead up to the third level.

Upon reaching the third and final level, he stopped and just stared. Lying on the bed on the mattress framed in gold was a naked woman. A beautiful naked woman. An outstandingly, take your breath away, naked woman.

He removed his shirt, and somehow without falling, slipped out of his pants. Unconsciously he placed his hand on his heart. She was sooooo beautiful.

She smiled at him and beckoned him to come closer.

He sat and as soon as he could, reached out to touch her and was stopped because, all of a sudden, out of the blue, his tzitzit stiffened and reached up and slapped him in the face.

The shock was too much. He fled. Down to the second level, down to the first level and collapsed in a corner of the room where he curled up in a fetal position holding himself and breathing hard and shuddering.

She followed him to the floor and confronted him saying, "By all the gods of Rome is there something wrong with me? Did you see any blemish, anything which would cause you to flee?"

"No fair lady", he replied. "You are by far the most beautiful woman I have ever seen."

"And probably the only woman he has ever seen", the rabbi quipped. "Have another sip and continue, "This is fabulous wine," he said smiling.

"Then why did you flee?" she asked.

"I desired you but when my tzitzit, my fringes, slapped me, I realized who I was and how God wanted me to behave. Intimacy is a gift, this was just, lust. I couldn't be that person", he said softly to himself." I couldn't and shouldn't be that person."

She smiled and looked at him. One of his hands covered as much of his body as possible. The other attempted to encompass his face. He looked up and she was gone.

No, she had just moved towards a table where she extracted a writing instrument and a piece of paper. He peered at her through his fingers. She reached toward him, grasped his hand and place the paper and pen in his hand.

"Write your name and the name of your teacher upon this paper," she demanded.

"Is he gonna get in trouble?" Eddie asked. "Is she gonna tell on him?"

"Sip, breathe and drink, and let me finish the story for you," David replied soothingly.

Sometime later, a woman arrived at the Yeshiva of Rabbi Hiyya. "Rabbi," she said, "I wish to convert." He looked at her and smiled saying, "Which of my students has caught your eye?" She handed him a piece of paper upon which was his name. And sometime later the bed which was first arranged in lust was filled with love.

"This was more than just a simple story," Eddie said smiling as he returned the paper he had been reading to the rabbi's desk. "And you're right, I've never tasted wine like this. It is great wine." Is all of the Talmud like this?"

"Sadly no," the rabbi responded, "but I suppose if people studied Talmud or most of the Talmud this way they'd be happier people. I think we're just about finished for the evening. Did you enjoy yourself Eddie?"

"Rabbi", he paused, "David, I'm not sure how to say this. I liked it. I didn't think I would. I only came because I promised, and a promise is a promise. But," he scratched his head, "this has been good. No, it was fun. I haven't had so much fun in a while. I doubt I'll get lucky tonight, but I'd like to try this again. Say next Thursday same time?"

"Same time," David responded.

"Should I bring the wine?"

No, that's my job, I'm the teacher. "Oh, Eddie, one more thing."

"Yeah"

"Tell Diane that we met, and that we're meeting together again next week"

David stood up, picked up the glasses and carried them into the kitchen. He turned on the faucet, added some soap and began to wash. "This might be the beginning of a friendship," he thought. "But I wish I could have shared the wine with an old friend."

Two Wednesdays later

"What's this?" Diane asked, it's not my birthday, why are you showing up on a Wednesday night with a bottle of wine?"

"This is not just a bottle of wine", Eddie said proudly smiling as he entered the kitchen and placed the bottle on the table. "This is a special bottle of wine, which we are going to drink after Marty goes to bed. It's a Burgundy, believe me," he grinned, "we are going to enjoy it."

"I think we should start calling him Martin," Diane replied as she closed the refrigerator door with a push from her elbow and maneuvered towards the sink where she carefully unloaded an arm full of vegetables. As she straightened up, she breathed deeply, turned around and raise the bottle to eye level. "After all, he's almost a bar mitzvah and if we don't start referring to him as Martin, he'll be Marty for the rest of his life. Is this wine expensive?" she asked. "It's French."

"Let's not talk about money."

So, it was expensive, she thought. "Eddie? Did you get a raise? Did something special happen at work?" she said as she closed her eyes and shook her head. "Did you get fired?"

"No, it actually was a normal not very exciting day."

"Did you win at cards?"

"No", he said as he walked to the sink, turned the water on and began to wash the vegetables.

"So", she hesitated and then responded in a soft cautious tone, "You just felt like buying us a fine bottle of wine? I don't get it. You don't know anything about wine, who put you up to this?"

"The rabbi."

"The rabbi?"

"The rabbi."

He lowered his head and looked at her with a sheepish expression on his face. She watched him take a deep breath as if he had been hiding something and finally needed to get it off his chest. He raised his chin and met her eyes and began.

"Well, I wasn't going to tell you about this till after Marty, I mean Martin, went to bed and we had tasted this wine. I thought once you tasted it, it would be easier for me to explain. But I guess…"

"I guess you'd better tell me everything right now or there isn't going to be supper."

"Okay," he sighed. "Last Thursday night and the Thursday night before, I didn't work late. I kinda lied, well, it was more of a white lie, a fib."

"You what?" You lied to me?" She said as her voice began to rise.

"Not, exactly," he countered, "I just more or less withheld information from you for a week or two until I was ready to share it."

"Well," she said stamping her foot, "you damn well better share it with me now!"

"Don't get excited, it's not like I'm fooling around. I didn't know how to explain it. I was confused and needed some time to figure it out. Ya see two weeks ago, I went to see the Rabbi and last week I did it again."

Tapping her foot, arms crossed against her chest she continued. "Why? How?"

"Diane," he said as he walked toward her and grasped her shoulders. "Calm down."

She took a deep breath. "What did you do which made you go to see the rabbi?"

"Don't get so excited. I didn't do anything," he replied soothingly as she pushed him away. He raised his arms in defense.

"You know you don't like it when I get mad," she said in a menacing tone.

"Diane! Breathe, calm down. This was and is a good thing. Try to lower your voice and drop your arms, this was a good thing. I am going to tell you everything when you're ready," he said backed away and lowered himself onto a chair in the kitchen. "I'll tell you everything. Just give me a minute and relax."

Diane turned away from him and breathed deeply. "Eddie," she said as her voice began to return to normal.

"Relax darling, you're gonna like this. You won't be upset. I promise. And you know that when I promise."

"A promise is a promise," she replied as she dropped her shoulders, lowered her arms, turned around and flashed a weak smile.

"I am not gonna make you upset… trust me… trust me," he said as he stood up and grasped one of her hands and lead her from the kitchen into the dining room. He placed his arms on her shoulders and gently pushed her into a sitting posture on the couch.

"The first time," he began, "was because he wanted to speak with me about Marty's, I mean Martin's behavior. You knew about that as a matter of fact, you told me to go see the school principal. But instead when I got there I met the rabbi," he paused, "we never spoke about Martin, we just talked."

"Talked? Talked about what?"

"I don't know, we just talked about stuff. We took a walk together and he told me about his family and his work and asked me questions about my work. Stuff!"

"Don't sound so bad", she said her voice still controlled.

"Yeah it wasn't. but, then… get this; it got, well somehow, I agreed to go back and to uh," he scratched his head as if trying to find the appropriate words.

"Come on baby, Spit it out."

"He got me to agree to study Talmud with him and I did it. And it was fun. And we drank wine and I loved the wine and so before I go again tomorrow, I thought we could drink the same wine, because I really had a good time and I didn't feel stupid, and I liked the wine and I brought it home, so we could drink it and it cost seventy dollars."

"Hush, Hush", she replied as she covered his mouth with her hand. "Hush, I get it," You had a good time with the rabbi and you're going back on tomorrow to study Talmud. I get it… it's fine."

"You won't tell anyone will you?"

"Of course, not, why would I do that?" she said smiling.

"I don't want the word to get out. It could be embarrassing," he mumbled in a low voice as he lowered his face

"Martin's got practice tonight and won't be home for another hour, why don't we try this amazing wine of yours?"

He smiled back and reached into the kitchen drawer for a corkscrew.

"Where the fuck is the corkscrew" he grumbled as he searched through the drawer. "I know I had one someplace. We got knives and spoons and I don't even know what this is" he said as he raised a meat thermometer. "Aaah here it is"

He pulled it out and proceeded to open the bottle.

"Honey, can you find the wine glasses? I think we have a couple in the back of the hall closet."

"I'm on it, "she said.

Pop! The cork sounded as he pulled it from the bottle. He poured her a glass.

She raised her arm and was about to sip the wine when he stopped her.

"Look at the color?"

"Huh?"

"I said look at the color."

She looked at him quizzically but did as he asked.

"Now smell the wine, don't drink! Just smell."

She did as he instructed. "Hmmmmm," she murmured,

"Now sit down and take a deep breath and sip the wine. No! Not yet, it needs time to breathe. Go get some cheese or some nuts, something we can nosh on, while we drink"

"It needs to breathe?"

"Yeah, it's kinda old. If you were stuck in a closet for twenty minutes, wouldn't you need some time to readjust. Well this bottle has been stuck like this for twenty years. Show some respect," he said with a smile.

"You're crazy," she replied grinning. "I'll go get the cheese,"

"Not the Velveta," he said with a raised voice as she exited the room. "Real cheese."

She returned a few minutes later carrying sliced cheese and a sliced apple on a plate. "I saw them bring fruit and cheese in a restaurant once," she said softly.

"Just like the movies," he said as he poured himself a glass and sat opposite her.

"Now tell me about your day."

They sat and talked and by the time Marty, soon to become Martin, came home. He found them on the couch in the den. An empty bottle of wine and the remnants of a cheese platter rested on the coffee table. She was lying on the couch with her head in his lap.

"That's disgusting," he said upon noticing their positions.

"Did you finish ya homewoik?" Eddie asked in his Brooklyn drawl.

"Not yet." Marty replied.

"Well sit at the table and finish it while your Ma and I watch a little tele."

Martin did some homework while they watched TV. Around 9:30, their usual time, they got into bed and went to sleep.

Eddie woke up the next morning at 6 AM like he did every day. Something was different. He felt a weight on his chest. He slowly opened his eye and saw her leg was draped over his body and her hand brushed up against his chest. He smiled and slowly extricated himself from the bed. He tiptoed quietly to the closet where he gently opened the drawers to his dresser and removed the necessary clothes for work. As he left the room, he looked at his wife, smiled and gently closed the door behind him. As the door closed she rolled over unto her side and sighed, "I love Talmud night."

Early December

"Leonard?" Madelyn asked as she lifted her head and placed her hands on the old wooden desk in the President's office. "Do we have a kiddush club?"

"Not that I know of", Leonard responded as he sorted through a pile of bills. "Bills, bills, bills, when I am going to have to wait for the Passover appeal before I see any checks? Why?"

"Because", Maddy replied, "I just opened an envelope and in it are a series of checks totaling Five Hundred dollars from a group of people who call themselves "The Kiddush club."

"Hmmm this could be interesting, do we know any of the people who made the donations?"

"I think so," she replied, "I recognize Harold Brown, and oh, this is one is Rene Rodriguez, you know, the carpenter, and look here's one from someone named Morty Kassoff."

"I know him," Leonard commented as he ripped up a flyer and threw it into a wastepaper basket next to the desk, "he has that little barber shop on State Street."

"Well, it seems all of these people," Maddy said as she continued to shuffle through the checks "are, no I don't know this one. Albert Kahn. He is definitely not a member. Do you know him?"

"Take the money<" Leonard answered, "My pappy always said, "take the money. Ten minutes ago, we didn't have a Kiddush club, now we do. Put it on the website. It clearly is generating revenue."

"Len, these are three-day, no two-day, possibly not even one day a year Jews. We never see them."

"That's not true, if they have children, you see them until the day after the bar mitzvah, after that," he shrugged, "they are gone! just like mice when it gets warm or someone washes the floor in the kitchen."

"Wait a minute," he said, slowly as he leaned back on his chair and began to thumb his chin, "I think I saw Rodriguez at Friday evening services last week, He was with a few people who didn't look familiar."

Maddie closed the checkbook, organized the papers on the desk into piles and then placed them in file folders in the lower desk drawer. She carefully locked the drawer with a set of keys that had been resting on the desk.

"I think this is one for the rabbi," she said as she stood up and walked towards the door. "Maybe he knows something about this kiddush club. Will you help me with my coat?"

"Of course," he responded as he stood. "I'll ask some of the guys. Maybe some of them know something about as well."

"Oh!" and speaking about the rabbi, she said, "remember we need to set a date for that January review."

Also Early-December

"You guys are nuts", Marty said. "It's Thursday night. Thursday night! And you guys are making Shabbat! Shabbat is on Friday night." Friday night is when you drink wine and have a great meal and dress up real nice and say blessings. Thursday night is for football. You drink beer and eat chips and sit by the big screen and munch. You guys are nuts."

"Well," Eddie, replied, "you're partially right and partially wrong. Sometimes I have to work late on Fridays and I get home late, but we still light the candles."

"Yeah," Marty responded smartly, "and then we eat Pizza or hotdogs."

"I wouldn't mind making a nice meal for Friday night," Diane chimed in. "We already light the candles and Martin you could say the blessings. It would be good practice."

"My name is Marty," he said, "why all of a sudden Martin? I've always been Marty and practice for what?" he responded firmly.

"Martin," Diane replied firmly. "You've got an edge to your voice. Your father and I felt it was time for you to be called Martin. People will respect a Martin more than a Marty and the practice is for your bar mitzvah. She replied in a teasing tone, "silly."

"But we never did Friday night Shabbat before. We only did it when we went to class Shabbat dinners. Why do you want to do it now?"

"I just said, I wouldn't mind doing it," Diane responded as she brought the roast to the table.

"I kinda would like to have it as well." Eddie chimed in. "It would make it a special family night."

"Oh, by the way, what are we drinking tonight dear?" she asked with a smile, will I like it?"

"It's what they call a Bordeaux", Eddie responded as he poured the recently opened bottle into a tube-like pitcher. "This is what they call a "decanter", he said, "I'm supposed to pour the wine into it and then rotate it like so," he murmured as he cautiously rotated the bottle in his hand, "The man at the store said it improves its breathing, whatever that means. But he also said we would like it."

"I still don't get it. Why do we have to start having Shabbat on Shabbat?" Marty snapped.

"Don't' be rude to your mother," Eddie inserted with a slight tone to his voice.

"I don't get it, I said I don't get it!"

"Do you think you'll like the roast Martin dear?"

"Of course, I'll like the roast. I'm hungry and it smells wonderful."

"Then shut up and enjoy it", Eddie responded. "Hmm I think it's time to pour the wine and say the blessings."

"But it's not Shabbat. Shabbat is tomorrow", he said stamping his feet.

"Well" Eddie said," I guess I could probably come home a bit early and we could do this on Friday nights as well."

"And", Diane added, "Martin you could start spending Thursday evening with friends."

Marty hesitated, "I could spend Thursday night with friends and we could have a great meal on Friday night? Did I hear that correctly?"

"Yes, of course", Eddie replied." That's what your mother just said. But the deal is you'll have to lead the blessings, all of the blessings."

"Okay, okay," he said. "Let's eat. And I'll do it. But you're both crazy."

Mid-November

"Knock, knock, hi rabbi," Eddie said sheepishly as he opened the door to the rabbi's study and gestured to the extremely large man who looked like a former linebacker who accompanied him. "This is Larry, Larry Kahn."

Larry stood around six feet two. He was wearing a blue suit and carried a large cardboard box in one of his arms.

"And this is Bobbie," he continued while turning his head in a gesture of acknowledgement to the tall red headed man who stood behind Larry and was also carrying a large wooden box. "Larry and I work together and the four of us, Mikkey isn't here, he lives in the next town over. We grew up together. We commute together."

"And", David responded thoughtfully as he raised one hand and seemingly scratched his chin, "you, all of you," he said gesturing with one hand, "are here because?"

"Because they want to join the class." Eddie walked in and pointed to the gentlemen holding the boxes indicating where they should be placed.

It's like he owns my office, David thought.

Eddie continued, "I know I should have called and asked but I was kinda embarrassed to do that and I hadn't planned on inviting them. They just kinda made me do it, if you know what I mean?"

"No, well maybe yes", David responded. "You're telling me that your friends," he looked at both of them, noticing that both of these men who even though they were dressed in business attire looked more workers from "On the Waterfront."

"friends"

"Since High School", the one called Larry said interrupting as he placed the box on the floor and gave the rabbi a gee-whiz-why- is- this- guy- asking- a- stupid question. "We've been taking the trains to work and playing cards together," he gestured with a meaty hand toward Eddie and Bobbie, "for many a year and we know you?"

"You know me?" David asked?

"Sure, we come to hear you speak on Yom Kippah."

"You're members?" He said incredulously. "Oh, I'm sorry it slipped out, I've only been here a few months and haven't..."

"We know", the one named Bobbie said cutting him off. "Not a problem. So, can we join? Can we learn?"

"Why of course, but, look at this room, it's too small for four of us to study.

I need another chair, let's go into the Boardroom and I'll make some more copies of the text."

"Text?" Larry said, whatsa text?"

David looked at him quizzically. He looked at Larry and he looked at Bobbie noticing the confused looks on their faces.

"It's nothing. The Text is the material we are going to stud, ..." he paused and said, "I mean read. Maybe Eddie will be our reader and I won't have to make copies but," David continued as he looked at the men "I don't think we will have enough wine and I have only have two glasses. He shook his head and began to frown, I might have to use plastic."

"Naah," Larry retorted, "I brought you a case of wine. I have a cousin in the business and when I told him what the two of you have been drinking, he gave me this case and said we might enjoy it more."

"And", Bobbie added interrupting Larry, "I have a brother who imports and sells china. I got the glasses. Burgundy glasses," he said triumphantly as he ripped the case open and theatrically removed a glass and waved it over his head.

David, looked at the glass. "May I see it?" he asked.

"Sure", Larry responded as he handed him the glass.

"This is a serious glass," he said as he placed the glass on his desk and bent over to read the wording stamped on the side of the case. "And this is some serious wine."

"Don't worry about the glasses", Larry said, "if this works for us the way it seems to be working for him," he said gesturing Eddie's direction with his face. "I'll wash the glasses and put them on a special shelf in the kitchen every week. And if there isn't a shelf, I'll build one."

"What's it doing for Eddie?" David thought, he does seem happier, he hasn't missed a class, he straightened up, took a breath and announced, "Gentlemen, let's go to the Board Room. Oh," he said as he reached toward a shelf and grabbed two yarmulkes in his hand, "take these."

"We got our own," Larry answered, "what kind of Jews do you think we are?"

Eddie and Bobbie, each picked up a case and exited the study while Larry, reached out and placed a hand on David's shoulder forcing him to remain while the men proceeded to the Boardroom.

"Rabbi, "he asked?"

"Yes,"

"Before we begin, I gotta question."

Who is this guy David thought as he stopped and turned to look at him, very aggressive? I don't even know him and he's, well he's, well I don't know what he wants, he thought. Just relax and roll with it. You might have two more students.

"So," he answered smiling, "ask."

"It's the wine, it's about the wine, isn't it?"

"What are you talking about?"

"The secret sauce, the reason we're here. We've known Eddie all our lives but in the past few months, he's changed. He's happier, He jokes, he's the old Eddie we grew up with. We watched him miss our card game on the train on Thursdays. He/we love that game and all of a sudden, he won't play on Thursday. And he's the old Eddie at work. It's about the wine, isn't it? The wine is the secret."

David looked at him and shook his head, "No Larry it's not about the wine."

"Then it's the Talmud right. I thought it might have been the Talmud, but then I said to myself, all those Hasidim and other rabbis I've seen never smile. It can't be about the Talmud. But if it's not about the wine, it's gotta be about the stuff you two are studying. He nodded his head in a knowing way, that's gotta be it".

Once again David shook his head from left to right, "No Larry it's not about the Talmud."

Larry, looked David right in the eyes, He must have played football or wrestled in High school, David thought, and said. "Rabbi, I might not speak too good. And I might not read fancy books, but I'm not a dummy. Bobbie and Me took a big risk tonight. We let people we've known our whole lives, see us not playing cards. Our wives think we are working late and I don't know what my wife is thinking. If it's not the wine and it's not the Book… he reached out as if he was going to grab his shirt and then hesitated, "sorry," he said, "this is a big thing."

"If it's not the wine and not the book, what is it?"

"Well," David gasped, (that was a bit close) "I guess it's the method."

He reached out and placed his hand on Larry's shoulder, (this guy has muscles).

"Let's see if it works for the two of you," as he maneuvered himself around him and reached for the door. "Let's see if we can manage in the Boardroom."

He walked down the hall feeling them trudging after him. He opened the door and switched on the lights.

"This is better than my study, but not as festive as one could hope. The two of you are new so let me bring you up to date, no," David said haltingly.

"I think I'd rather Eddie did the dirty," he said with a smile.

Eddie grimaced and then shrugged his shoulders. He looked at his friends, took a deep breath and said, "We always begin by taking a few deep breathes."

"I can do that," Bobbie quipped.

"Me too", Larry chimed in. "Uhm, this ain't gonna be like pilotes is it. My wife has been busting my," he hesitated, "really wants me to do pilotes with her." I ain't gonna go nowhere in shorts."

"You don't have to," Bobbie said interrupting. "My wife and I go every Sunday."

"Guys, shut it, we're not here to kibbutz. We're here to learn from the rabbi," Eddie added. "let's cut to the chase. Breathe, Breathe," he said nodding to David.

David smiled winking at Eddie. "Then we pour the wine, check out its color and inhale."

Got it.

"And then we say a blessing. The blessing over wine. Do any of you know the blessing?"

"You think we don't know the words for Kiddush?" Larry said, "I know how to say, "Borei peri hageffen"

"It's gaffen" Eddie gently added correcting him. "Geffen is Geffen records, gaffen is vine."

"Sooorrry," Larry said,

"Larry get serious, remember this is serious." Bobbi shoved him.

"Rabbi?" Eddie said turning to him, "can you take it from here?"

"Of course, I can, this is my job. The words of the blessing are very important. They tell us we Bless You Lord our God who is King of the Universe, because you brought forth, you created the fruit of the vine. It means more than just growing grapes. Think of it this way", he continued.

Every fruit has a different taste and every type of grape tastes a bit different as well. You can plant the same type of grapes in two different places and when you taste and compare the fruit it can taste differently. That's because the roots of the vine, draw the minerals that are in the soil into it and that shapes the flavor. The rabbis of old, those living in the time of the Talmud used to make wine that was so good, the Romans always tried to obtain it."

"Rabbi", Larry interrupted, "are you telling us a long time ago rabbis worked? I don't mean it that way" he said quickly recovering. "I mean they had jobs and didn't study all the time?"

"Kinda like women and perfume," Bobbie added as he held the wine to his nose and inhaled. "This one must have been a redhead."

"Correct," David continued ignoring Bobbie's comment. "they had shops, and trades and farms. One was even a gladiator and one of our greatest commentators a man who we refer to as "Rashi" was a winemaker in France during the Middle Ages."

"I've said enough," he continued. "Breath, smell and then, yes, finally, taste."

A feeling of quiet contentment filled the room as each man, slowly opened their eyes and smiled.

"The topic for the evening comes from one of the six books of the Mishnah. It focuses on the Sabbath, Shabbat. Tonight, we are going to ask what types of candles can be lit in honor of the Sabbath."

Two Weeks Later

"Leonard did you have the house committee install a new cabinet in the kitchen?" Maddie asked.

"Don't be ridiculous, why would I do that? You know we have procedures, committees, and processes before anything as simple as installing a cabinet could occur. Why are you asking?"

"Because we have a new cabinet, filled with expensive Burgundy glasses in our kitchen", she replied.

"Must be the kiddush club," he quipped.

"We don't have a kiddush club", she snapped.

"Well," Leonard answered, "maybe we do and if we do, I think I'd like to be a member."

The New Volunteer

"Honey can you get the door? I'm in the bathroom."

"No, can do, my hands are filled with soap and I can't find the dishtowel. Eva! Eva, please get the door, Dad and I are indisposed."

Don't worry, I'll get it, just a minute."

Thump, thump, thump, "Any idea who it might be?" she asked as she ran down the stairs.

"it's probably the rabbi," Frank called from the bathroom.

"The Rabbi?" Sophie said.

"The Rabbi?" Eva said as she stopped in front of the door and quickly tucked in her blouse and smoothed her hair.

Frank's voice floated across the room, "Just open the door and smile. I'll be there in a second."

Eva took a deep breath as Frank appeared in the hallway. "Why is the rabbi coming to our house?" she asked. "I didn't do anything wrong."

"No one said you did," he said smiling. "The rabbi's coming to see me. We have a meeting."

Sophia turned off the faucet, clad in an apron with her sleeves rolled up to her elbows, she firmly placed a hand on the door, blocking Eva from opening it.

"Why didn't you tell me the rabbi was coming to visit? The house is a mess. I would have put up some coffee or at least offered him something to drink? Frank! How could you? We've barely finished dinner."

'We usually have finished by 7:30. I had no idea you were going to work late and you, "he said motioning to Eva, "had drama rehearsals. Sofia, take your hand off the door, the rabbi is waiting to be let in."

Sofia removed her hand and blushed as Eva turned the knob and opened the door.

"Rabbi," she said. "What a surprise."

"Rabbi," Sofia said, "please come in. Let me take your coat. Frank neglected to inform me we were going to have a guest this evening," she said giving Frank a withering look.

He blanched, swallowed and said. "Well, the rabbi called me today and asked if I had any free time because he needed some assistance and I thought we would have been finished with dinner by 7:30. Rabbi, I'm sorry for the mess and the disruption your presence seemed to have caused."

"Not a problem," David replied as he removed his coat and entered the home. "thank you for allowing me to drop by on, what seems to have been a moment's notice."

"Not a problem," Frank said with a smile, "Let's go to my studio. It's quiet there and we won't be, (he looked at his wife and daughter), "interrupted."

"Not the studio!" Sofia whispered. "It's our basement!"
"It's really fine with me," David replied with a smile. "We just need a place to talk. I need some advice. You're welcome to join us, Sofia if you'd like."

"No, no," she replied. "I have things to do and obviously. You want to speak to my husband."

"Sophia, "Frank said, "prefers not to go into the basement."

"Mancave,"Sophia said with a smile, "I'll fix us drinks and we can enjoy them after you finish your meeting," she said with a menacing smile towards Frank, "after you ascend from the playroom."

"Can I go upstairs?" Eva asked.

"Of course, you can," Frank said smiling weakly. He opened the door which lead to the basement. They descended the stairs and all of a sudden, Frank heard the word, "Wow".

"This is great!" David said as his eyes took in the scene. What you've done with the walls, the illustrations on the ceiling. Like Michelangelo. And look!" he said as he ran to an easel, "comic book covers! Dr. Nero, my favorite."

"I didn't realize you were a comic book aficionado," Frank said.

"Yes! I certainly am."

"But that's not why you're here is it?" He gestured to a chair next to a stool. David sat.

"Is this about money?" Frank asked.

"Why would you say that?' David asked.

"Because," Frank continued, "whenever the synagogue calls, it's about money."

"Well," David replied shaking his head, "someday when the synagogue calls it should be about what the synagogue can do for you, not the other way around."

"Agreed," Frank said as he reached into a refrigerator, "Beer?"

"Sure."

Silence. David looked around the room and then began to stare at the floor. Frank looked at him and waited and waited. And waited. After what seemed like forever, but probably was less than a minute, Frank asked. "Rabbi? What can I do to help you?"

David raised his head and met Frank's gaze. "I could use a little help with something and I thought you would be the best person for the job."

Frank raised an eyebrow, "really?" he said. "What kind of a job?"

"It won't take a lot of time. I know you're extremely busy but it's important and I don't know who else could do it in a creative interesting way."

"Rabbi. What are you asking me to do? I travel a fair amount and my work and family takes a great deal of my time. And since I rarely attend religious services, you know, I'm not big on prayer."

"I know," David said in a desultory tone. "But I am not asking you to come to services. You've got a great kid, and she's involved in religious school and…"

"Yes," she is," he added. "Quite surprising. I hated Hebrew school when I was a kid. You must be doing something right. The few classes I attended when you teach sexual ethics were actually quite intriguing."

"Me too, "David added.

"You too what?"

"I too, hated Hebrew school," David added with a smile.

"And," Frank paused and took a sip, "that's why you became a rabbi?"

David nodded affirmatively. "if you want to know more about that, you have to take me drinking."

Frank smiled, "rabbi, I welcomed you into my home. You seem like a person I might want to spend some time with, he hesitated, some other time. My wife is upstairs glaring at me and wondering why you came to see me. My daughter's in her room texting all her friends that you came to visit her Dad and she's not in trouble for whatever she thought she would be in trouble for. Why exactly are you here and what are you going to ask me to do?"

David met his eyes once again. "I said it's a small job. You can make a big difference if you accepted. I," he paused. "I would like you to redesign our website. Will you do it?"

Frank hesitated. "That's a big job," he said. "Is there a deadline?"

"Three months," David replied.

"Let me give it some thought," he said. "I'll get back to you in a few days. Now if you'll excuse me, he said as he took another sip of his beer, "I have some apologizing to do."

"Not a problem," David said as he looked at his watch, smiled and reached out and took Frank's hand. "Thank you. I can find my way out. Please apologize to Sofia and Eva for my leaving without saying goodbye."

"Not a problem, "Frank repeated as he followed David up the stairs. "Be careful on the driveway. It's icy."

He closed the door, turned around and exhaled deeply. A moment later he was joined by his wife.

"I forgot to put out the wine and cheese."

"I can see that. You were listening at the door, weren't you?"

"And what if I was? It's my house too! What did he want?" she asked.

"I guess you should have opened the door a bit more, so you could hear better. He asked me to volunteer."

"Did you accept?"

"Not yet, but I probably will," he replied.

"Why?" she asked.

"Because he didn't have a clue how to ask." He shook his head. "Not a clue."

EARLY DECEMBER

"Rachel! Rachel!" he yelled as he strode into the house. The door closed with a slam. "Rachel! Where are you?"

"Shhhhh!" he heard a whisper along with the sound of someone descending the stairs. "I just put Ari to bed. How many times have I asked you, no, told you, not to let the door slam." She grabbed his hand and on tiptoes dragged him into the kitchen.

"Rachel, I have four students! I started with one. A few weeks later, four! four!", as he gleefully thrust his hand in front of her face. "Four! And they came back after the first lesson."

Her face filled with joy and she smiled back at him and said, "Does that mean you will fix the door?"

"What", he said making a face trying to figure out what she had just said. "Oh sure, I'll do it tonight, Rachel four students and they liked me. They really liked me" he said as he turned from her opened the refrigerator door and began rummaging through it. "Where's that cheese sandwich, I know it must be somewhere? Where? Where…"

"Maybe this will work"", she murmured to herself as she raised a hand and brushed back a strand of her brown hair. She stood about five feet six still in her late thirties. Long dark brown hair, hazel eyes and a comely figure.

"Maybe, just maybe, this place will work."

"What are you going to teach them next week?" she asked smiling.

"Found it," he said as he pulled a wrapped sandwich out of the fridge and closed the door. "Found it." He placed his hand on his chin, lowered his head and started to pace, "I don't know I need to give it some thought."

"Not so loud", she murmured.

"Maybe, maybe."

"Next week, I'll teach them about Hanukkah. It will blow them away when they learn the story of the miracle of oil didn't happen. They'll go crazy and the week after that we will learn about Purim. Oh my god", he said placing his hands on his face. "They will plotz when they learn the rabbis had a sense of humor and asked questions like, "Did Esther keep kosher in the harem? Or did she and Achashverous do the dirty. "They will ….plotz."

She walked over to him placing her hands on his shoulders. "David, I think you should sit and maybe calm down."

He looked at her hands and smiled, "you have beautiful hands."

"Yeah, right", she answered with a chuckle. "And the messiah is coming tomorrow."

He looked up at her as she more or less forced him to stay seated.

"I haven't seen you this excited in a while," she said. "I like it."

"I like it too," he quipped. "I like it too. Rachel, they liked me. I think they could even become friends."

Her look changed. "Don't you remember what happened last time?"

"Of course, I do but this could be different."

Her face darkened. She dropped her hands turned away and began to walk towards the stairs.

"Last time we weren't able to choose where we lived," she said shaking her head. "And, once again, we're living in a dump."

"It's a congregational parsonage," he said. "We didn't have a choice."

"Or the money to buy our own house," she said in a whisper. "Not that there's a house in the neighborhood near the shul, where I would want to live." She shook her head slowly.

"These people might be different. One of them asked me if I liked basketball."

She turned, "and you said you hated it?"

"No, I told them I loved the Knicks. I do read newspapers you know."

She sighed, "and...and"

"And he asked me," he stumbled, "they have season tickets and sometimes someone can't make it and they asked me if I would be interested in filling in."

"And you said, "

"Well, I said", he said proudly, "as long as it is not on Friday evening."

"You shouldn't have done that", she turned and walked toward him. "That's distancing. They know you won't attend on Shabbat, a simple yes would have sufficed."

"Hmmmm, You're right. "I'll try to do it better next time. But Rachel, I think we could be sort of friends and they have wives and children and we have

Ari and …"

"'David,'" she responded tartly. "I don't want to be friends with them. Have you forgotten what happened with our so-called friends last time? Last time when your contract came up? Do you remember what they said about me? Do you remember, how difficult it was to find a non-Jewish obstetrician in the next town because I refused to have your congregants talking to one another about your wife's vagina?"

She bit her lip, "I won't go through that again. It was bad enough that my father told me I shouldn't marry you because you would never be successful. That successful rabbis had to be scholars!"

"Do you remember," she said raising her voice, "he told me in front of you that you would always be too gullible, too nice, and not academic enough to serve successfully in a congregation?" She stamped her foot. "David, I won't go through it again! No friends and I mean it. This is your job and it's the third time. No friends, no weaknesses."

She reached out and grabbed him by the shoulders. "If you want our marriage to survive you have to succeed here or you'll sleep alone for the rest of your life. Do you understand?"

"Okay, you don't have to be friends but will you …"

"Act like a rebbetizim?"

"No," he responded quickly. "I want you to act like you, but I think we might be able to stay here. It's a nice community. I know they aren't all intellectuals and artists, but they are nice people. We could make a difference."

She sighed and looked him straight in the eye. "I don't want to be friends with them, but I want us to be happy and I want Ari to have friends and I want you to be successful. What do you want me to do?"

I'm not one hundred percent sure. Could you teach a course?

"What kind of course?" I'm not a scholar, I'm an artist."

"You're a rabbi's daughter and know more about Jewish life and Judaism and just life than most people. Teach them with food. Get them to bake challot, and Hamintashin for Purim and then fabulous food for Passover. And make it a schmoozing class, so they can talk about what they like and what bothers them. Make it fun. Would you do that?"

"Let me think about it," she said. "If I do it, I want you to promise me you'll revisit your relationship with, she hesitated, "your students. They are not," she said raising her voice and looking at him, "your friends. They are congregants. Remember that, they are congregants. Promise?"

David nodded affirmatively, "Okay," she said continuing. "This will require a plan. I'll have to be more than just nice to these women and," she shrugged, "being nice, hasn't always been my forte. I've watched these women interact. They're not kids anymore. They struggle and play all sorts of stupid games. And, and they can be hard. Not just harsh. Let me think about it."

Two Years ago

"Maybe you should spend more time working with the teens," the older man said. "You're young and perhaps, your skills will be more appropriate with children than in the sanctuary."

"But Rabbi Rabinowitz, they loved my sermon. I watched the expressions on their faces. They smiled, they nodded. Some of them actually approached me afterwards and told me how much what I said meant to them."

"They were only being polite," the elder man replied as he nodded wisely. I've been the senior rabbi here for almost forty years," he continued. "Believe me, I know my people".

I looked at him, an immaculately conservatively but elegantly dressed man of about seventy. Gray thinning hair with a handsome goatee, a trifle too thin with delicate hands. He was the perfect senior statesman. But he was wrong. I knew he was wrong.

"I worked extremely hard on that sermon. I knew it was important to explain to the congregation that the rabbis of old new that the miracle of Hanukah never occurred. I knew that if I told them they created the miracle story in order to prevent further rebellions it would resonate with a majority of the congregation.

He shook his head from side to side. "It was inappropriate for you to destroy the myth, the story of Hanukkah in a public forum. Think of all the people who were raised to believe in miracles. Think of what you did to them!"

"Do you really think that a majority of your highly educated congregation really believes that a flask of oil that was intended to last for one day actually lasted for eight? Do you really think your people, never considered if there was a miracle it was the Maccabean victory, Come on Judah, you know better and did you really have to stand up and criticize me in front of four hundred people by saying, "there are many theories about Hanukkah; Rabbi Duvin's is just one of them?"

"David, I've never given you permission to call me anything other than "rabbi." And I find your, your, (he hesitated,) your outburst inappropriate. I'm telling this to you as a friend. Perhaps you should spend more time with the children and their parents, and in a month or so, you will have the opportunity to deliver another sermon, one that is more appropriate. I'm telling you this as a friend."

"Rabbi?" The intercom blared, and David opened his eyes.

"Rabbi?" Shirley called out. "Rabbi, Mrs. Mansour, the Chair of the school committee is here to see you.

"Thank god, Rebecca," he said as he stood up and walked to the door. "Thank you for coming."

"You called the meeting the woman known as Mrs. Rebecca Mansour replied. "What's on your mind?"

"I'm concerned with one of the teachers and I don't know what to do."

"Which one?" she asked.

"Mrs. Mankowitz."

Mrs.Mansour just smiled. "She taught my children when they were in religious school. What a lovely lady. Did you know she's been teaching the aleph/bet class for twenty years?"

David grimaced, "Yes," he said. "And I was hoping you could advise me how to handle this situation. I've never fired anyone before."

Mrs. Mansour's back stiffened and she responded a little too firmly, "You want to let her go?"

David, looked at her and continued. "No matter what I say to her, she just smiles and says "yes rabbi" and continues doing what she has been doing for the past twenty years. I suggest new textbooks, films, field trips, and she just smiles and says, "yes rabbi" and continues doing what she does. I'm not sure she can actually hear me when I talk to her. I'm certain we could find a replacement who could follow directions."

Mrs. Mansour shook her head. "Rabbi, everyone loves that woman. She's part of the fabric of the Temple. She's irreplaceable. You simply cannot replace her."

"But?"

"No buts," she replied as she stood up and prepared to leave. "you asked for my advice and I gave it to you. Don't do it. I doubt you could survive what would follow."

Slam!

"Thank you for coming Mrs. Mansour," David said weakly.

The intercom blared loudly.

"Rabbi, Mr. Kaplan the teacher is on the phone."

"Shirley," he replied, "ask him to hold, I'm, I'm thinking."

"He says its important," Shirley yelled back.

"It doesn't sound good," David replied looking at his watch. "It's 3:30. Religious school starts In fifteen minutes and it almost time for me to greet the parents at drop-off."

"He says he was in a car accident and he's waiting for the police and won't make it to class," Shirley screamed.

"Really not good," David said that's the eleven and twelve-year old's and it's too late to call a sub. Six girls and three boys." He shrugged and removed his jacket and walked to the classroom, nodding and smiling at students who were in the process of entering their respective classes.

"No parents this afternoon," he said to himself. "What am I going to do? Bible, History? Holidays? Naah, I won't know til I see them." He opened the door quickly scanning the room.

Five girls were standing together texting, the sixth was in the corner facing the wall, trying not to cry and furiously pushing the buttons on her phone. Two boys appeared to be using snapchat or Instagram to photograph the girls and upon seeing the rabbi enter the room, John quickly shut his iPad and blushed. "Must have been porn," David thought.

The door closed with a thud and everyone froze.

David walked to the front of the classroom and stared at them. He looked from one to another while furiously thinking. "What should I say? What should I do?"

The kids began to fidget. Jonny took out a pen and began to draw. Tiffany picked up her phone and was about to text.

"Let me ask you a question." David blurted. "Have any of you had a boyfriend or a girlfriend stolen from you by one of your friends?"

The kids sat up and looked at one another. Tiffany, the most physically mature young women in the group weakly raised her hand. "Last summer in camp, my best friend stole my boyfriend."

"How did you feel about it?" David asked.

"We're still not really talking to one another. I think she felt bad and," she said nodding her head, "I felt worse."

"We're a little young for that rabbi," one of the boys added. "But," he said turning his head to another young man, "we do compete for their attention."

"I remember that," David said with a smile. "and whoever gets that attention is really cool."

The rabbi said "cool." Someone whispered.

"Another question," David added, "Do any of you know the story of David and Bathsheba?"

One of the girls raised her hand. "I saw the movie."

"But do you really know the story? Do you know that David sent one of his oldest friends to the front line to be killed so he and Bathsheba could do the dirty." He looked at them with a smile and said, "Yes, I said, do the dirty."

"Let me tell you the story and afterwards let's see if anyone can find hints that reveal what really happened in the text.

An hour and a half later the kids were still talking.

One Hour Later

rrrrrrrng!

"Rachel," David shouted. "Rachel! Come downstairs and answer the phone. I'm cooking."

"I told you we should have gotten rid of the landline. It's a nuisance," Rachel yelled back as she came down the stairs, entered the kitchen and reached for the phone. "We both have cellphones. Why do we need this?"

"For shul calls, "he said as picked up the frying pan and placed it in the oven."

"Hello," Rachel said as she answered. "Duvin residence who's calling?

Just a minute," she replied politely as she handed the phone to her husband. "Big surprise it's for you and it's dinner time."

"Can I call him back? The fish is almost ready?"

"No," she replied, "first it's a her, and second she has a tone in her voice, rabbi," she said with a wicked grin.

"Okay," he said, handing her the oven mitt, "switch."

"This is Rabbi Duvin, to whom am I speaking?"

"Rabbi it's Nancy Schweitzer, Tiffany's mother."

"Of course," David replied. "She's a great kid. How can I help you?"

"Rabbi," she said. "I'm extremely disturbed. Why are you teaching twelve-year-old girls sexual ethics?"

"What?" David answered.

"Tiffany came home from your class this evening, just thirty minutes ago, and all she could talk about was how unacceptable it was, she used the word "unacceptable" for girlfriends to steal their friends' boyfriends. Believe me it was quite a dinner conversation. Somehow it was connected to a Bible story?"

"David and Bathsheva," he replied.

"Rabbi, I don't think it's appropriate for you to be talking to children, to my daughter about sexual behavior."

"Mrs. Schweitzer, please give me a minute to digest this. I wasn't teaching sexual ethics. I was teaching Bible. Give me a minute to organize my thoughts and then I will explain."

"I hope you would rabbi, because we were considering starting to attend services on Friday night but if this is what the kids are learning in school, well," she said. "We just might reconsider our Temple membership and I've already received phone calls from some of the other parents."

OY!, David thought. Gotta do this, gotta do this, gotta do this right! He took a deep breath and responded in a slow thoughtful voice. "I want to differ with you. Let me ask you a question. Was Tiffany happy and engaged when she returned home?"

"Yes, but"

"Please let me continue. Did she say anything about her personal life or behavior other than she had difficulties last summer with one of her friends over a young man?"

"No, she said that one of our Kings, the Jewish King David, did something that wasn't right and then she ran upstairs after dinner telling us she needed to find a Bible and learn about someone named," Abigail."

"That's the classes homework for next week. Her class was so successful I want to teach the kids again. Mrs. Schweitzer, my goals for the class were two-fold. First to teach them about some of our Biblical ancestors in a manner that made them realize they were real people with the same strengths and weaknesses we have today. The second goal was to engage them in text analysis, well let's call it textual study," he said correcting himself.

"Learning how to approach a text, any text is a key Jewish value. It trains the mind to analyze and ask questions. If we're successful with our children, and Tiffany is a smart young woman, the skills she learns in my class will help her succeed in the future."

"That's all very well and nice, Rabbi, but I'm having enough trouble keeping her hands off herself and others right now. Do you know what's it like to live with a hormonal young woman? All she can think about is her body and boys!"

David sighed and replied. "I have an idea Mrs. Schweitzer. One you can share, if you wouldn't mind with the other parents. I asked the class to attempt to figure out how many wives David had and how were they treated for the next session. How would you and any of the parents of children in that class like to sit in this coming Sunday when we meet again. If the kids can do the research I 'm going to tell them the story of David's first wife, Michal.

All of the parents will be welcome. The only rules will be they can't interrupt me. They will have to behave as if they are members of the class. After the class has concluded if any of you think I've overstepped line. We can talk about it in my office, and I will do whatever you desire. How does that sound?"

"Mrs. Schweitzer are you still there?"

"Yes," she answered. "I just wasn't expecting that kind of a response."

"And?"

"And I'll call the parents and see you on Sunday," she paused. "I think I have to thank you rabbi, for being so receptive. But I'm not sure I want too. I'll see you Sunday," she replied as she hung up.

Days Later

rrrrrrrng! rrrrrrnnnng!

"I'm coming, I'm coming, Diane shouted as she put her cigarette in the ashtray, dropped her magazine on the floor, placed her hands on the arms of the chair and pushed herself to a standing position.

rrrrrrng! rrrrng!

"I said I'm coming!" She repeated with more force as she ran to the kitchen "Now where is that phone? I know I put it someplace."

rrrrrng!

"AAah, the table," she said as she grasped it in her hand raised it to her ear and pushed the accept button.

"Lo? This is Diane, whoze calling?"

"Mrs. Lankin, this is Rachel Silverstein."

"Rachel who?"

"Rachel Silverstein, the rabbi Duvin's wife."

"The rebbetizin?"

"Yes," she sighed, "the rebbetizn."

"But you kept your last name."

"That's right Mrs. Lankin I…."

"That's gutsy. You can call me Diane."

"Thanks, please call me Rachel, I really don't like being referred to as the rebbetzin. It makes me think of a bossy old woman in early seventies and that's not me."

"Whadda ya want?"

"What makes you think I want something?"

"Because whenever the phone rings and it's the shul, they always want something and its usually cash."

"Well", Rachel responded somewhat flustered, "that's not why I called. I called, because your husband told my husband you are a first-class baker and you like to bake with cinnamon and chocolate."

He told the rabbi I was a first-class baker? Diane repeated the phrase to herself. "First class baker?"

She smiled and swaggered over to the refrigerator, placing the phone between her neck and shoulder, opened it, removed a pitcher of ice tea and slowly poured herself a glass.

"Well, it's true," she said. "I like to bake, but my repertoire is very limited."

"Well, actually, that's why I'm calling. I enjoy baking as well, but I like to do it with company. I haven't really met very many people since we settled here, at least people with whom I had much in common, you know what I mean, don't you?"

"Absolutely," Diane responded simultaneously making a quizzical face.

Rachel continued, "I was wondering if you would like to get together and bake a chocolate and cinnamon babka with me."

"Never made a babka before", Diane said, "but I know how to use a rolling pin and I like nuts and raisins. Uhm," she said hesitantly. "We don't have a kosher home. I mean it is really not kosher. Are you sure you still want to come?"

"Do you cook with lard?" Rachel asked.

"Of course not," but the plates, dishes, I remember my grandmother's house and believe me my house is nothing like that."

"Neither is mine, I can assure you," Rachel replied. "How about I bring a cutting board. I assume you're cooking utensils are stainless."

"They are," Dianne nodded.

"Great, "Rachel answered. "when do you want me?"

"Why don't you come over tomorrow afternoon, Wednesday afternoon around 2 PM and we can work in my kitchen."

"Why, thank you," Rachel said, "I'd love to. I'll bring the supplies and the screwdrivers."

"Screwdrivers?" Why are you bringing a screwdriver? My house doesn't need fixing."

"To drink, silly. To drink."

Christmas week

The Board room is too small. The Sanctuary is too big. Well, he said to himself, the class will probably be tiny this week anyway. I assume most people will be out of town. But, he said scratching his chin. I will need to start another class. Who do I ask for permission? Madelyn? The Board? Or, do I just let them know. Or, should I just do it?

If I go to the Board, should I make a formal presentation or just simply make a request? Yicch, I never do that sort of thing very well, he muttered as he pushed the message button on the office phone.

"Rabbi, Its Alex from three weeks ago, I just joined the shul, and was wondering could I bring a friend to the class? I had such a good time studying with you. I can't explain it, I'm sleeping better, I feel more relaxed. Give me a call if you have a chance, no I'll call back later. Oh, yeah, Merry… forget I said that, I'll call back later."

"Rabbi, its Larry, just checking to see if we have enough glasses. I'll call back, no. I'll drop another case off at the shul before candle lighting. Babs said, she wouldn't mind if we went to services on Friday."

"Rabbi, its Moishe. You know me as Mike, Mikey, I'm part of the friendly four. Eddie, Ronnie, Larry and me. I was wondering if I could come by a little earlier, I'll meet you at minyan and perhaps before class we could talk for a few minutes. My daughter is ….., I'll tell you later."

He shrugged his shoulders, I have to either do this on my own or ask. Or, he said thoughtfully. I could just move the class, not tell anyone, and looked surprised if I get found out. "Good idea, David," he said. "Now, how should I re-arrange the room?"

The Friday evening disaster

"David? What are you doing?" Rachel said. "Services begin in less than an hour. It's almost time for you to leave."

"I'm practicing," he said as he stood in front of a full-length mirror occasionally gesturing with one hand. "I've been working for weeks on this sermon. It's complicated and I want to be able to explain all of the details without looking at my text."

"Like we did when we were starting out," Rachel said with a smile.

"Exactly," David replied as he raised his left hand and pointed with one finger to an imaginary audience.

"I can't believe how involved I've been with this topic. Jacob and Esau. It could have been written at the same time as the Romulus and Remus myth concerning the founding of Rome."

He turned from the mirror and looked at her. "Preparing for this sermon has been a fascinating experience. I've found Syriac and Ugaritic references to similar stories. The rabbis who lived in Roman times and the Church fathers all had something different to say." He picked up a bunch of papers and began to shuffle through them. "Even Aristophanes and Plato joined in. This is going to be a great session. I can't wait til this evening. And to think I've crammed hours of research into a little more than a thirty- minute lecture."

"Thirty minutes! David, you know the old saying if you can't strike oil in fifteen minutes you're boring. You've got to cut it down."

David paused and looked at her. "You are always so right about things." He picked up the text, grabbed a pen and began to cross out paragraph after paragraph. "I don't want to forget this just in case I need to refer to a source," he said as he finished the quick edit and placed the papers in the inside of his brown sport jacket.

"I'm sure you don't," she said as she playfully pushed him. "Now take a shower, shave and get dressed or you'll be late. And don't eat too much at the kiddush. Dinner will be spectacular."

"Okay Captain," he responded as he walked towards the bathroom and began to remove his shirt.

Ten minutes later, she shouted, "David hurry up! You're going to be late."

"No, no I'm not," he replied as he descended the stairs fully dressed and entered the kitchen. wearing a brown sport jacket, blue tie and gray pants. "How do I look?" he asked with a smile and slight dramatic turn.

"I'm looking for a recipe," she said. Holding her Ipad in two hands, she quickly glanced at him "Blue jacket with that tie. Get rid of the brown one."

"Yes Captain," he chirped as he returned upstairs and exchanged one sport jacket for another.

"See you around nine," he said as he exited the house.

"Knock em dead," she shouted as the door closed.

The third week of January

"Good morning Meyeroff, Kaplan Winig and Schwartz, how may I help you?"

"Yes, this is Leonard Skoff. I'd like to speak with Madelyn Schwartz please."

"May I ask what this is in reference to?" the receptionist responded.

"I'm a friend, just tell her Leonard is on the phone."

"Of course, Sir, just a moment and I'll see if she can take the call."

"Leonard, I'm in the middle of a hundred things, what do you want?"

"It's January, I promised I'd call a meeting in January to discuss you know who, but I can't. My mother needs a hip replacement and I need to go to Florida to take care of her for a week. Did you know they can perform hip replacements these days and you leave the hospital walking the same day?"

"Of course, I know that," she replied. "My mother had one of hers replaced two years ago. But, I think we still need to meet. Something is happening, I can't put my finger on it but," she paused, "people who I haven't seen in years are beginning to show up at services. Donations are arriving from unexpected sources. I think we need to figure out why this occurring and…"

"Use these items as an opportunity to get rid of the rabbi and engage one with more talent?" he said interrupting her.

"What?" She laughed and responded, "no, of course not. We need to figure out how we can capitalize on it."

"Look, Maddie, this could be just a blip, a reaction to what's going on in Washington for all we know. Don't you remember? We need a super star to keep this place alive. This might be the moment to turn it around and if it is we need to seize that moment! We both knew he wasn't a super star. I know he was the best we could find at the time, but maybe," he continued thoughtfully, "maybe we can use this blip, as a teaser."

"A teaser? What do you mean?" she asked.

"It's a marketing thing," he said. "You develop a little nothing, a blip into a real something. I think," he continued his voice rising with his excitement.

"Then we can start a new search and use this blip, to attract some real talent. We can post something like, "Don't you want to be part of a growing Jewish community?""

"I don't know", she said thoughtfully. "That doesn't feel right, and he might be the reason this is occurring. You know what the poet said, "something is going on and we don't know what it is.""

"That's right Maddie, we don't. So, let's make it into something! Let's use this blip as a catalyst to attract some real talent to this sleepy, nearly dead congregation in hopes that with the right person it can live again."

RRRRng! She paused, "Barbara, hold that call! Tell whoever it is, I'll return it in five minutes. I don't know Len, maybe he's the right one, maybe he is the catalyst we need, but a different type of catalyst than we thought we needed."

"Naaa, you're just being soft, who would have thunk it? Maddie Schwartz the barracuda of Park Avenue", he teased. "You're getting soft in your... young age."

"Stop it Leonard, he's the Rabbi and he has a family."

"And I think he is kind of a shlub. But you're the president and you wanted this meeting. It's your decision. Hello? What? Maddie, I have a call I have to take. Why don't you speak to some of the newbies and ask them?"

"And why don't we have a meeting with him and ask him how he perceives what's going on?" she added.

"Not a bad idea. I'll set it up and talk to you later."

"Leonard call me when you get back and good luck with your mother."

February 2018

"What a great view," David said as he looked at midtown Manhattan from the fifty-third floor of an office building. "I can see Saint Patrick's, and Central Park and, how do you get any work done when you have such amazing views?"

"One gets used to it", Maddie responded in a matter of fact tone. "One learns to look at the material on the desk not to look outside. One learns," she said with a sigh, "to use the conference room when one doesn't wish to be disturbed. Would you like some coffee?"

"No,"

"Some water?"

"I suppose," David responded, still gaping at the floor to ceiling glass windows that composed two sides of the room. The rest of the room was bare. A mahogany wooden table surrounded by six chairs. Nothing on the walls, with the exception of the modern wooden cabinet and some shelving filled with books.

Maddie pushed a button on the telephone and said, "Some water please."

"It will be here in just a minute, Aaah here's Leonard. Just about on time", she said rising as she walked to the door as it opened and reached out and grasped his hand. "Almost on time, she said, "not bad for you."

"It's that lousy number 6 train. Stalled again on fiftieth street. But I'm here, Hello Rabbi, glad you could make it," he said as he unbuttoned his sport jacket and hung it on a clothes rack near the door. "I'm glad you were able to break away. Sometimes it's easier for us to meet in the city. Less distractions," he mumbled as he walked toward the table and slowly lowered himself into a chair. "Must be getting old, sitting is becoming more enjoyable than standing," he said.

"Glad to be here, but I wasn't exactly clear of the meeting's purpose," David answered. They want to tell me to start packing, he thought. They just didn't want to do it in the building. Maybe, there's a suggested pay off if I leave early, Rachel will be furious, she was just getting settled.

"Let's call it a personnel review," Maddie added. "We wanted to speak to you as friends and as synagogue officials. We think it's time to learn what you have been doing, what you think is working, where it isn't working, and where if you might need help, and…," she added while tapping a pen on the table.

"It's happening again," David said. "Just like the last time. Just like last year."

"David, thank you for coming. I appreciate you taking time out of your very busy schedule."

"Well Norman, he replied. "You are the president of the congregation and," David said as he gestured at the wine and cheese on the kitchen table, "and a

fabulous host. Rachel and I have enjoyed our time with the two of you. But why are you home and not at the office?"

"It's Wednesday and I am one of the few Doctors in town who doesn't play golf," he said with a smile. "I wouldn't dream of working and embarrassing my colleagues by going to work, so I use the day to take care of synagogue business."

"Oh?" David replied. "I guess I'm here on business."

"Yes, Yes, its business but come into the kitchen and let's have a drink. I know its early afternoon but its always six o clock somewhere," Norman said smiling as he walked towards the kitchen. He approached the wine, lifted the bottle and poured two glasses. "Italian Chardonnay," he said as he inhaled. "A perfect white for a warm Spring day. Sit down David and enjoy."

David sat. Norman sat. David looked across the table wondering why the successful fifty something physician had brought him to his home in the middle of the day.

"Norman?" David asked. "Have you asked me here because you want to talk about something private? Is it about your or Maggie's health? Are any of the kids in trouble? Would you like me to reach out to them?"

"No, no," Norman replied with a smile. "Thank you for asking, Rabbi. I appreciate your," he hesitated, "your sincerity. No, my family is fine. I didn't invite you to my home to because of my situation. Yes, I have, no, we have elderly parents but that's not unusual. Hopefully, they will remain healthy for years to come. No, David. I asked you here because I want to talk to you about your life. Please tell me what you think about the wine."

David sipped. He reached out and placed a piece of fruit in his mouth and sipped again. "Its good," he replied. "very good."

"Yes, it is. Tell me," Norman asked, "how long do you planning on staying here?"

David gulped. "You mean, he replied, how long would I like to remain with this congregation?"

"Exactly," Norman said with a smile. "I see we are beginning to understand one another."

"Well," David replied thoughtfully. 'Rachel and I are beginning to make friends and Rabbi Rabinowitz is approaching retirement age and..."

"I'm your friend, aren't I?" Norman said interrupting.

David nodded affirmatively.

"You're like a son to me, you know that don't you?"

David nodded again and continued. "As I was saying, I hope when Rabbi Rabinowitz retires I could be considered as a primary applicant for the position. I'm learning a lot. I think people like me. You brought me here to engage young families and I believe I'm doing that quite well."

"Yes, yes, Norman added, "you are. And that's why we have a situation.

"A situation?" I don't understand. What situation?"

Norman shook his head. "David, we have a serious situation because of the Sokol bat mitzvah."

David hurriedly sipped the wine. "I don't understand. I helped a family who had a twelve-and-a-half-year-old daughter who completely lacked the ability to learn to read Hebrew and provided her and her family with a meaningful experience."

"Too meaningful," Norman added. "Too meaningful."

"Wait a second," David said. "I went through the process. The Rabbi agreed. The ritual committee agreed. We created a Saturday afternoon/evening experience for the family that brought people into the sanctuary for the afternoon and evening service who rarely attend that service. It was a win/win."

"It was too successful," Norman said. With our support you have created a monster. The Rabbi has been besieged by parents who desire to have a similar experience."

"And what's wrong with that?" David replied.

"The Rabbi is unhappy. He wants to have all the b'nai mitzvah ceremonies in the main sanctuary on Shabbat morning. And he wants to continue to officiate at those ceremonies."

"But I know the kids! I know their parents! I did what you asked me to do?"

"Yes," Norman said wistfully. "I know but the rabbi isn't happy. And it might be in your interest to start looking for another position."

And, Leonard added, "we wanted to make certain you understood our expectations."

David's heart missed a beat. Just like the last time," he thought. It always begins with the word, 'friend.' "I'm suggesting this as a friend. As a friend and someone my son's age, I'm concerned about your future. I/we want you to succeed. Just like last time, only this time, they are better dressed.

He walked to the table and took a seat next to Maddie directly across from Leonard. "How would you like to begin?" He asked with a shit eating grin on his face.

"Tell us what you've been doing, we" he said with a smile as he extended both of his hands palms up, "want to know how you've been spending your time."

Mr. Nice Guy will be the hatchet man, I remember when we first met, I knew enough not to take his offer of friendship. I've been down that road before. But it's different this time. My classes are more than filled. People who never attended Friday night services are just showing up. And, their coming back. The school is growing. It is different this time. This is my place! I'm not going to let this happen again. I should be able to play this game too, he thought as he lowered his face and began to scratch his head.

I have to own this, Rachel will go berserk. I am doing good things. I know I am.

He took a deep breath, "that's easy", he replied as he raised his head and stared back at Leonard. "I know all the parents and all the children. I think the school can grow. We're beginning to attract new people."

He raised his arm and unconsciously scratched behind his ear. "Something is happening to the school. I can't put my finger on it, but the kids are happy, and their parents are starting to attend some of the classes. The religious school was such a mess when I arrived. No curriculum, poor teacher morale, but the teachers have asked me to work with them after school. We've had a few sessions and, it's not like I've done anything unusual, but after the first session they insisted that we have more. I've never heard of anything like this occurring before. Teachers insisting on study."

"Tells us about it," Leonard asked leaning forward.

"It all began when Shirley received a call from Mr. Kaplan fifteen minutes before class was supposed to start indicating he had been in a traffic accident and wouldn't make it to class. It was too late to find a substitute, so I took over."

"It was the eleven and twelve-year olds. Six girls and three boys. The worst age. I glanced at the group and partially froze.

Five girls were standing together texting, the sixth was in the corner facing the wall, trying not to cry and furiously pushing the buttons on her phone. Two boys appeared to be using snapchat or Instagram to photograph the girls and upon seeing the rabbi enter the room, one of the young men, I hesitate to tell you his name, quickly shut his iPad and blushed. "Must have been porn," I thought.

I walked to the front of the classroom and stared at them. "What should I say? What should I do?"

The kids began to fidget. Jonny took out a pen and began to draw. Tiffany picked up her phone and was about to text.

"I didn't know what to do. If I yelled, I knew I would lose them. If I forced them into a traditional frontal classroom setting, they would grudgingly comply. Marty, Eddie and Diane's son and I had a relationship. He has an inquiring mind and is extremely thoughtful but he's not a leader. At least not yet. I knew I could count on him if I could gain some additional support. The kids were starting to fidget. I was on the verge of panic and then, and then, I had an idea."

I asked them, especially the girls who, well you know at that age their all legs and glands. Twelve year old girls are …. never mind, I'm sure you remember what they are like. I asked the girls how they would react if one of their best friends stole their boyfriend? And then all hell broke loose."

"Everyone had something to say. I had a few of them find the appropriate verses in the books of Kings and then asked them to form groups and reinterpret the story in their own language and substitute women for men so that it was the girls who were sending someone away so they could steal another's boyfriend. By the time the class ended all of them asked, no, demanded more. And I agreed."

That evening I received two phone calls from agitated parents demanding how could I be teaching sexual ethics to twelve- year old's. I tried to explain that wasn't what I had intended but they were so irate, I invited them, if their child agreed, to attend the next class. A week later four parents, three mothers and one father, Frank Aronheim, did you know he was a house husband?

Leonard shook his head back and forth.

"Well, apparently he is an illustrator for comic books and magazines and his wife works in the city. She's a dentist."

Maddie responded thoughtfully, "Sofia Aronheim is a dentist. I didn't know that."

David raised his glass and sipped. He cleared his throat and continued. "the next session, I asked the class how many wives did David have? Once they found the answered I told them the story of Michal, his first wife." He shrugged his shoulders, "It was difficult keeping the parents quiet but every so often, I would let one of them ask a simple question. The dialogue which followed between students and parents was really good," he said.

"The parents are still attending that part of the class and the teachers, well we only have three, have me telling them the same stories. Ideally, they will adapt them or those which are less sophisticated to their classes."

Maddie leaned forward placing her hands on the desk. "David? I mean rabbi, are you telling us that our children want to go to Hebrew school?"

David shrugged his shoulders, "Yesterday I heard Melinda Furer yell at her mother for making her late. I simply don't understand. I mean I know the kid. I've been to every parent's home in the last three months. I have even begun to work with a few of the families in their homes when I visit, but this," he paused. "I just don't get it."

"Let's try to unpack this," Maddie said, "when do you think this began?"

"I'm kind of thirsty and this might take a while, Could I have a drink?"

"Waters on the table," she said.

"No, I mean a real drink. (you're going to fire me anyway) I always seem to think better after a glass of wine. Its mid—afternoon, would you mind?"

"You want me to serve you a glass of wine at 1:30 in my office?" Maddie asked.

"If it's not too much trouble," he replied. "This might take some time to explain."

"I certainly don't mind Maddie, if you don't," Leonard added. "After all I used to work in a three-martini lunch culture. A glass of wine would be nice."

Maddie shook her head, "Okay, Okay, just a minute. If that's how we need to do this nicely; I mean right, I guess the rabbi is worth a glass of wine," she said as she rose from the table and walked toward a cabinet standing against the wall. She removed three glasses from the shelf, and a cork screw and returned with a bottle.

David looked at the bottle admiringly. "Good stuff," he said.

"At Four hundred dollars an hour it better be," Leonard added with a smile.

Maddie poured. David smelled and sipped.

"Well rabbi, you were about to explain." Maddie continued.

"Very impressive," Maddie replied.

"I," he paused, "I regularly visit the sick and make hospital visits, and …"

"We know you make hospital visits," Leonard interrupted. "To a great extent you're doing what we asked you to do when you were engaged and what you said you would be doing. And it seems you are turning the school around. But what I really want to know", he interjected his voice hardening, "is what you are doing that we hadn't expected?"

Right for the throat, he thought. He's the bad cop.

"David shrank into his chair, "I wasn't finished," he responded meekly. "I was about to explain I have been calling people on their birthdays and…."

"You call people on their birthdays?" Leonard interrupted.

"Regularly" David responded with a smile, "Yours isn't til next week, if I remember correctly".

"Oh," Leonard answered softly. "That's actually very nice."

Maddie raised her hand dismissing Leonard's smile. "What else are you doing Rabbi? Tell us something we don't know?" she continued as she raised her head and met him eye to eye.

David sighed inwardly, now she's the bad cop. He raised the glass and swallowed. "I'd like some more if you don't mind," he said, casually wiping a few drops from his lips. "I've been working on the Friday night service to make it warmer and friendlier. It's taken a lot of time."

"How so?", she inquired

He noticed her foot had resumed tapping.

I'm losing this, he thought. I need to take the initiative. I know I can turn this around.

"Well, I'm not exactly certain how it happened but our attendance is growing. When I arrived it was basically a dead service. One could say it was a *mate-Mitzvah*, that is to say, a Cohen wouldn't touch it."

They stared at him blankly.

"It means it was a dead body and Priests aren't supposed to come into contact with the dead. It was sort of a joke," he replied in a weak voice. "Not good," he thought once again raising the glass to his lips and taking a very large gulp.

"The service," he paused. "Sucked. The same fifteen people always attended and the way they prayed, well actually, mumbled, didn't add to the atmosphere. If I tried to lead them in song, I felt like all of us were stuck in a closet. Rob Cantor likes to lead the singing. If he ever even considered finding the appropriate, any appropriate key which would allow us to sing together, he would fail. I would say "Rob change the key." And his reply was as effective as kicking the wall.

Leonard smiled. Maddie didn't.

"It was", he made a face, "painful. I went to Mr. Mirsky because he was head of the ritual committee and asked him if I could introduce instrumental music on Friday nights." He told me all the ritual committee did was hand out honors on the holidays, and I could do whatever I wanted as long as I didn't change the tunes.

"That's Sam", Maddie sighed. "So, what did you do?"

"Many years ago," he dropped his voice with a smile, "a long long time ago, one of my teachers, a very wise man, published an article addressing how to institute change without losing one's head, my head," he said smiling.

David leaned forward, "I spoke with each of the elders and asked them for permission to introduce instrumental music at that service, as an experiment. They told me I could do what I wanted as long as I didn't change the tunes. It was a start."

"So", Leonard asked, "you, did it?"

"Not right away," David shook his head from side to side. "I needed more involvement. I called a meeting. I called four or five people who never attend Friday evening services and asked them to come to a meeting and tell the group what it would take for them to find the Friday night service meaningful. One person, told me hated the Friday night service."

Maddie nodded.

"I told him," David answered as his voice began to rise, "that's why I invited him. He came to the meeting."

Maddie gave him a puzzling look. "Let's me make sure I understand what you just said. You invited a person who didn't like,

"Detested, was the word he used," David said interrupting.

"You," she continued, "invited a person who detested the service to come and share his or her thoughts about the services with the group."

"Precisely," David replied. "You see there are only a few things one can say about the service. It's too long. No one ever said it's too short. The Rabbi speaks to much, I can't remember when anyone would have said, the rabbi doesn't speak enough! And, there is the time services begin and how the space was being used."

"Wait a minute", Leonard interrupted, "it's a Chapel, the space is fixed."

"Not exactly", David responded "but I'd rather not get into that. Well, maybe I do, because I know if you don't like what I have to say… I know what you're going to say," David said with a serious tone as he looked at Maddie.

"Leonard, no disrespect intended. Look at it this way. Everyone likes theater. No one likes bad theater. What was taking place in the Chapel was very bad theater. My job was to transform it into very good theater."

And then I found Linda Kurfitz."

"Kurfitz?" Maddie asked, "the pharmacist?"

"Yes, her daughter is eleven years old and in the religious school. One day, I heard humming. I told her she had a good voice and was musical. She looked me and said, "if you think I'm musical you should listen to my mother."

"Barbara Kurfitz?" Maddie commented, "musical?"

"Not just musical," David added "a former music student. She plays the piano, clarinet and has a voice. It took a little persuading but between Linda and me, we convinced her to work with me on an occasional Friday night. That was three weeks ago, and she has a friend who has a kid, who plays the drums.

We started slowly. Traditional tunes, with one or two new ones. Instead of a traditional sermon I substituted a four -five-minute teaching. The clincher was once we agreed on what changes would take place, everyone was asked to come to shul as critiques and to advise me after Shabbat how the changes were received. Last Friday night forty people were in attendance and I think the number will continue to grow in the coming months because my music team of two are bringing their families and their friends."

"Wait a minute," Leonard interrupted. "Are you telling me that the number of people attending Friday evening services has increased dramatically just because you added music?"

David moved his head to the side and raised one of his hands. "I'm glad you asked that question. I've spoken to colleagues who have introduced music on Friday night, and they told me attendance worked like a sign curve."

"A what?" Maddie asked.

"A sign curve," David replied. "When its first offered a lot of people come and almost all of them respond positively. But the second and third time music is added to the service, in other words, when it becomes standardized, attendance levels off. I can't figure it out but for some reason attendance hasn't dropped. Not only has it maintained itself but its continuously increasing. I really can't figure this out."

"What about Saturday morning", Maddie interjected.

"Hold on, Maddie," Leonard said. "Don't distract him. We need to stay on topic."

"That's another project", David responded. "Much more complicated and I don't have a clear picture of what I need to do, yet. It might involve… no, I'm not ready to discuss it. Frankly, I'm still not certain why these people are coming to services on Friday night. It can't just be the music."

"David," Leonard continued, "I mean rabbi, has anything else changed in the service?"

David shrugged his shoulders. "Well, I had been working really hard researching and writing what I thought could be a major sermon. I spent hours in my library and an equal amount practicing my delivery in front of a mirror. It really was a fine piece. The Torah portion focused on Isaac giving his blessing to Jacob and Esau. I spent hours attempting to learn if the words he used in his blessings reflected Ugaritc and Syriac texts.

Maddie yawned, "that would have been a winner," she said.

"Stop it, Maddie," Leonard said in a forceful tone. "Did you deliver the sermon?"

David shrugged his shoulders once again. "I had planned on it. I didn't want to leave anything to chance. I was afraid of losing my text. So, the night before I printed it out and placed the sermon in my brown sport jacket. Believe me, I was prepared."

"And?" Leonard asked.

"It's kind of embarrassing. The next day when I was getting dressed to go to shul, I put on a blue shirt and a striped tie. I reached for my Brown jacket and began to leave the house. I kissed my son and wished my wife a good shabbas and she said, 'David your jacket doesn't match your shirt and tie. Wear the blue blazer not the brown one.'"

"And?"

He smiled weakly. "I was a good husband. I listened to my wife and changed jackets. Unfortunately, I forgot the sermon was in the pocket. It wasn't until I arrived in shul, fifteen minutes before the service was to begin that I realized I didn't have it. It was nerve racking. I broke out in a cold sweat. What was I going to do? What did I have to say?"

Leonard and Maddie looked at one another. Neither spoke.

David stood up, walked around the room and reached for the wine bottle. "I'm a little tipsy," he said to himself as he proceeded to pour himself another glass of wine. Maybe I should have gone to law school, I don't seem to be able to change their minds. Well, at least the wine's good. It seems they like what I've been doing, even though they called this meeting committed to giving me notice. I doubt they're willing to reconsider. He raised the glass to his lips and drank. They want a dynamo and I'm, I'm just not that type of a guy. Well, since this is my last moment I might as well let them know how I really feel. What the F! he thought as he cleared his throat.

"Would you like to hear what else I've been doing?"

"No rabbi," Leonard continued. "We want you to tell us what you did when you couldn't find your sermon."

"Really?"

"Yes, really."

"Not much, I guess. I just looked at the people and wished them a Shabbat Shalom and then asked them if they have ever felt that they had to masquerade as someone else to gain their parents love?"

Leonard and Maddie just looked at one another.

David continued, "I mean that is one of the messages of the portion of the week. Jacob had to dress up and impersonate his older brother in order to receive his father's blessing. I asked the question and then we talked about it. A lot of people had something to say. Someone said his father never told him that he loved him. Another said his children don't understand why he does things. A third was in business with her sibling and felt they were always competing for their parent's affection. I listened, and they talked for quite a while, that is until I brought them back to the concluding prayers." This could be going better, David thought to himself as he grabbed the wine bottle and lifted it to his lips. "What the fuck," he thought.

Leonard and Maddie looked at one another. Maddie had a puzzled expression on her face, her feet no longer tapping. Leonard's was leaning forward both hands on the table. Maddie reached for the bottle and shook her head as she realized it was empty. She looked at Leonard, he nodded and gestured with his hand for David to continue.

"Rabbi?" Leonard asked. "What happened after the service?"

"Well, there was a lot of discussion. On Sunday I received a bunch of emails asking me to raise similar questions the following Friday evening. And since they asked, I did it."

"Thank you, Rabbi," Leonard said, "and oh by the way, what's the kiddush club? We have been receiving checks and there is a new cabinet in the kitchen filled with expensive wine glasses. What's the kiddush club?"

David exhaled slowly, "It's more or less a Talmud class. We meet Thursday evenings. By invitation only. It started with one person, and it's grown to about eight. I will probably have to open another class because I'm developing a waiting list. Oh, and my wife has organized a group of women who meet somewhat regularly and bake. She's making friends and some of these people are starting to attend Friday evening services. I think the baking is just a first step. Many of these women are Jewishly and spiritually interested but no one's ever reached out to them from a Jewish perspective to help them meet their needs. If we had the financial backing….."

He paused looked at them through what had become an alcoholic haze. I'm angry, I am really angry, he thought. They schlepped me into the city to tell me my life is hanging by a thread and they didn't even know what I've been doing. He turned to them and said,

"You know, you could have just called every so often and asked how things were going? You didn't have to drag me into the city to tell me you were going to let me go." He shrugged his shoulders, bury the anger, Rachel always said I don't wear it well. The hell with that, if I'm going down, it's with a clear conscience. "Is there anything else you would like to know?"

"We didn't know," Leonard said, sounding slightly flustered. "We simply had no idea you were so engaged. I heard you had attended a few interfaith events, we expected that. But," he said as stood realizing David was on the verge of ending the meeting and walking out. "But frankly we didn't expect everything else. David you're much more dynamic that we ever thought you would be."

'I'm not dynamic", David responded tersely. I'm really angry, he said to himself.

"I know who I am and what I can do and if a few people offered a little support and believed in me. "

Too much anger, slow down, can't, I'm on a role, and not a good one.

"I'm a person who is seriously committed to this community. I've never had the opportunity to try to shape a community the way I always wanted. There were always too many people who wanted to tell me what to do. Too many people who always wanted someone with more talent who was more dynamic, more inspirational and who were ready to let me go, if I didn't meet their unrealistic expectations. And for some reason, whatever I'm doing in this community is working but the two of you decided that it's time for someone else. Leonard did I get this right? That's why the two of you really called this meeting. You want me to resign."

Leonard placed his hands firmly on the table and looked at the angry young man standing in front of him. Maddie caught his eye and nodded affirmatively. "Tell him Leonard, "she whispered.

"Yes, you got it right, that's why we brought you here. To read you the riot act. But we were wrong. You're doing everything and perhaps more than we could have hoped. I'm sorry, I doubted you."

I'm sorry too," Maddie quipped.

David glared at them, as he swayed to the left. "I like it here and more importantly my wife is beginning to like it here."

"Rabbi", Maddie rose and walked toward him hand extended. She reached out and gently removed the wine glass. "Rabbi, you've had enough. I know when a mistake has been made. We want you to stay. Keep up the good work and let us know if you need our help. "

Leonard grabbed his jacket and walked toward the door. "I've got to get back to work, thank you, Rabbi" he said. I'll see you."

"Friday night?" he mumbled with a smile?

Leonard shook his head and smiled. "Yes Rabbi, Friday night."

"Gotta go too," David mumbled as he staggered towards the door.

"You first," Leonard added. "Glad you're taking a train."

"Me too," David replied with a burp.

They waited until the door had closed. They looked at one another. Maddie shook her head, "He really has no clue what he's doing,"

"No clue at all," Leonard responded. "But it's working, really working."

⌣

Part Two: Can the Fox steal the Chickens?

DRAGONS

February 2018

"Rabbi,!!!!!!

"Rabbbbbiiii!!!

"Shirley, Shirley," he said as he ran out of his office as if it was on fire.

"Shirley, why are you screaming? Stop screaming!" He said as he opened the door and ran into the reception area in the congregational office. "Shirley, why are you?"

He stopped suddenly as he noticed the young man in the black middle length coat, with the white shirt, black hat and fringes hanging from his waste. "Excuuuuse me," he said as he slowed down and skidded to the left. "Hello, can I help you?"

"Yes" the man in black responded with a slight European accent said. "Are you Rabbi Duvin?"

"Yes," David said, as he straightened up and turned to him, "I'm Rabbi Duvin and you are?"

"I'm Rabbi Luria," the young man replied as he extended his hand. "I'm Rabbi Yehuda Luria and I hope we can be friends."

"Oh shit," he mumbled as he extended his hand in greetings. Just what I need a Hasid and a young one at that.

"Come into my office, I'm sure there is a way I can help you," he said as he turned around extended his arm pointing to the office entrance and bowed slightly.

The Hasid not sensing humor, smiled as well, squared his shoulders and marched into the Rabbi's study.

"Sit down, sit down," the David said gesturing to a chair positioned opposite his desk.

He scratched his chin and said, "Rabbi Luria, my first name is David and yours is?"

"Yudah", the young man answered, "Yuda Luria."

David smiled and said, "I get it. It's a nickname, short for Yehuda. So, you're Achka/sefarad?"

"I'm sorry rabbi," the Hasid said quietly, "I don't understand."

"Ashka/sefarad," David replied with a smile, (why is he here? What does he want?)

"Your first name is western European, and your family name is Sephardic so I called you ashke/sephared. Just a joke."

Yudah's face lit up with a smile. "I like jokes," he said as he reached into his jacket pocket and removed a pack of cigarettes. "Do you mind if I smoke?"

"Actually, yes, I do. This is a no smoking environment. We don't smoke in shul." He must be in his late twenties. Probably already has a couple of kids.

"Oh, sorry," he replied as he returned the packet to his pocket. "You play the drums?"

"Yes, mostly when I need to let off some steam." Thin beard, but a nice face. Yes, he seems pleasant enough.

"I get that way sometimes too," he said as he shifted slightly in his chair, "but then I study Psalms." he mumbled as he removed his hat placing it on the desk revealing a head with thinning hair under a simple black yarmulke.

"Oy" he thought, "he wants to show off his piety."

Yudah stood up and walked over to the bookshelves. The bookcase was close to seven feet high. He stood about 5"6. He raised his toes and skimmed the titles on the top of shelf. He dropped onto his heals and his hands went to the shelf that was a bit lower.

"This is kind of rude," David thought.

He ran his fingers over the spine of the books on the third shelf. He paused and reached out and grabbed a well- used book.

"That's my Mekilta."

Yudah opened it noticing the markings around some of the words on the pages.

 "Yours?" he asked.

"Yes, mine."

"Your comments?"

"Yes, my comments."

He brought the book to his lips and carefully replaced it on the shelf. He dropped to one knee and scanned the books on the shelf below. He removed another book opened it again browsing the written comments in the margins.

"You studied Tanya and you are not a Hasid."

"I study Judaica," David replied. "History, Law, philosophy and kabbalah."

"You are a scholar?"

"No, I'm just a student."

"What are you studying now?"

"Zohar, have you studied Zohar?"

"No, it says in the Talmud that one cannot study kabbalah until they are forty. I'm just twenty-nine."

That's not what it says in the Talmud, he thought. It says one must be a person who understands oneself. Enough of this. "Yudah," David said with a smile. "What brings you to our little town?"

"Oh," he said smiling, "I thought it might be a good idea, a real mitzvah, if I opened a library."

"That's very nice," David replied, "but I think we have enough of a library to service our community in this building. You wouldn't be thinking of starting another synagogue, would you?"

"Of course not, Rabbi, I just thought maybe a library where I could teach a few classes".

"Is this your first posting?" David asked.

Yudah smiled and nodded affirmatively.

Rrrrrrrng

"I'm sorry Yudah, I've been expecting this call. It was a pleasure meeting you. I look forward to seeing you again, could you," he said as he picked up the phone and motioned to the door. "Could you."

"Of course, rabbi, we'll meet again, very soon. I'm so glad to have met you. Next time I'll call for an appointment." He picked up his hat and placed it on his head.

"Just a minute," David said to the person on the line. "Someone's leaving. Yes, do that," he called out.. "Just call my secretary and make an appointment."

"You're a very busy man," David heard him reply as he was exiting the office. "I'll do what you ask."

David gently returned the phone to its cradle. He stood up and shook his head from side to side. He dropped his chin and didn't move for several breathes. After a few moments he slowly raised his head to a normal position and exhaled, "Just when I thought we had turned a corner. Shit," he said. "Shit."

Hours later

Bam dddabam,ddda bam bam bam. Bam dddbam ddda bam, bam, bam.

The sounds of *Oh Come All Ye Faithful.* were barely heard as Rachel's phone continued to sound.

Bam! DdBAM, dda Bam, Bam Bam!

Oh come all yea faithful….

Bam, Bam ! Whew, that was tiring, David said to himself as he wiped the sweat off his forehead.

Oh come all yeah Faithful,

"Ok, Rachel, I hear you," he panted. I'm coming, I'm coming. "

"David? David? Where are you? Dinner's been on the table for an hour and I've been calling and calling, and you weren't picking up."

"I'm sorry, darling, I've had a last-minute crisis and had to stay in the office. And, I think I'm going to be stuck here for a while, at least, (deep sigh) until I get everything straightened out."

"Do you want to talk about it?"

"Not at the moment," he responded. "It's, it's," he hesitated. "I need to work through something. Once I do, I'll come home. And yes, we'll talk about it. Just not right now, I have too much to consider. I'm sorry, but I don't know how long I'll be here." Bdam.

"Okay, I hear the drum. I understand work sometimes interferes with life. Just don't fret too much. I'll leave something for you in the fridge."

"Thank you dear," he replied in a distant voice, as he hung up.

Bam, dda bam, dda Bam, Bam, Bam!

The COOKING CLASS

"A few of my friends will be joining us this afternoon." Diane said as she slipped a "Go Mets" apron over her head. Their names are Madge and Karen. Madge and I grew up together, Karen moved here after she got married maybe ten years ago. Her husband works for a Moving company. Likes to watch football and play cards. When the card game starts, she usually comes over here and we drink a beer and watch the soaps. Madge is a single mother. The marriage just didn't work out. I think she had him as a waz-bund for a while and…

"Waz-bund?" Rachel asked.

"Was bund," she repeated slowly as she opened the pantry and began to remove the necessary objects for baking.

"Yeah," she continued, "he wasn't much of a husband and wazn't around very often, and then one day he just told her he had found a twenty something. I saw a picture of her once, she looked more like an almost twenty something.

Anyway, Karen got the house and takes care of Joey junior. He's a good kid. She's a good mom. She started a referral business from the house and is making a good living. What do you got in that bag?" She said pointing to the one which Rachel was carrying.

"This is heavy," she said as she plunked the bag on the kitchen table." I bought some extra things and I thought we could try to make rugelach."

"I love rugelach"

"It's not that different from a good babka, we just have to change the shape. I brought enough raisons and chocolate for an army. If we don't like them, we can give them to the kids at religious school."

"Ha!" Diane said, with a snicker, "you're bad, rebbetzin, a bad rebbitzen.

"What did I tell you about that word?" Rachel responded with a smile.

"Just kidden, just kidden," was the reply.

"Well, I'm looking forward to meeting them. I need to get out more, and this is better than it's been for me in years."

She hesitated and put a finger to her lips. "I only hope it continues," she whispered.

Diane moved closer. Rachel suddenly became aware of how much larger this woman was. "Rach? Are you okay?"

She took a deep breath, lowered her shoulders and smiled, "yes, well, not really, David had visitor a few days ago that left him unsettled," she said as she looked into Diane's eyes. "It concerned him and so it concerns me. I don't think I'm ready to talk about it. At this point it's David's problem. She shook her head, "there's nothing to talk about, at least not yet. I guess," she shrugged "I just absorbed some of my husband's anxiety. I'm sure you know what that's like."

"Yup", Diane replied as she opened the refrigerator and pulled out an ice bucket. "Now where did I leave the bitters," she mumbled as she began to move things around in the cabinet. "Ya know my husband doesn't talk. He just sits down and stares at the window. Well, at least that's the way he used to behave. He's changing. Becoming more relaxed."

"Funny you should say that," Rachel commented as she twisted on an angle,

"I don't know if I should say anything but, David used to be like that until things get very hairy. He holds everything inside until he feels overwhelmed. I'm not like that at all. If something happens I just spit it out."

"Me too," Diane added, 'but ya know what really bothers me?"

The doorbell rang. Rachel turned away from Diane and said, "Who's got the sherry?"

"Time to play," Diane said as she went to greet her friends.

"Diane?" Rachel called. "You didn't finish what really bothers you?"

Diane just smiled. "If somethings important, I have to sit Eddie down and say, "we need to talk."

Rachel stopped moving. Her eyes fluttered open and her jaw dropped. "Me too," she said in a whisper. "That's exactly what I do. And David gets all flustered. But now, he rarely gets defensive, it isn't easy for him. I wish he would be the one who says those words."

Diane looked at Rachel and softly said, "Put it away girl. It's time to play."

The Meeting at the Seminary

The desk was covered with piles of papers and the computer resting upon the desktop, was surrounded by newspaper articles, loose sheets, yellow pads filled with scribbles in Hebrew, Aramaic, Yiddish and French. A pitcher of water rested on top of a stack of loosely arranged papers. Next to it two clear juice glasses were precariously placed on a stack of papers. He reached out and grasped the pitcher and carefully poured water into each glass. He handed one to the young man sitting across from him.

"Drink up," he said. "The tap water in Manhattan is still good."

David gratefully took the glass and swallowed deeply.

The rabbi sat at his desk absent mindedly shuffling papers. He was wearing a sweater and a purple scarf was wrapped around his neck. A thin leather glove covered his left hand while the right one shuffled papers. He peered over the papers. Searching, searching.

The old circular clock most likely designed in the 1940's, was probably installed to remind past teachers, it was time to leave their books and do what they were supposed to do, teach. His little cubby of an office was probably last painted when the clock had been installed and clearly could not be repainted because what passed for walls were floor to ceiling bookcases. The once white walls could barely be seen and had aged over the years with its occupant. The shelf behind his desk revealed a window similarly stacked with journals and books and a series of pamphlets successfully limiting any natural light from entering the room.

The clock read 2:15.

"He's dead. He must be dead. I haven't heard his name spoken since I was a student and that was more than a decade ago and," he added, "that was after he retired."

"He's still alive", the older man replied. He was wearing a recently pressed but faded white shirt. A blue corduroy tie hung loosely from his neck. His hair, what remained of it, was gray. His face, thin. His hands, delicate. A simple black yarmulke covered his head.

"I'm sorry to contradict you Professor Mintz," David said. "But why do I need to find him?"

The man placed his hands on the desk and pushed down as he attempted to rise to a standing position. He hesitated stopping midway. His hand reached around and placed a hand on the small of his back, "AAh, he said with a grimace, "standing will have to wait."

He slowly lowered himself back into the chair. "David my friend," he began. He cleared his throat and sipped the water. "You called me. You told me you needed help. Needed advice and you told me why. I responded indicating your request required me to do some serious thinking. That's why I couldn't answer you on the phone. That's why I told you to come and see me the following week.

"You're here. I've thought about your problem, no," he hesitated. "Your situation." He reached up and massaged his chin, "I realize the seriousness of the situation. You are not the first person who has encountered them. This has been going on for decades and it has grievously hurt our communities."

"Thank you, Professor," David responded with a flutter in his voice. "But even if he's still alive, how could he help me? Why would he help me? We used to read his essays and books in Rabbinical School, not that they were ever required, but many of us appreciated his insights and ability to affect change."

"I needed to remember his friends, most of whom are no longer with us. I needed to recall the students who followed him around, many who became successful rabbis. "Yes," he nodded while continuing to scratch. "Things certainly would have been different if he hadn't been around. "He used to tease me about my obsession with French Provençal culture, telling me it was just because I liked wine and truffles," he mused.

"Professor, I don't want to appear to be rude, but I have to catch a train back to town. I, I have a class to teach in a little more than two hours. I can't spend as much time with you as I'd like. But tell me, why him?"

"Why is he the person with whom I need to speak and how do I find him? Hold on! What's this" David said as he picked up the water pitcher and moved it a few inches to the right. He reached under a stack of papers and slowly, carefully removed a pamphlet that had been buried. "Is this the most current directory?"

"Yes, it is," the professor said, "but you won't find his name in the directory. He resigned from the Assembly years ago."

"But, why"

"I don't know. I don't know. We weren't that close, but I think our colleague Barukh Greenberg was. He might know how he can be reached. They were and perhaps still are friends. Well, more like teacher and student. He mentored Barukh, advised him on placement, helped him develop his pulpit and marketing skills. If he's alive, Barukh would know how to reach him. He was one our stranger and more interesting students. Not as strange as his mentor. No, not at all. He didn't live with the rest of us in the dorms or on the Upper West Side. He lived downtown. In the village or Chelsea. The Professors didn't know what to make of him. The way he dressed. His long hair, no beard. No beard. And then there was the time he made the newspapers. I remember, it read something like, why is this rising star dating this Rabbinical Student. Almost got him expelled. And then there was the time he organized a boycott because every teacher kept on adding classes and the students were in class thirty hours a week."

"Professor! How do I find him?"

"Use the directory. Call Barukh. He's serving in a large congregation in Chicago. I'm sure he would take your call. Use my name or better yet, use his name. Call him. Ask him if he has his phone number and address and if he does, go to see him. Don't send him texts, emails or anything else. He's old style, one on one. Yes," he said affirmatively, "you need to find him and believe me if you can, spend time with him. It will be worth it."

"Thank you, professor", David said. "I knew I could count on you. But tell me, you still haven't answered my question. Why him?"

"Because, my boy. If anyone can help you. He's the one."

First Meeting Could it be the beginning of a beautiful friendship?
March 2018

"Thanks for the ride," David said to the Uber driver who dropped him off in front of monstrous apartment building on Alton Road in Miami Beach. As he walked toward the entrance he couldn't help but notice a strikingly attractive woman wearing a tank top and some very short shorts exiting the lobby with a cup of coffee in one hand and a leash which lead a very small dog on the other. She had long black hair, they certainly dress differently here than where I live, David said to himself as he straightened his tie and tucked his shirt into his pants.

He removed a phone from his pocket and said, "Call Rachel's mobile". It rang a few times. She picked up.

"I just want to let you know I'm here. I'm standing in front of his apartment building. Rachel, I haven't been to South Beach in years. Boy has it changed."

"How so?" she asked.

"There aren't any of those three and four stories apartment buildings anymore, the ones they used to call, "low rises". Every building is huge, modern, and fancy. Very fancy. The place is crawling with restaurants and almost every woman looks like a model".

"Well, don't get to know too many of them," she said with a chuckle. "You know why you're there."

"Don't worry," he said. "It's kind of nice here, and if I, I mean if we, can get through this," he hesitated, 'situation', maybe we could take a long weekend. We haven't been away together for years."

He walked towards the building and pushed through the revolving door and proceeded toward the concierge's desk. "Well, here I go, talk to you later."

"Later, call me when you're done."

"Will do," he said as he placed the phone in his pocket

"Wow, nice floors," he murmured. "Great colored glass windows and the chandelier rotating softly without a breeze. Striking."

"I'm here to see Rabbi Talbot", he said addressing the person at the desk.

The gentlemen behind the desk looked at him quizzically. He wore a name tag that said, "Luis". He responded to him speaking with a slight Spanish accent. "I'm sorry, we do not have any one living here named "Rabbi."

"It's a title," David answered, "Maybe you know him as Mr. Talbot? He's probably around eighty years old, that's all I can tell you about him. Apartment 36B."

"Oh, Senior, you mean, Mr. Talbot, yes we call him Sandy. You can go right up, the elevator it is over there, around the corner," he said pointing to his left.

"Thank you, "David responded, "but his name isn't Sandy."

"That's what we call him," Luis answered. "All of us call him Sandy."

"Really, well, I've come a long way to see him, even if he goes by the name of Sandy. His name is Shmuel and before that is was Samuel. He published under the name of Samuel Talbot, but his friends referred to him as Shmu," David told the concierge as he walked toward the elevator bank.

Who is Sandy and why is he going by a pseudonym? David thought as he entered the elevator and pressed the button for the thirty-sixth floor.

The door closed the elevator rose and opened at thirty-sixth. David stepped out noticing each floor contained just two apartments. Each apartment sported a mezuzah. The one on right was an elaborate piece of art. The one affixed to the doorpost on apartment thirty-six B was the classically non-descript one that has been around for more than one hundred years.

He walked to the door with the more traditional mezuzah covering and rang the bell. He waited. A few seconds later he heard movement and the sounds of the door being unlocked. It was opened by a dark haired tall Latino woman wearing tight jeans and a colorful blouse. Tanned by the sun her skinned glowed.

"Rabbi Duvin?" she said in a calm and measured voice. "Please come in Sandy is expecting you."

He just looked at her.

"Rabbi Duvin?"

"I'm sorry," he mumbled, "I wasn't expecting the door to be opened by someone else, I apologize for staring, I was just surprised."

She smiled back at him and said, "You were staring at me. I wasn't offended. Lots of men stare at me. At least you weren't luring. Staring is okay. Luring is not. One gets used to staring, we do that as well," she said with a slight smile. "Let me take you to Sandy." She turned and began to walk down a long brightly painted hall.

"Excuse me, why do you call him Sandy?"

"Because, he asked me to," she responded. "He'll be with you in, she looked at her watch," about five minutes. He doesn't like to be disturbed when he's writing. Please," she said gesturing to a chair, "sit down, I'll bring you some refreshment."

David sat, and surveyed the room. No books! No family photos. A few remarkably interesting paintings in a room filled with shades of blue and brown. A glass wall with a door leading to a terrace filled with a lounge chair and a table that over-looked the Ocean. It was a spacious room which yielded nothing about its owner.

I suppose one could meditate or daven here, he thought.

A door which probably lead to the kitchen opened and the woman entered carrying a tray upon which were two bottles of wine sunk into ice buckets, two glasses, and several slices of different types of cheese.

"Thank you," David said, "uhm I don't know your name."

"I'm Adriana", she said as she placed the tray on the table.

"And you are his daughter? His niece? His…

"No", she said smiling, "I'm a boarder and a friend. I live here. I'm one of the women who takes care of Sandy when we're not in school."

"School?"

"Yes, I'm a Law student and I take care of Sandy."

"I'm," David reddened, "a bit confused, perhaps I shouldn't have asked."

"No, it's all right", Adriana replied smiling." I can explain."

"It will have to be another time; he's mine" a voice interrupted.

David turned to his left and saw a man of approximately eighty years old entering the room. He was thin weighing approximately one hundred and thirty pounds and stood about five feet 7 inches. His hair was grey and thinly covered about ¾ of his head. His face was clean and angular. He sported a colored Hawaiian shirt and pair of blue checked Bermuda shorts. His hands were bare of jewelry. He wore an old battered watch on his right wrist.

Reminds me of a beach bum in the 1960's, David thought. All that's missing is a battered air force or a discarded motorcycle jacket.

The man David knew of as Rabbi Talbot approached him briskly. He reached out extending his hand. "You must be David Duvin. Glad to meet you. Thank you for coming."

"Thank you for allowing me to visit, Rabbi"

"Stop! No titles here, we are colleagues. I always used to tell the rabbinical students, first names only. We are colleagues. We shouldn't need titles anyway, they're all stupid. You can call me Sandy."

"But, Ra," he stopped, "Sandy, that's not your name?"

"It is now", he chirped as he sat in the chair opposite David. He dropped his eyes and reached out with his left hand and softly touched the watch. "It is now," he murmured. "new life, new name."

He looked at the tray and the items it held and clapped his hands, "Beautiful job, Adriana my sweet. It works! It all goes together. You chose the exact wines we needed this afternoon."

My sweet? David gulped. What could be going on?

"You do like wine, don't you?"

"Yes", David replied, "I take my wines very seriously."

"Good, Kosher or real?"

"Real please", he answered with a smile.

"Good because we don't have any kosher. Just these two, a dry Bordeaux followed by an Alsace Pinot Blanc. You come highly recommended," he said as he nodded his head and gave him a once over. Very few of our colleagues come to visit or actually call," he said shaking his head a little, "let alone take a plane in order to spend some time with me. Let's try the wine, pour the wine please?"

David reached out and grasped the Pinot Blanc in his hand. He raised his eyes as he looked for Sandy's response.

"Good choice young man," he replied with a grin. If we had the Bordeaux first we would never have been able to taste the Pinot. Please," he gestured, "Pour."

"Adriana appropriately opened them some time ago in order to let them breathe. Even white wines could use a moment," he said smiling at her. "You did good kid, now get along you'll be late for class and I expect a draft of that paper on my desk before dinner."

She smiled, blew him a kiss and exited the room.

He turned back to David, "Lovely girl, keeps me smiling. We can talk as we drink."

His head isn't covered, and he is about to drink. I guess, I don't have to cover my head either. He's so informal. I feel I can talk to him. He lifted his glass and brought it to his lips. He closed his eyes and sipped, drawing it into the back of his mouth and inhaled bringing in a little air. "This wine is fantastic! Really good sir."

"In this climate the whites stay longer. It's just difficult to find the one's you want. I have an acquaintance who drives people's cars back and forth from New

York. Whenever he goes, he picks up and delivers what I want. Now," Sandy said as he nibbled on some cheese. "Why are you here and how can I help?"

I'M ON A HIGH

She was standing at the cutting board with a knife in her hands when her phone began to pound out the words of *Come All Ye Faithful*. It startled her. It was almost dinner time and very few people had the number and those who did, knew that at 5pm during the week she was usually occupied preparing dinner or working on a project. It took her three repetitions of the verse before she was able to clean her hands and pick it up. It was David.

"Hi hon, I'm at the airport."

"How was your meeting?" She asked in an excited tone.

"It was," he hesitated. "Great!! It was great! He was great! I can't wait to get home and tell you all about the meeting. I feel so much more confident. We can beat this guy."

Rachel sighed with relief, "I'm so glad, what did he tell you?"

"He told me I needed a plan, and then I talked, and he listened, and we drank wine, really good wine, and he asked questions and then he told me I already had a plan I just didn't know it. We made a list, and I have a lot to do, but it will be successful, I ...

"David, darling, slow down, you're ...

"I'm on a roll. I 'm on a high. I can't wait to be home., Oh there's the gate. Gotta go. Don't wait up. We'll talk tomorrow, Kiss the kid for me. I'll be home late tonight and need to be out of the house very early tomorrow morning. We'll catch up over dinner. By."

Rachel hung up the phone and froze. After a few moments she took a deep breathe and continued to chop the vegetables in front of her. "I'm glad you're excited hon," she said. "But we have to talk."

First Thrust: THE BAKERY

The morning began as it always did. Up at 5:30 in the store by 6:00 AM and baking by 6:30. The ovens had been scoured the night before, as usual. The floor had been washed, and all the preparations for the following day had been completed, as usual. The breads looked beautiful as usual, the rolls smelled outstanding, as usual and the cookies and the cakes would be ready by 10.

The construction workers arrived on time at 7. Always on time. Their coffee and buttered roles were waiting. Mrs. Petrone arrived punctually at 7:45 and her biscotti had been placed on the little table by the door and wrapped just the way she liked them. He wasn't exactly certain what she did with two dozen Biscotti every Monday, Wednesday and Thursday. But he did recall seeing the ancient women sitting in the park draped in the same black shawl. Perhaps she gave them to the young women who were taking their young children to school or she fed them to the squirrels. She was always polite, and the money, as little as it was, never hurt.

The morning began as it always did but at 8:15 everything changed. The rabbi walked in. He had heard him speak at a church a few weeks ago but they had never spoken. "Wonder what he wants," Angelo thought.

"Good morning Mr. Scarlati, I'm Rabbi…"

"I know who you are rabbi, I heard you speak about interfaith cooperation at St. Anthony's a few weeks ago. Welcome to my store."

David, walked around the store, eyeing the counters, the pastries, breads, and cakes that were harmoniously displayed. "Everything smells wonderful," he said.

He smiled, "Thank you, here," he said, as he reached into a cabinet and withdrew a small cream puff. "It's a gift, I love making cream puffs."

David reached out and accepted the gift. He paused, he didn't eat sweets but knew it would be inappropriate to say, "I'll save it for later." He popped it in his mouth and then replied with a smile, "It's very good. Delicious!"

Mr. Scarlati beamed and said, "What can I get you, Rabbi?"

"Well, actually, I'm not here as a customer, but, let's say, (he hesitated) I'm here in the interests of interfaith cooperation. I have an idea how you and my synagogue community could mutually benefit, and I wanted to learn if you would be interested."

Mr. Scarlati's expression changed. This was business. He leaned forward placing his hands of the counter. Still smiling but obviously extremely cautious, he said, "I'm listening."

"It's really simple, do you know what a challah is?"

He nodded, "yes, it's a Jewish bread. You can make it with eggs or without. Sometimes it's round and has raisons and maybe a little honey, but most of the time it's more loaf shaped. I grew up in Brooklyn."

David smiled and then said, "I've never done any business, and I'm really very bad with numbers, so let me just share my idea and if you like it. We can work out the numbers to your satisfaction later."

"Go ahead," he nodded. "I'm all ears."

"I want every member of my community and then some to receive a challah every Friday. At least for the next few months. If this is successful I want to make this a community activity. I have a bunch of women who can do it. I want them to bring their children, from about 10 years old through high school and to teach them how to bake. If any members of your church wished to join us. That would be fine and I", David took a breath and continued, "I want them to bake it here under your supervision."

Scarlati, shook his head slowly, his hand reaching up to touch his mustache. "And what's in it for me?"

"A couple of things. First, I'll pay for the materials, my people will do the cleanup, up to your," he looked around, "very serious standards. In addition, I want you to prepare pastries under my supervision which the synagogue will buy from you on a regular basis. After religious services on Friday evening we have what's called an 'Oneg Shabbat' and we serve coffee, tea, fruit and sweets."

"In addition, you get publicity, and you also, though I can't promise, should get a heck of a lot of new customers. Right now, my people probably aren't buying your breads and pastries because they shop at the supermarket. But I think if they are in your store and saw your merchandise that would change. What do you think?"

"He nodded his head, "you said you would pay for the supplies?

"I did."

"For how long?"

"Let's just say for the first month and then we will discuss it again."

"Okay, I'll work up a budget and call you when I have the numbers. How many tchallahs do we need to bake for the first batch and how big do they have to be?"

"Challah's" with an "H" not a "T", he said correcting him. "About eight inches long 3-4 inches high and let's say we start with two hundred."

"Good number," he said with a big smile as he watched the rabbi turn and walked towards the door.

"All I have to do," David said to himself, "is find and convince the crew to give us one night a week for four nights next month and to find the money. Piece of cake, no, he said with a smile, "piece of bread."

She heard him locking the front door and turned over to look at the clock beside the bed. It was almost 9:15 in the morning. Even though he told her we would be home late and had to leave early and probably wouldn't go to the office until much later in the day, returning at this hour was extremely unusual. She remembered hearing him when he unlocked the door last night. He had not wanted to disturb her and had slept in the guest room, not that it mattered, she slept very poorly last night, if at all.

It was President's day, a school holiday and Ari was still sleeping.

She turned on the light, and groggily walked toward the bathroom to wash her face. The light was on in the kitchen. She reached for a brush and quickly straightened her hair. It was chilly outside, and the house was old and poorly insulated. She entered the bathroom and removed the robe which was hanging on a hook. She pulled it close and carefully knotted it, so it would remain closed. She quickly freshened up and after wiping her eyes walked toward the kitchen. His head was in the refrigerator.

"David you're home", she said as wrapped herself around him and pulled him close.

"Umph, wait a second, I need to eat. Give me a moment," he muttered as he reached into the refrigerator and removed a plate wrapped in cellophane.

"I need to put something in my mouth. All I've had to eat in the past fourteen hours was a pastry. I'm starving, could you open the Cote de Rhone that's on the shelf next to the cabinet?"

"David! It's 9 o'clock in the morning!"

"I've seen the French do it, and right now it will be better than coffee."

"I know where it is silly," she said with a smile. "Stuff your mouth, I see you found the cheese sandwich on the second shelf. I'll open the wine and wait til you can speak."

"Okay, sure, mmmm, that's good. There wasn't a thing on the plane I could eat. It was either meat or something fried and I couldn't eat last night, my stomach was upset, and I was too hopped up because of my meeting with Sandy. How can people, mmmm, this is good," he said as he took another bite, "eat airplane food."

"Slow down darling", she said as she handed him the wine. "I'll wait."

"Can't wait," he answered between mouthfuls. "I know I sound hyper but barely slept last night. I was over stimulated from my time with him. So many ideas it, He was amazing! There was a lot going on in his apartment which I didn't understand, some of it was, well it made me feel a bit uncomfortable, but he treated me richly. He listened, and we spoke, and I felt I had known him my entire life. We drank some excellent wine, and, you know, some of the older Cantors when asked about him referred to him as, "not like the others." Mmm, I needed this sandwich. Thank you darling."

"Not a problem," she smirked. "What did he say about our situation? Can he help? Did he help? Is he coming to help us?"

"Slow down," gulp, "slow down Rach. He told me we needed a plan and he told me most of it I had already figured out. I told him about your baking group and he smiled and asked me, if I knew what would be the first thing he would do if he was trying to establish himself in our community?"

"Well," I said, "I would visit everyone in the hospital."

"But you're already doing that David?"

"Exactly, I'm already doing that."

"What else could he do to establish a presence?"

"He could deliver challot to all of our members"

"Yes!" He said his voice rising.

"Ssshhh you'll wake the kid."

"Oh, right, yes," he whispered smiling. "And what are you doing with your women? Why we're oooh," she said as her hand went to cover her lips.

"Right, exactly. We need a plan and all we have to do is anticipate his next steps. We just have to cover all of the bases before he gets up to bat."

"David, I'm getting excited. We could make this work, I can expand the group…"

"And," she said, "we could engage the pre b'nai mitzvah and teens."

"And," he added, "if we do this right we can grab the juniors in high school and call it "community service."

"We can do a lot more. But (he burped), right now I need to calm down and then tomorrow I need to make a few calls and I have to try to see a few people."

"I think I know how to calm you down" Rachel said with a smile, "it might take a longtime but come to bed, I'll see what I can do. Let me help you with your coat. What's this?" she asked. "Where did you get the pastry?"

"Oh," he said with a full mouth. "I had a meeting with Mr. Scarlati the baker this morning. He makes quite a creampuff."

RABBI BUSINESS

"Good morning B&D Insurance company, this is Marjorie speaking, how can I be of service?"

"I'd like to speak with Martin Ezring please."

"Just a minute and I'll connect you. Who should I say is calling?"

"Rabbi Duvin."

"Thank you, sir. I'll put you through."

Rrrrrrng

"Hello this is Martin speaking"

"Good morning Martin, its Rabbi Duvin."

"Rabbi! Rabbi? What a surprise. What can I do for you?"

"I'd like you to go to see Mr. Scarlati, the baker in town. Do you know his shop?"

"Well, I've never been inside but I know where it is, why?"

"I want you to tell him, I sent you and I'd like you to find out what type of insurance he has. I'm planning on running a program in the Bakery which might involve both adults and children and I want to make sure he is well insured. Can you do that?"

"Why sure. My pleasure. I'll stop by there tomorrow on the way to work. I can take a later train."

"Great, thank you and by the way, Sasha's a great kid."

"Thanks rabbi."

A FEW DAYS LATER

Rrrrrrrrng

"Good morning Temple Beth Tzouris, Shirley speaking."

"This is Frank Scarlati, the baker. I'd like to speak with the Rabbi."

"He just walked in, I'll connect you."

"Rabbi? Rabbbbbi, telephone."

"Shirley, Shirley, you don't have to yell. I told you use the buttons."

"Rabbi, there's a Frank Scarlati on the phone for you."

"Thank you, Shirley," he said, "Try whispering. I told you, use the buttons."

David picked up the phone, "Good morning Mr. Scarlati."

"Rabbi, please call me Frank."

"My pleasure and Frank please call me David."

"Don't think I can do that, you're a rabbi."

"Give it a shot. I promise it won't hurt."

"Okay, Okay, I'll try. Your guy came by yesterday and this morning he called me and told me he can offer me a better policy, more insurance for less money. Can I trust him?"

"He's a member of my congregation and I assume he is honest. Why don't you ask him to send me a copy of the policy and why don't you drop off a copy of what you are currently using, and I'll compare them. How does that sound?"

"It sounds great! I think I'm gonna enjoy working with you."

"I hope so, now send me the estimate."

THAT EVENING

"Really Rachel?"

"David we need to talk."

"Rachel," David said. "Can't this wait?"

"No, David, it can't."

"But I'm so hopped up planning. I have a lot to do if I'm going to overcome this, this situation. And it's 9 o'clock in the evening. Can't this wait til tomorrow,?" he said as he poured himself a glass of wine.

"That's one of the reasons we need to speak," she said as she reached out and took the glass out of his hand. "You're drinking too much."

"No, I'm not," he said. "Just a glass or two every evening."

"More like four glasses which is as I count, a bottle every evening."

David slumped, "That much?" he asked.

She nodded affirmatively.

"It's the pressure, I have to succeed. The shul is such a mess and I'm way over my head. You know if I'm not successful, the downside will be more difficult."

"Yes, I know what you're going through. And I know how hard you are trying to make this work and you know I'm being as supportive as I can but," she hesitated. "You haven't exactly had much time for me these past few weeks or is it months, I don't know anymore."

"Know what?"

"Oh, when you'll be around, when we will have time to really spend some time together. The usual things. I guess you want me to fade into the shadows until I'm needed, like the cooking class."

"Rachel!" he said as he moved forward to approach her. "You know that's not true."

"When was the last time you asked me what I was doing? What I was feeling?" she replied as she retreated from his arms.

His arms fell to his sides. He dropped his chin his eyes looking at the floor. He moved from side to side as he worked at taking in what he had just heard.

"I'm sorry," he said. "You're right. I have been ignoring you. What have I missed?"

Rachel grinned, "You might want to sit down for this one. And even though you might want the wine, please don't reach for it."

David nodded glumly and sat.

"I have two things to say. First, people, in your congregation have been wanting to invite us to their homes. Social invites are usually for Saturday nights. As it stands right now, since we're observant, six months out of the year we can't make it until after 8pm and If its summer time 9:30."

David nodded.

"If you want us to have a social life in this community, if you really want us to make friends and you know how I feel about that, then we need to begin to travel on Shabbat."

"What!"

"We have to go to their homes when they invite us. Don't worry they know enough to ask us what we will eat." But you have to decide what you really want. I think if we accepted social invitations you might be able to encourage some of them to take your classes, come to services you know, the Jewish stuff."

David listened and nodded. "You have a point. I don't have to decide right away let me think about it," David said as he started to rise.

"Wait a minute!" Rachel said, "we're not finished. I'm bored. Very bored. So bored that last week I went to the city and visited galleries looking for work and, was offered a job selling Art in a gallery."

"Why that's great!" David said weakly.

"Yes and no," she replied reaching out and placing an arm on his shoulder. "It means I have to work weekends. Saturday and Sunday afternoons from 1-5pm".

"But its….."

She covered his mouth with her hand, "hush."

"I know. I've never done something like this before; but if I don't, I think I'll go batty. I figured it out, we can still have people over on Friday evenings. I can go to shul with you in the morning, but I'll leave at 11. You'll have to take Ari home after services and I'll be home by 7, unless we have a dinner engagement. It's up to you darling. I won't do this without your consent and I know how difficult making this type of decision is. Its your choice. We don't have to have friends if you don't want to, but I still need to get out of this town on a regular basis."

David looked up at her. "could you find a job where you don't have to work on Shabbat?"

She shook her head. "Not in the Art world."

"Are you finished," he asked. "Is there anything else?"

"No, she replied. "that's it."

"I, I, I need to think about this." He just looked at her. "You know I love you and want you to be happy. But what your asking is huge! It will disrupt my life, our life," he quickly added. "Rachel, I'm glad you forced me into this conversation. I'm sorry I wasn't more sensitive to this before. I need to think this through. I need some time. Is that okay?"

She smiled at him. "It's more than okay."

First Parry

"I made a deal with the Baker." David said. "He'll let us use his shop and I will allow him to cater dairy events and Ongei Shabbats in the synagogue."

"Rabbi, what's an Ongei?"

Oh, sorry. It's the plural of "oneg". It the plural form of the work "joy.",

Leonard looked at Maddie and shrugged his shoulders, "Keeping the kitchen Kosher is the rabbi's responsibility. It's his right. That's why you called a meeting, to tell us what you could have told us on the phone?"

"No, this was just a brief progress report because we have a problem and I need your help." David said as he looked at each of them. "And this is a problem I wanted to "discuss with both of you in private. I need help in two areas, first the problem, or let's just call it a situation which, if we don't handle properly, will most likely put us out of business. The second item directly relates to the "situation" but requires immediate assistance."

Maddy glanced at Leonard, he shrugged his shoulders. "Look, rabbi we're very busy.

"I said this is important. Do you think I would have insisted on this meeting and schlepped into the city because I wanted to schmooze with you? This isn't something like the school where I more or less fell into a successful strategy. This is serious.

Let me ask you a question, what do you know about a certain sect of Hasidism, that has tefillin trucks, is on most college campuses and organizes massive events on Jewish holidays like Chanukah where they fight with the local officials until they are allowed to erect a giant Chanukah Menorah?"

"They seem like nice people," Maddie said, "and they do tremendous outreach all over the world."

"Yes," David said as he shook his head. "You're right they are all very nice people and they reach out to college students and feed them and drink with them and try to bring them closer to Judaism. Not our Judaism. Their Judaism."

"Sooo," Maddie said.

"Have either of you ever been inside one of their synagogues?"

Both Leonard and Maddie shook their heads.

"Well, if you ever did, you would notice, no you wouldn't notice something special, but you might wonder why an Israeli flag is not displayed in their synagogue."

"It's not," Leonard asked quizzically?

"No" David continued. "It's because they don't acknowledge Israel as a legitimate state. When our children get involved with them, that's one of the things they are taught." He shook his head, "I'm not getting through, let me put it another way."

"Who would you rather have your children marry? A Chasid or one of the Clintons"?

"That's very funny," Maddie said, "but I still don't understand where you are going with this."

"Just think about it. You would have a lot in common with the Clintons. You both like theater and art and music. If they were careful you could eat in their home and they could certainly eat in your home. You support charities as do they. You would possibly like their friends and they would similarly enjoy yours.

Now, if your children, no Maddie, your daughter married a Hasid. She would have to shave her head, could never go the beach with you if Men were present. If her husband was very flexible she might not have to wear a wig, and possibly could eat in your home if you made special, very special arrangements, but forget about going out to dinner in the restaurants you currently enjoy. And forget about her children ever reading Shakespeare, or Melville, or any real literature, or even going to the Movies."

He paused and took a breath and looked at them. They were following his line of reasoning but not far enough.

"I know you're wondering why is the rabbi providing me with all this interesting information? You're probably thinking this would make a great adult education course. But let me tell you what happens when one of these very nice people moves into your community. They come to the rabbi and introduce themselves and inform he or she that they will be opening a library. A library, not a synagogue. But it so happens that when it's time to pray the evening service or if the library is open on Friday or Saturday, they will just happen to hold services, so they can pray. And everyone who is visited in the hospital, nursing home, or who has birthday, or whom they meet on the street will be invited.

And a few days later those who attended will be visited and asked to support the religious school teacher whom they have just hired. Probably the Rabbi's wife, also a very nice person. And since this is going to be a free religious school, the rabbi needs financial support. And this is just the beginning. And this is what is about to happen in our community. And that is why I called this meeting."

"Free religious school?" Leonard said, "it will undermine our membership."

"Free b'nai mitzvah?" Maddie commented nodding her head, "that could impact on our newly developing youth program and Hebrew High school."

"I wish I wasn't smiling," David said, "but you're beginning to understand. This," he sighed, "brings me to the second item. Last week I went to one of my legendary teachers and asked him, how to respond to what I know is going to occur. He helped me devise a strategy and the first step in this strategy is the challah baking effort. I told Mr. Scarlati, the baker, that we would cover the costs of the materials for the first three months, after which, if the program was successful, we would revisit it."

Leonard looked at David, smiled and said, "And you want us to cover the costs."

"It's not exactly in the budget, David responded. "Here's the bill."

Leonard reached out and accepted the piece of paper. He scrutinized it and sighed. "It's really not that much, Maddie. I'll take care of the first month, Maddie" he said looking at her, "she'll take the second and we will split the third."

David breathed a sigh of relief. "Thank you. Both of you. If this is successful it will only be a deterrent. There are a number of entry points that will need to be addressed. I have an idea, I think it will work, but it will require Board approval and engagement. Can I have thirty minutes at next week's Board meeting?"

Maddie, stopped taping her pen, "What will the topic be?'

David, sighed and scratched his head, "I have an idea. It's pretty much off the normal spectrum. I think it should work. I shared it with my mentor and he encouraged me to share it with the Board. I've been thinking about this for years but could never get the support I needed. Now that I've gained your trust, that is, until I mess up and lose it," he said with a smile, "if it is going to work it could work here and put our little community on the map. Originally, I was hoping to bring this up and to begin discussion in a few months; but because of our new neighbor," he shrugged, "I think it's time we addressed moved up the agenda."

"Rabbi?" Maddie repeated, "what will the topic be?"

"What? Oh, sorry, the topic will be retaining our post b'nai mitzvah children."

The not so Coffee Klatch

"Your house looks just like my house," Madge said as she entered Rachel's home and began to casually look around. "Only your house has more books," she said as she handed Rachel her coat.

"Not surprising," Diane quipped as she followed Madge and removed her jacket.

"Yup," Karen quipped bringing up the rear. "We used to wonder what would happen if one of our husbands came home late and was a little bit soused and drove into the wrong driveway and got into the bed with wrong woman."

"We decided, that it probably wouldn't have mattered," Diane added. "They would just usually fall into bed in a stupor and maybe get a little bit horny in the morning."

"Then, they'd be too embarrassed to stay around. They'd open their eyes suddenly realize the colors or the furniture were different, and they would scoot out hoping we were still in that deep womanly sleep, that they all think we need in the morning." Madge added with a smirk.

"Sounds like you've rehearsed that one," Rachel said meekly. "Welcome to my/our home. This is the first time we've had guests."

"Humus, olives, and pita, fabulous." Diane said as she walked into the living room and sat on the couch.

"First time for me to be invited to the rebbetz...whoops sorry Rach, to the Rabbi's home."

"It's okay," she responded with a smile, "I can handle it from the three of you. Make yourselves comfortable I made a pitcher of gin and tonic. Just something to help us get through a rainy Wednesday."

"Diane poured herself a glass and sipped. "not bad, I kinda like it. Not too sweet, not too sour. Just right," she said with a smile as she raised her glass. "Here's to Rach! If it weren't for her, we wouldn't have Talmud night."

"Certainly changed, Mikey," Karen replied raising her glass. "After fifteen years he has finally begun to clean the sink after shaving."

"Ronnie has learned to sit on the toilet when he pees." Madge added.

"I got one better, my Eddie took me to a wine tasting last week," Diane added. "All because of Talmud night. And, she added as she took another sip, "he showers and shaves before he wakes me up in the morning." She giggled. "I gotta say, we've become a lot closer in the last few months since he began going to that class."

"Me too," Madge added.

"Me three," Karen giggled. "Here's to Rach!" Karen said raising her glass.

Rachel poured herself a drink and sat on one of the dining room chairs she had brought into the living room. "I have to say," she said as she looked into the eyes of the women surrounding her. She started again, "I have to say, who would have thought a baking group would have so much fun?"

"Are we going to make hammantashen today?" Madge asked.

Rachel cleared her throat and replied. "Yes, but we need to make two different batches."

"Ya mean prune and apricot?" Diane asked.

"No," she replied. I mean one for the children and a special one filled with brandy and sherry for the husbands."

"oooh, Karen replied with a giggle, "was Jewish living this much fun when you were growing up?"

"No, actually, my childhood was very controlled and monitored. It was fun on holidays and sometimes just being with family. My mother liked to get my father to let down his barriers, so she would make them for my father and never tell him what was in it." Rachel said with a smile. "But it was David who filled almost everything with joy."

"And then they had their own Talmud night!" Diane added with a laugh.

"Pass the pita, pass the pita," someone said.

Talmud Class 1 week before Purim

David walked into the congregation's Board room holding a handful of papers. The lights were already on. "Some of the group must have arrived early." He opened the door. He looked at the room. "Oh my God!" he said, "this is just as I imagined it. Rachel and crew, I love all of you."

There were at least twenty-five people in the room. And the room, it was no longer the long narrow dark Board room. It had been transformed into a charming dining room, sporting placemats and cheese and crudité plates, laid out in the center of the table. Each placemat hosted a paper plate, knives and forks. A glass wine glass was strategically placed on the upper right-hand corner.

"My class, how we've grown," he said as he walked towards his seat at the head of the table. "Who's new?" he asked.

Two gentlemen sitting in the back timidly raised their hands.

"And you are?" he asked.

The overweight slightly bald man sporting a wildly growing gray beard wearing overalls raised his hand and said, "People call me "Spidey"

"Spidey? "

"Yes, it's a long story."

David looked at the man. He could have been in his early fifties, about five feet nine inches and at least thirty pounds overweight. "I don't mind calling you "Spidey," but just for the record, "Spidey," he said. Would you mind telling me your birth name?"

"No, not at all," he glanced at the people sitting at the table. "Most of the people here are used to calling me Spidey," he replied with somewhat bashfully. My name is Arthur. My mother was from Tennessee and where they have different naming traditions. My true name is Arthursue.."

Someone snickered.

"Okay, er, Arth… I mean Spidey," David replied, "Glad to have you with us. But how did you find us?"

"I brought him," Mikey said. "We kind of overlapped in high school, and my office uses him for copy editing."

"Really?" David responded thoughtfully. "Glad you're with us. Do you live in the neighborhood?"

"No, actually I live in the next town just over the river, but I've been coming to Friday night services. The music called me."

"Really," David responded. "Welcome" he said warmly. "Mikey," he said with a smile, you should be on the Board."

"I am on the Board, Rabbi, and I brought him because I thought if he enjoyed your class, well, Spidey's single and I thought if he came to class and got more involved it might, you know help his social life."

"Mikey," David said. "I had no idea you sat on the Board. We study together why didn't you tell me?"

Mikey dropped his gaze along with his voice. He looked around. "I didn't want the guys to know I was involved. You know what I mean."

David nodded. "Yes," he responded. "I guess I do."

"And who are you," he said pointing to a thin man of roughly the same age, He was dressed like he worked in a clothing store. Well pressed pants, a perfectly tied solid colored tie.

"You can call me Bob."

"Noodles," someone called out. "It's Noodles from around the cornah?"

"Uhm," David said, "should I call you Bob or would you prefer "Noodles" since apparently, you have a nickname?"

"Bob/Noodles," shrugged his shoulder. "I'm fluid. You can call me what you want."

"Okay," David said as he sat. "First let's fill our cups and say the appropriate blessing. Do I have any volunteers?" He looked around, "Eddie! I knew you would volunteer."

"But I didn't, Rabbi."

"Of course, you did. I know you know it and it's the short one. And we will help you, come on everyone glasses up and being…" Baruch Ata…Excellent! By the way what are we drinking?"

"Cote de Beaune Burgundy," Mikey answered. I got it from my cousin. He donated a case because he said having me in synagogue, I didn't tell him I was on the Board," he whispered, "would keep the crime rate down."

Everyone chuckled

"Well," David said, "hold onto your hats this evening we are going to be introduced to a volume in the Talmud called, Megillah and among other things it has to do with scrolls, megillot."

"Esther," someone offered.

"Yes," he replied ". But there are five scrolls that are read on festival or fast days and the text addresses a lot more than that. But this evening we are going to learn many things, one of which being why did the rabbis in the Talmud ask whether or not Esther kept kosher while she was in Achashverous's Harem and what did she do if he desired to consummate the relationship?"

Interlude

"Rabbi," Shirley said, "Rabbi Luria is on the phone. What should I tell him?"

David, paused and looking up from the books that filled his desk. His secretary who was obviously uncomfortable with the caller.

"I told him you were studying, and I didn't know if you could be interrupted."

"That's very thoughtful of you Shirley," he said as he shook his head and took a deep breathe. "This is one call I really have to take and Shirley, he's really a very nice person and," he smacked his lips, "he most likely will be visiting and studying with me on a somewhat regular basis."

"I don't like the way, he speaks and the way he dresses," she said.

"Well," David answered, "tell him to hold and I'll explain away your fears."

"Okay, Rabbi," she said as she exited his office and returned to her desk.

He noticed the red light on his phone was flashing as Shirley returned.

"He's dressed the way Polish gentlemen dressed about three hundred plus years ago. That's because the man or men who started the Movement in which he was raised, dressed in that manner. It's a sign of identification and of tradition. The reason his English is so heavily accented is because his first language, the language his parents and their friends and their community speak at home, in school and in business, is Yiddish. Actually," David continued, "and we can speak more about this later, but, don't worry. He is a nice young man. Oh? The phone, tell him I'll be right there."

David returned to his office. He took a deep breath and said to himself. "I'm ready for this. I anticipated this. I'm ready." He picked up the phone, "Yudah, Yudah, how are you?" he said in a cheerful voice.

"I'm fine, thank you Rabbi. I'm fine," the voice on the other end of the line answered.

"To what do I owe the honor of this call?" David responded.

"My honor, rabbi. I was just following up on our last meeting and was wondering if you were serious about our *leoining* together?"

"Yudah, my friend, it will be my pleasure for us to study together. What would you like to study?"

"Well," he stumbled. I thought you could choose, maybe some Gemarra? Or some Tanya."

"Talmud or Hasidic mysticism, sounds very interesting. I study Talmud somewhat regularly," he answered. "But I haven't studied Tanya for at least a decade. Yudah, I think we should do this differently. Why don't we meet on a regular basis and each bring a text we wish to teach? You will teach me, and I will teach you and then we can learn about our differences. What do you think?"

"I'm flattered Rabbi. That sounds like a very interesting idea. What would you teach Rabbi?"

"Me? I was more of a Bible student. I will teach some Bible," David replied.

"Bible? Isn't that for women?"

"Yudah, I know you were raised in an education system, where the boys and girls learned separately. If I remember correctly the girls studied Bible and the boys studied Talmud, right?"

"Yes, that's how we learned."

"Well, don't you agree the Bible is holier than the Talmud?"

"Of course, it is."

"So, you wouldn't mind studying Bible with me, would you?"

"No, I guess not," was the grudging answer.

"Good," David replied. "And what would you like to teach me?"

"Well, Yudah replied. There is Tosophos in the first chapter of Sanhedrin, that I think is interesting. It focuses on lucky and unlucky numbers. Have you studied Tosphos before?"

"He's testing me," he thought. "I seem to remember that the Tosaphot were French and German Talmudic scholars who lived between the 10th -12th centuries. Is that correct?"

"I'm not certain, rabbi about the dates, but they did live in France and Germany."

"Fine, we have a deal. Come see me Wednesday morning say 10 AM?"

David carefully placed the phone in its carriage. He raised his hand and gently, thoughtfully placed in upon his desk. His fingers gently moved in a circle. And now it begins, he said to himself. Sandy, I hope you're right.

Thursday evening

He locked the door the synagogue and began to walk home. It was brisk, and snow was in the air. The Talmud class had been a major success and after drinking one glass of wine, he was alert and feeling alive.

"Good class, good group, can't wait til next week. I'll bring the blessings after meals booklet and we'll begin to learn how to recite the grace after meals. No, I think it would be preferable if we began, not at the beginning, it will put people off. Aaaah, I've got it. In the middle of the class, after the first glass of wine, I'll begin to sing a niggun. Most of them won't exactly know that a niggun is a song without words. They'll think it's a drinking song and will join me. Aaah, I can see the smiles on their faces, and it will lift them up."

Bobbie Kantor seems to be less angry than usual. Arthur Smilowitz told me he brought flowers home for Shabbat and his wife loved it. He smiled as he turned the corner, "the children and their parents are enjoying the school. Friday night attendance continues to increase. I'm not certain why this is happening but whatever I'm doing seems to work. I'm so happy."

It was just a short walk, a block and a half to the very very middle-class house in which his family lived and the congregation owned. "It's a good think the grass has died. I'd hate to ask the house committee to take care of the lawn. They take care of their lawns and I'm supposed to take care of mine. But what if something goes wrong with my house? I can't fix my house. I don't know who to call. Then again," he mused, "there is the Yudah situation. Not a great way to refer to him. Bad term, he thought shaking his head, not appropriate. I think I should refer to him in a more rabbinic way. I'll refer to him as 'Acher.' "That feels right," he muttered.

"Acher or "that one" was how the rabbis in the Talmud referred to Elisha ben Abuya in the second century. According to the Talmud he was one of four sages who entered into a mystical moment and as result became an apostate." He smiled, "I remember attending a Hasidic wedding and the rabbi began the ceremony by reading a letter to the bride and groom wishing them well from the Lubavatcher Rebbe, a man whose been dead for nearly thirty years. And when the rabbi finished his little talk, he wished the newly wedded couple a happy, healthy and Hasidic life. Now that doesn't exactly foster Jewish unity. That certainly reflects an "acher" type attitude."

"It's not the worst house in the world," he mused. "A lot of my members live in similar dwellings. I could get used to it. It could be fixed up. Rachel would like a garden and the kid could use some swings. Maybe this Spring if things continue to work out. This isn't the worst place to raise a family," he thought as he arrived at steps leading to the front door. "I can handle this guy," he said to himself. Sandy put me on the right track. I can do this. I know I can."

He walked up the steps and opened the door. It wasn't locked. It was Thursday evening and somethings was different. He breathed in deeply. The smell of the coming Shabbat was missing and it was Thursday night. Where was the smell of tomorrow night's dinner? Where was the Shabbat spice?

"Rachel? Rachel? Are you here?"

No one was in the kitchen. He turned and went to the stairs which lead up to the bedrooms on the second floor. He hit the stairs two at a time. "Rachel? Rachel! Where are you?"

And then he heard it. A slight sound coming from the bedroom. "I'm in here David".

He hurriedly opened the door. It was dark.

"Rachel? Rachel! Where are you?"

There was a spark, and a candle was lit. The candle rested upon an end table upon which was a bottle of wine and what appeared to be slices of apples and pieces of cheese.

"What's going on?" he asked. "Where is Ari? I thought I would have smelled what you were making for tomorrow night's Shabbat dinner?"

"Sshh," she said. "He's having dinner with the Mirskys. One of my cooking class parents. I told them I needed a few hours alone with you without him."

"Why?" What about Shabbat dinner?"

"Darling, trust me it's all taken care of. I did this because I needed to get you alone for a few hours."

"Why?" he asked

"Because, dammit, I need to know everything which happened in Miami."

"Okay, okay, I get it," he said as he took of his sport jacket, removed his shoes and removed his tie.

"I wish you would torch that horrible tie," she said.

"What's wrong with it? It's clean, I've had it since I graduated," he replied as he sat on the chair opposite Rachel.

"You've had it for twenty years and it looks old," she replied with a smile. "It makes you look like an old academic with your herringbone jacket. Don't you understand that for certain people clothes make the man?"

"These people?"

"Yes, even these people." She continued, "You don't have to look like you work on Wall street. But you do need to look like you're living in the present."

"Okay," he said with a slight blush. "I'll get a new tie tomorrow."

"No, David," she replied. "I'll get you a new tie and a new sport jacket tomorrow and you will come with me. I'm free around noon. We can go the Mall."

"I", he grimaced, "you know I'm rather store phobic."

"Of course, I know that, but you can take an hour or two at lunch tomorrow and put up with me. Now what happened in Miami?"

"Didn't we already speak about this?"

"Yes," she said with a smile, "but in depth. I want you tell me everything. I'm certain that you left out important details, the culprits always do." she said with a wicked grin on her face.

"Can I at least have a glass of wine, while I tell you?"

"That's why it's on the table," she quipped. "Pour, drink and tell."

"Before we begin, I want you to know that I've been thinking about our conversation the other night. My stomach was upset for days." He looked at her and smiled. "I thought about everything you said and if our congregants invite us to dinner on Shabbat, I trust you will handle it appropriately. Anything you agree to is fine with me."

He smiled, "I'm still having trouble with job thing. How much time do I have?"

"Two weeks," she replied. Two weeks."

"There's not another alternative?" he asked.

She shook her head.

"I'll get back to you."

Rachel gave him a little push and said, "what happened in Miami?"

David's started slowly, "He," he swallowed, "was amazing. A little weird I have to say. There were these young gorgeous women who appeared to be living with him and he seems to have changed his name. He did say something about a new life, but I wasn't certain what that meant. Anyway, we sat and drank he challenged me to articulate exactly what I thought could happen if Reb Yudah was successful."

"And?"

"And then he forced me to think of how I could counter, no," he hesitated, "not counter, anticipate what I should be doing to ensure whatever he did would not be successful. It was brilliant."

"And?" Rachel continued.

"And then we mapped out a plan. The first step, was owning the outreach effort with the challot."

"That's all fine and good," she responded, "you anticipated he would begin distributing challot and owned it before he could begin. But that can't be enough, what's next?"

"You're good," he said with a smile. "I need to develop a way to retain the post b'nai mitzvah families and I need to raise the level of volunteerism in our community in a way that attracts others. This is really good wine? Where did you get it?"

"Don't ask", she replied. "Just enjoy. I'm enjoying plying you with wine after I almost put you on the wagon. You'll tell me everything I want to know and then," she said with a smile, "I will have my way with you."

He returned the grin, "You know you don't have to do that to have your way with me."

"Don't be such a guy," she replied with a smile.

"Ah, excuse me," he said, "how much time do we have until the kid comes home?"

She looked at her phone. "Not enough time but it will have to do."

He stood up and began to undress.

"Wait" she said. "We've got the Challah and you, somehow think you can solve a situation that no rabbi has been able to solve for fifty years?"

"Yup."

If you're successful will that be enough?"

"Nope" he said as he removed his shirt.

"What comes next?" she said with a smile as he moved toward the bed."

"We shall see. We shall see."

The Board Meeting:

"Hello, Leonard,"

"Good evening Madame le president," he replied. "It's the first Tuesday of the month."

She smiled at him as she entered the Board room. It was a long rectangular room that was completely dominated by a long oak table surrounded by faded office chairs that had seen better days. "Well," she commented as she entered, "we have new carpeting in the sanctuary, I suppose one day a few angels will arrange for this room to be painted."

"Right now, those angels", Leonard added as he took a seat next to her at the head of the table, "are pretty involved with challah and by the way it's pretty good."

She shrugged and said, "it's the same old people. I don't have any idea if we will ever be able to find new and younger men and women to fill next year's vacancies. Did you bring the agenda?"

"Well, actually, no. I spoke with the rabbi last night and he indicated that he hoped he could accomplish what he desired in thirty minutes. But he requested an hour, just in case. If he takes an hour, the group will be too tired to conduct real business. I did order some fruit and cheese for later and the rabbi said the kiddush club would send over a few bottles of wine."

"Food at a Board meeting?" Maddie commented. "That's an innovation."

The door opened, and several men and women filed in. Within about five minutes the room was filled.

"Where's the Rabbi?" Maddie asked.

"I'm right here," he said as he entered carrying a small projector. "I'm ready as soon as we do an opening prayer."

"An opening prayer?" Maddie said raising an eyebrow.

"Yes," he responded. "We're a shul. Next month, assuming you permit it. I will teach for a few minutes. It's important that the Board learns."

"Okay, okay rabbi," she murmured. "I'll call the meeting to order and then it's yours. What's the projector and the screen for?"

"Interest. To keep their interest. And besides some people will understand my presentation better if they can see it. I'm ready."

"Look at the Rabbi!" Mrs. Kantor commented to the man sitting next to her. "He's all dressed up like he was going to an important meeting."

"Well," he should, "A Board meeting is an important meeting. We manage the affaires of the synagogue."

"Jonathan," she said putting her hand on his arm in a loving way, "we haven't done anything more important in the last ten years than painting the parking lot."

"He asked to address us," he replied. "And after only seven months, it must be important."

"Do you think he is going to resign like the last one?" A purpled haired lady asked who was sitting on the opposite side of the table.

"No", Jonathan replied. "He could do that in a letter."

"Well", she said, "he is the only item on the agenda. I can't wait to hear what he has to say."

"Ladies and Gentlemen, this special meeting of the Board of Directors is about to begin," Maddie said in a formal manner. "Does anyone have to leave for any reason?"

No one moved.

"Is the secretary prepared?" she asked.

The man sitting next to her turned his head and nodded affirmatively.

"Very well", she said. "I want to remind everyone not use their phones or computers. This is a special meeting and the rabbi will need your attention. Rabbi," she gestured. "The floor is yours."

David rose and looked at the twenty or twenty-five people sitting around the table. He cleared his throat and began.

"I'd like to thank all of you for coming this evening. What I am going to share with you has the potential to change the nature of our community." He paused, "but if what I am going to share with you is to succeed, I am going to need your help."

A quiet groan accompanied by a huge exhale floated through the room.

"All of you know how difficult it is to retain the post b'nai mitzvah families."

A nodding of heads and a few whispers followed.

"I think I have found a way to retain these children and their parents." The whispers rose in intensity.

"I'm going to explain the way I understand this situation and my plans, no my hopes, that with your support, it will succeed." He looked around. He had everyone's attention.

"I envision this as a marketing challenge. Bob, you're a marketing person, would you agree if we want to keep the families we need to provide both the parents and the kids with a reason and a need which will make them to want to stay."

The bald man who appeared to be in his eighties, nodded his head in agreement.

"Good," David responded. "I asked myself, what are the things that most high school students want? That's a question," he said, "Anyone want to hazard a guess?"

The man who was in advertising shrugged his shoulders and responded. "Well, they want to get into a good University. They don't feel the pressure until they are sophomores, that's when they start taking tests. "

"Good answer," David responded. "Anyone else?"

"They want to get laid," Sadie said. "They're teens all they think about is sex."

"Right again," David said with a smile. "You are such a good class. Okay, now let's look at this from the view point of the parents. What do they want?"

"They want their children not to have sex," Sadie said. "And they want their kids to get into a good school."

"Yes!" Yes! David replied as he began walking around the room. "Our challenge is to figure out a way to give both groups at least one of the things that they need, and this is how we are going to do it."

A man of approximately fifty years wearing a herringbone jacket and a pair of corduroy pants raised his hands. He cleared his throat and began. "Rabbi, I don't think we've met, I tend to travel a great deal and am not what you call a good Jew. But it seems to me that your suggesting you've found a way to address one of the most serious issues confronting the Jewish community. Something which our greatest minds has failed to do for generations and you," he smiled, "think you have found an answer?"

Not a person in the room spoke.

David looked at him and cleared his throat. "I'm sorry, you're correct we haven't met. Mr. or Dr. ...."

"Kaminer," the gentleman added.

"Kaminer," he said to himself. "Before I respond to your question. I want you to know that I'm not offended by what could have been an accusation," David replied. "I'm puzzled, why do you define yourself as not being a good Jew?"

"Why, I practically never attend services, I don't keep kosher and I consistently violate the Shabbat. As matter of fact if I actually didn't violate the Shabbat on occasion it would have been because I either spent the day in bed or was in the hospital."

David raised hand and stroked his chin. "Mr. Kaminer, do you support any charities?"

"Of course, I do," he responded.

"And you choose to sit on this Board?"

"Well, I'm here, aren't I?"

"Do you vote?"

"Of course, I do."

"Am I correct that you either teach or have published on some post high school level?"

"Well, yes," he said somewhat expansively. "I just published a book about crime in the ghetto. I'm a sociologist."

David kept stroking his chin. "Well I'm sorry to disappoint you Sir, but it seems that you serve as a volunteer on religious Board, concerning yourself professionally with the poor, vote and support charities. How can you be anything other than a good Jew?"

David took a step back and flicked the switch on the power point projector. "Now I would like to explain my idea. It might not solve, what Mr. Kaminer called "the great challenge" but on some level with a little bit of this groups' support, I think we can minimize the exodus of the post b'nai mitzvah families."

"Let me begin with a question. I really am new and am just beginning to learn about the wonderful not for profit organizations that exist within our communities. Can you help me make a list and if anyone knows someone who is employed at these institutions, let us know? Who wants to start?"

David looked at the group and each one of them looked at him.

"Hmm," David said, "I'll start. I saw an advertisement in the local paper for an organization called the Coalition for the Homeless."

"That's Bob Rubell's organization," someone quipped. "It's been around for a long time."

"What about, the United Way?" Someone added.

"I know one of the project coordinators," someone else added.

"The food pantry!"

"The Salvation Army!"

"Our Federation!"

"Is there a junior or local college within this community or one of its neighbors?" David asked.

"Yes, of course," Rita Tobin added. "My nephew is one of the Deans."

"Great, Great! This is great," David added. "Now let me tell you how I envision how this could work."

"Maddie, you're the synagogue President so I need you to call a meeting of all the parents who have children going into Tenth and Eleventh grade next year."

"But, we've lost many of those families after the b'nai mitzvah," she said.

"That's correct and that's why we need you to call them to this special meeting. I don't know them, but you do. You are going to tell them we are developing a special initiative that will increase their children's possibilities for college acceptance. It's almost springtime and our goal is to convince them to enroll their children in the special two- year program in the Fall."

"What program is that?" Mr. Kaminer asked.

"I'm getting to that," David replied looking at the Board, "I want everyone in this room to give Mr. Kaminer the names and positions of anyone you know who is active in one of the not-for-profit organizations we just listed. Mr. Kaminer, can I call you Stephen?"

He just looked at the rabbi and nodded his head affirmatively.

"Stephen, you ask good questions, are clearly an intelligent, sophisticated and educated person. I am asking you in front of this group," he paused and gestured to those sitting around the table, "to accept the chairmanship of this effort for two years."

"I.….

"It won't be a lot of work, just calling these people and offering them the opportunity to meet with high school students, and then arranging the schedule with me. Do you accept?"

Stephen looked at the rabbi and then at group sitting at the table. "How can I refuse," he said with a smile, "you did that so well."

"Thank you," David replied. "it will be fun working with you. I won't waste your time and it will make a huge difference to our community." He turned to the group and continued.

"Our job is to convince the parents this effort which will consist of only 6 Friday evening dinners a year, followed by a speaker, will increase the possibility of their children's acceptance to college. Once we have parental support, we will hold a special dinner for our emerging young adults in May or June and we will explain how our synagogue is going to help them increase their chances of obtaining their goals."

"Rabbi", Bob called out, "I'm sorry to interrupt, but you still haven't told us how this program is going to help us retain these families. What's the secret?

Why will they want to take part in this effort?"

David took a deep breathe, smiled and answered. "Every parent and every child wants to be accepted to the school of their choice. The competition is brutal. Every little item think will help them increase their chances somehow finds its way onto the college application."

"We are going to give them something unique. Possibly with the support of a local college, but even it that cannot be achieved, our students will be able to indicate on their applications they have completed a two- year course in not-for-profit management. Any questions?"

Leonard reached across the table and shook David's hand.

"Does this proposal have Board approval?" she asked.

It was unanimous.

INTERLUDE DINNER AT CAPRESE'S RESTAURANT

Eddie, Diane, Mikey and Karen are sitting at a table in a local restaurant. The waiter has just distributed the menus.

"What looks good?" Eddie asks Diane.

"I had the clams casino when I waz here last and it was delicious" Karen offered.

Eddie made a face, "I don't know," he said, I tink I will have," he softly chewed his cheeks as he read the menu. "Da striped bass."

"Striped bass?" Diane responded quizzically, "Eddie, we've been married eighteen years and now you order fish?"

"Well," he said, "I've been thinking about my health and too much meat isn't good for you."

"So, it's okay if I bring home more fish from the market? It's almost lobsta season and...."

"No lobsta, please," he said raising his hand.

"But you love lobsta, "she replied.

"Yeah but, I've been thinking…and

"The rabbi got to him, didn't he?" Mikey interjected. "Admit it! He got to you."

Eddie blushed, "It's not like he told me what to do, matter of fact we haven't even discussed keeping kosher, I just thought with me," he glanced at Mikey, "with us studying Talmud and with the bar mitzvah just a few months away, and" he looked at Diane, "and with us making Shabbas dinners, it might…"

"You're making Shabbat dinners?" Karen asked.

Diane smiled and nodded, "Yup, and we make the blessings."

"Been a good idea." Eddie said. "Boy you guys make it hard to finish a sentence."

"Don't be embarrassed," Karen added. "Mikey here, loves his shellfish and his BLT's but he won't allow them in the house."

"It's my background," he said, that's how I grew up. "

"It wasn't like that in my house," Diane added. "In my parent's home they ate everything, except on Passover, no bread. No cereal. My motha used to eat ham and cheese on Matzah."

The waiter came and took their orders. The appetizers arrived almost immediately. Diane and Eddie were eating roasted garlic.

"We should make this for our cooking class," Diane said as she dropped a clove into her mouth.

"Mikey, how's the Talmud class going?"

Mikey looked at her and smiled. "its still great. Getting a bit too large for my tastes but the wine is good, the conversation is lively, the text study continues to be interesting, though the rabbi is beginning to look tired. Real tired."

"I noticed that too," Eddie added as he popped a clove towards his mouth. "I wonder what's causing it?"

"Must be because Rachel got a job," Diane interjected

"The rebbetzin got a job?" Mikey asked. "And where is that?"

"In the city someplace, I think downtown, and she has to leave services on Saturday early so she can get to work on time."

"She's working on Shabbat? The rebbetzin is working on Shabbat?"

"And," Diane continued, "it means the rabbi has increased child time."

Everyone at the table stopped talking. After a few moments Karen began,

"The women's cooking group thinks its fine. Rach, discussed it with us before she took the job."

"Maybe that's why he has his hand on his stomach almost all of the time," Eddie suggested.

"Stomach tension?" Karen suggested. "Not a good sign."

"Yeah, Mikey added. "He's working real hard. Lots of new things going on. Maybe they need the money? We're not paying him much."

"You're on the Board?" Diane asked.

"Shhsh," Karen said, "He don't want too many people to know."

Diane raised her hand to her shoulders and began to make a cross, "whoops," she said. "Knock on wood." We're not supposed to do that anymore."

"Ya shouldn't do that eithah?" Eddie said. "When you "knock on wood," You're knocking on the cross."

"Lotta pressure," Eddie said. "Lotta pressure."

"Yup," Mikey added. "Just like the rest of us."

The following morning – An Offensive Parry

"You begin."

"No, you are the Rav," Yuda said gesturing with his hand, "You begin."

"Sorry," David replied, "Since I'm the Rav and your senior colleague, I insist that you begin."

Yuda smiled sheepishly and replied, "Okay Rav. I selected a passage from the Gemarra (Talmud), Massechet (volume) Shabbat, which discusses the origins of lighting the lights on Chanukah."

Yuda began to teach and explain the Aramaic passage discussing how one knows the order of lighting the Chanukah candles. He explained the Talmud was wrestling with two different approaches to how one lights the candles. One approach explained one begins by lighting the eight lights the first night and the seven the second and so on, because according to the students of the school of Shammai, the first night was the most important.

The contrary view which reflects todays actual practice was put forth by the student of the school of Hillel who explained the lights should be written in ascending order. Yuda read, translated and explain the different reasons for the different interpretations of lighting the candles in great details. He concluded with the following statement.

"And today, we follow the school of Hillel."

David looked at him, shook his head and said, "Yudah, that was an excellent translation and description of the arguments. But why do you think both schools justified their positions by providing us with two answers?"

"I'm not sure," he said. I only know Shammai provided us with two answers as did Hillel and the Sages decided we should follow the school of Hillel."

"Do you have children?" David asked.

"Of course, you know I have two children, a four-year-old and a two-year-old."

"Yes, I did know that," David said slowly, "have you ever worked with older children, say maybe ten years old or even teenagers?"

"Of course," he replied. "Why do you ask? What has that to do with the material we are discussing?"

"Well," David responded in a thoughtful voice, "If I ask somebody a question and they respond with two answers, then," he paused, "I don't think they really knew the answer. Let's look at the text again but with that in mind."

"Someone asked what is the proper order of lighting the Hanukkah candles? Should we do it in an ascending or descending order? And some people answered, 'We do it this way. We light the candles in an ascending order and we have two different explanations why we do it that way.' And other people answered, 'We do it this way, we light the candles in a descending order and we also have two different reasons for our practice.'

Oh, and another thing. When I ask someone a question and they respond with two different answers, I'm not certain they really knew the answer to my question. Usually one question receives one answer.

I am suggesting both groups had forgotten why they lit the candles, the Hanukah lights, the way they did because both groups answered a simple question with two responses. I think that by the time this text was written, both groups were lighting the candles according to the way they had learned. Perhaps they even lived next to one another? Overtime, the followers of Hillel's way became dominant and that's why we light the candles the way we do today. But at one time, some people did it one way. And others another way."

Yudah shrugged his shoulders. "I hadn't really considered that, but it could have been possible."

David smiled and said. "Good. Now it's my turn. This morning we are going to study a little Bible."

Yudah snorted. "Bible? You want to study Bible?"

"Is there anything wrong with that? After all it is our oldest and most sacred text."

"No," Yudah replied, "it's just that we studied chumash."

"Bible," I said correcting him.

"Bible," he said continuing, "when we were children. We learned Torah, with the commentator Rashi."

"I know and maybe, if you were good, you also were able to study Ibn Ezra and Abarbanel, and others."

"Rabbi," he continued. "Rabbi, the way we usually learned Bible or Taanach is through the study of Talmud."

"Yudah," David replied gently but slightly intensified his voice. "I'm not an idiot. I know how you learned Bible. But you don't know how I learned Bible, and so I'm going to teach you. Is that okay with you?"

His shoulders rose slightly as he winced. "Yes, Rabbi. It's fine with me. What are we going to learn?"

"Well," I said smiling, "we are going to learn (he emphasized the word "learn") about one of the kings of Israel."

He smiled back. "Dovid? (David) Shlomo? (Solomon) Shaul (Saul)?"

David shook his head from side to side, "No Yudah we are going to learn about one of the great kings of Israel," he paused. "Manasseh."

"Menasheh!" he exclaimed as he placed two fingers in front of his mouth and spit three times. "You want me to learn about a man who was worse than Haman? A man who the Talmud says was denied a place in the world to come?"

"Yes," David replied with a smile, "let's see what the text actually says. He opened the bible on his desk. "Please turn to page 1004."

"I'd like you to read what it says about Manasseh in the second book of Kings.

"Don't glare at me. You should be happy we are learning Torah together."

Yudah glumly lifted the Bible in front of him and began to read.

"He did what was displeasing to the Lord, following the abhorrent practices of the nations that the Lord had dispossessed before the Israelites. He rebuilt shrines that his father Hezekiah had destroyed; he erected altars for Baal. He bowed down to all the host of heaven and worshiped them and he built altars for them in the House of the Lord.

He consigned his son to fire; he practiced soothsaying and divination and consulted ghosts and familiar spirits. And Manasseh led them astray to do greater evil than the nations that the Lord had destroyed before the Israelites. Therefore, the Lord spoke through his prophets and said,

Because King Manasseh of Judah has done these abhorrent things he has outdone in wickedness all that the Amorites did before his time and because he led Judah to sin with his fetishes, I am going to bring such a disaster on Jerusalem and Judah that both ears of everyone who hears about it will tingle.

I will wipe Jerusalem clean as one wipes a dish and turns it upside down. I will cast off the remnant of My own people and deliver them into the hands of their enemies. They shall be plunder and prey to all their enemies.

Moreover, Manasseh put so many innocent people to death that he filled Jerusalem with blood from end to end."

Yudah, completed the last sentence and stared at David. David could tell he was thinking, trying to find the correct words to express himself without offending him. He began to raise his right hand, and then shook his head and lowered it. He was panting ever so slightly. It took about thirty seconds before he regained his composure.

David watched him gather himself together and sit up straight.

"You. Want. Us. To. Study. About. That. Man!"

David waited. He waited until he thought Yudah had finished. He was wrong.

"That's the man who you called one of the great kings of Israel?" Do you hate Israel!"

"Of course not," David replied gently. "I love Israel."

"So, what's the point of learning about one of the most despicable people in our tradition? There are so many great people in the Bible why in the world would you pick this one?"

"Yudah," David said in a calm gentle voice, "relax. Take a breath, and I'll show you."

"Let's start with a few questions, okay?"

"Still obviously rattled, he replied glumly. "Okay."

"Do you know the name of Manasseh's father?"

"Of course, the text tells us. It was Hezekiah."

"Correct, and was he a good king?"

"Yes," he replied. "A very good King."

"Did you know he reigned in Judah for twenty-nine years?"

"No," he mumbled, "we didn't study dates when we learned Bible."

"It doesn't matter," he replied. "Let me fill you in. During his reign he attempted to restructure the government. The Assyrians were in the process of establishing an empire. They accomplished this because they created a technologically sophisticated army which was able to rapidly advance. They quickly conquered a series of smaller kingdoms and incorporated them into their empire as provinces. They deported the elite of these populations and settled them in other regions thus destroying their national identities and at the same time eliminating the future threat of rebellion. Damascus fell in 732.B.C.E. and Samaria (the Northern Kingdom) ten years later, that is to say, in the sixth year of Hezekiah's reign.

Egypt and some of the neighboring countries formed an alliance hoping to stop the Assyrian aggression and remain independent. They approached Hezekiah and threated to attack Judah if he refused to ally with them. The prophet Isaiah advised him not to join this alliance. His advice was ignored. In the meantime, forty-six cities were conquered, and the Assyrians continued to Jerusalem.

In order to resist the attack, Hezekiah attempted to reorganize the government. He invited all of the remaining tribes, after all, the Northern Kingdom had already been conquered and destroyed, to offer sacrifice in the Temple during Passover. He stockpiled grains, oils and wine. He fortified provincial towns and in order to assure that Jerusalem had a more than adequate water supply he diverted the spring waters of Gihon through a tunnel to the pool of Siloam."

"How do you know this?" Yudah asked.

"It's all in the text but one needs to know a little history and the context in which this was happening in order to more effectively understand it," he replied.

"The Assyrians continued to advance and Hezekiah rather than have Jerusalem destroyed surrendered and Jerusalem became an Assyrian province."

"No! that's not true!" Yudah said, "It can't be true. God saved Jerusalem."

"I'm sorry Yudah, maybe you're right. It is possible I suppose, that God inspired Hezekiah to make a decision that would save his people and his holy city."

"Yes, he nodded. "That's it. That makes sense."

"Well, to continue, it was into this world and after a decade of being mentored by his Father, that Manasseh became king."

"Hezekiah was a good King." Yudah said. "He did all the right things. He saved Jerusalem he tore down shrines to other Gods. But his son was...."

"Hey, this I my class,'" David said. "Let me ask you a question. What do you think makes a good King?"

"A good King? A good Jewish King?"

"Yes, Yudah, a good Jewish King."

"Well", he said. "He has to believe in God".

David nodded.

"And he has to observe the mitzvahs (commandments)."

Another nod.

"And he has to take care of his people."

"That's good. I agree with everything you said, so let me ask another question."

"How was the son of Hezekiah, going to keep the Assyrians from doing to his people like they did to every other people?"

Yudah shrugged his shoulders. "I don't know, "he said. "He has to believe that God would protect them."

"Like God is protecting us now," he asked with a smile.

"Okay, good point," he responded.

"Do you think if a king managed to avoid war and feed his people, that he could be considered a good king," he asked?

Yudah nodded, not exactly certain where this was going.

"Did you know that Manasseh managed not to go to war and to keep the peace, for forty years? The longest peaceful period in the history of the first

Temple."

"No, I didn't know that."

"Did you know that under his reign, in return for letting the Assyrians build Temples to their deities and for paying taxes, Manasseh was permitted to build roads to increase the country's ability to produce and export olives, olive oils and fruits? That under his rule, the population in the Beersheba and in the highlands grew and towns and cities were rebuilt. For example, Ekron and Gaza and the forts of Arad and Usa were rebuilt in order to protect the trade routes."

"No", he said. "All that information wasn't written in the Bible."

"Well, some of it was and the rest we learn from other sources. It appears the Manasseh was indeed a successful ruler."

"Stop!" Yudah said. "If that's the case why does the Bible say such horrible things about him! And why do the rabbis in the Talmud agree!"

"Excellent question! Yudah. Excellent. Let me tell you a little about how the Torah came to be written."

"God dictated the Torah to Moses and Moses wrote it down."

"Not so fast, my man. Who brought the Torah at least the first five books to Jerusalem?"

"I know that, he said promptly, Ezra, the Priest."

He nodded. "Very good. It was Ezra who in 459 B.C.E. brought the Torah with him from Babylon. Very good. But," David paused, "the Torah hadn't been stored or hidden from the time of Moses for almost eight hundred years. No, the Torah was compiled in Babylon by different groups of people. All of those groups wanted the people in Babylon to return to what today we call Israel and to rebuild their/our country. Some of those groups believed the way to do that was to insist on the importance of the Temple and the belief and practice of the one God and only that God. And some of those people, most likely priests wanted the people to follow them because they felt they were special.

In order for that to occur they had to discredit the king the same one who rebuilt a country and kept it at peace for forty years. Let's face it Yudah, politics hasn't changed that much in the past couple of thousand years."

Yudah was silent. He placed a hand on his chin and stood up. He paced around the room. He paused, looked at me and continued pacing. "Why are you doing this to me?" he asked.

"Doing what?"

"Presenting me with this material."

"This is how I learn," David replied. "It's how I study. I want to know the truth."

"The truth, but can't learning the truth," he paused. "Can't knowing the truth violate your faith in God?"

"Actually," he said. "No. For me knowing the truth or what we think is the truth, reinforces my belief in God. And I think it challenges me to be a better person. Does what we just learned challenge your faith?"

"I don't know," he said. "I'm not sure. This, that, what we just did, is so new to me. I, I don't know what to do with it."

"You don't have to do anything with it. I once had a teacher who told me that even if one could prove there wasn't a God, he would still believe in one. I'm puzzled, I thought you liked challenges. That's why I chose this text."

"I do, but the Bible, I always accepted what the commentaries said. I never really thought about it on my own."

"I'm sorry", He replied, (though internally he was chuckling). "Let's call it a session. We both learned something this morning. I'll see you next week."

"Yes, next week." He said as reached for his jacket and slung it over his shoulder. Next week," he said as he exited his office.

"Oh, Yudah?"

"Yes?" he said hesitantly.

"When I choose next week's text, I'll try to make it less, less challenging. Would that be okay?"

Yudah smiled and said, "Rabbi, that would be very nice."

David returned the smile. He waited until the door had been closed. The smile widened into a shit eating grin.

Knock, Knock.

"Door's not locked", David replied in a loud voice, "Come in."

The door swung slowly open to reveal a twelve-year-old boy.

"Marty? Marty! Good to see you," David said as he stood up and walked towards the boy. "You're lookin good. He let his eyes roam up and down. "You've lost some weight, no, you've gained a couple of inches. Gonna need some new clothes soon. I hope your parents haven't already bought your bar mitzvah suit," he said smiling.

The boy just stood there and smiled weakly.

"Come in, come in. Here take a seat, To what do I owe the honor of this visit."

The smile broadened a bit as he lowered himself into the chair.

"Hmmm," he said. "Everything all right?"

The boy nodded affirmatively.

"Problems with the bar mitzvah speech?"

He shook his head from side to side.

"Girl problems?"

"No."

"Parent problems?"

He shook his head.

"Hmmmm, but you came to see me. You must have a reason."

He nodded his head affirmatively.

"So, you came to see me. You're sitting in my office. We're staring at one another."

The boy's smile broadened he looked like he was about to laugh.

"And you're not going to tell me why you're here."

"No, Rabbi, I am going to tell you, I just wanted to see how far I could get without saying a word," he replied.

Interesting kid, he thought.

David leaned forward dropping his eyebrows and with his best James Cagney accent said, "so what's this about kid, give?"

"I got into trouble with my teacher and my parents a couple of months ago when I let a few inappropriate words slip out," he began. "And sometime later my father started to study Talmud with you."

David nodded affirmatively.

"And a couple of weeks later, my parents changed. We started to have Friday night dinners together. Shabbas dinners."

"go on,"

"And they started laughing more, having a better time together. And my friends' father's," he nodded his head as if he were piecing things together, "also started going to your class."

"Is anything wrong?" David asked.

"No," he said, "nothing is wrong, but something is going on and I'd like to know more about it. On one hand they're still the same jerky parents. The men talk about sports almost all the time, and the mom's they just," he shrugged his shoulders, "talk."

"So," he continued. "I think whatever is taking place in your class is changing them. And it's a good thing." he hesitated.

"Marty, you're a smart kid. I'm guessing you're a good student, aren't you?"

"Yes, I'm a very good student but I don't try to show it, if you know what I mean."

"I do," he responded with a nod. "And it's obvious you're intuitive, but you're still holding back. What is it you want to ask me?"

The shyness of a twelve-year-old vanished as if it never existed. He looked

David straight in the eyes and said, "I want to be part of it. Whatever they are doing, I want some."

"It's a Talmud class, Marty. We study. We schmooze a little, I ask questions. I introduce new ideas and new information about Judaism and about life and your Dad and the others think about it."

"Why has this class become so important to them? My Dad, changed bowling nights, which is a big deal in this community, so he could attend your class."

"Well," I replied, "on a certain level its more than a class. It's become a chevrah, a group of friends. Most of the men in this community, no, most men, don't have intellectual and independent social opportunities. They've been trained to work to support their families. For entertainment, they watch things. Some of them do things like carpentry or fishing but a lot of them rarely do other things. This class gives them the opportunity to learn in a comfortable relaxed way. They aren't competing with one another like they do in the market-place or on the bowling floor. Does that make sense to you?"

"Yes," he said, "and I want to join the class."

This kid ain't learning about Bordeaux, David said to himself. "Okay, I'll give you a few options. We can either study together or if you can get together a few of your friends, we can meet twice a month in a restaurant for a pizza dinner and we will study. Your choice."

Marty stood up and reached out and shook my hand. "I'll think about it," he said with a smile. "I'll get back to you."

David winced and placed his hand on his stomach as he stood and watched Marty leave the room. He turned and walked over to his drums. He slowly lowered himself onto the stool, slowly releasing his hand from his stomach as he picked up the sticks and started to strum. "What just happened? What just happened?"

The Morning After

"How much time do we have before he wakes up?" David asked as he rolled next to her in the bed.

"About twenty minutes," Rachel said as she turned into him and yawned. "You don't want to do it again, do you?"

"Yes, of course I do," he replied as he stretched. "But no, not really, I'm too relaxed to move. It's been a long time since we've had time to be this close. Thank you for taking the initiative."

"Well," she said with a smile, "I had my reasons. It pleases me to see you relaxed but it looks like you're in pain when you move in certain ways."

"I have been having some stomach discomfort," David admitted.

She smiled, "You could get up and rinse out your mouth, you're…

"Okay, Okay," he said, "I know my breathe, don't worry, I'm taking care of it right now," he said as he rolled to the other side of the bed and lowered his legs, grasped his stomach and quickly walked to the bathroom.

"I'm not kicking you out" she whispered. "I just want you to smell better."

"I know, I know," he said as he returned to the bed and slipped under the covers.

She moved into him and they both smiled.

"You know," he said, "you're more relaxed too. Could it be you're beginning to settle in? Maybe you're starting to like this place?"

David stared at her as she stretched and arched her back, "God, I love it when you do that."

She turned into him and began to play with his chin. "I think I'm going to turn the garage into a studio. What do you think?"

"I think that's a great idea," he said with a smile. "You are beginning to adjust to this place. Could it be that Rachel is beginning to make friends?"

"Let's not go that far," she said with a smile still cuddling. "But they are nice people. They're good people. I'm mostly being accepted. One woman asked if we could go to the city and visit a museum. She did it quietly, I think she was concerned she would be criticized. Another asked me if I played mahjong, and," she paused. "Getting away a few days a week has certainly helped me maintain my sanity."

"The mahjong thing," she guffawed. "I really had to control myself because

I wanted to say 'I hope to learn when I'm eighty'. But she meant it. Let's just say I'm adjusting."

David smiled, "me too." He said as he raised his arms and stretched. "hmmm, I don't want to go to work today. Let's just stay in bed."

"We have at max five more minutes and there is something I wanted to talk to you about."

"Ah, Ha!" he said grinning. "All of this, including last night was a set up."

She lowered her hand to his chest, and said, "not all of it. But I wanted to tell you I spoke to my father about," she hesitated, "you know who."

"Acher. That one," he replied. "And what did my scholarly nearly divine father-in-law say about him? Did he find an obscure curse in some ancient text that if I recited three times would make him disappear?"

"Stop it," she said playfully slapping him. "He's my father. I love him."

"Sometimes," he replied. "I can't help it. He was sooo supportive of our marriage."

"He's entitled to his own opinions but that didn't stop me." She replied turning away from him.

"Okay, I'm sorry. What did your father say?"

Rachel turned onto her side, was once again facing him. "He said, he was glad to be at the end of his career and it is much more difficult to be a rabbi today than it was forty years ago. He said, he wished you good luck and he hopes you can find a way to deal with," she paused. "Acher."

David exhaled deeply and replied, "Well, that's honest. Maybe a time will come when he will stop being so critical of my work and his daughter's choice."

"Maybe," she said smiling. "David?"

"Yes."

"I was wondering what I could do to help. There must be something."

He just stared at the bedroom ceiling. After a few seconds he inhaled and exhaled deeply.

"Rach, all of these things are happening. The school, synagogue attendance, new people" he paused, and I don't know what I'm doing. Things are just happening. I feel like a blind man reaching out and trying to touch something tangible. I feel that I'm constantly stumbling into or onto things. And every time I begin to feel that I'm standing firmly on my feet, something else happens. I don't know," he said wistfully, "what you can do to help me, other than being with me, he paused. "Well, maybe," he said in a low voice, "maybe you could share some of my concerns with the women. Tell them stories about how when these acher-like people enter a community they cause damage. Tell them they don't accept Israel the way we do. Tell them, what they do on campus. Tell them, they won't pray with us. Just tell them, gently what you've learned, what you've seen growing up, on campus and in life. Words spread, people can be influenced. It might stop them from going to 'his library.' Who knows?"

"I certainly can do that," she said smiling. "It will be like when we first started. Two against the world."

He grinned as they move toward each other. Each making a fist and bumping one against the other. "Two against the world," they said smiling.

A Offensive Parry

The bell over the door rang as he opened it and stepped into the bakery. The man standing behind the counter washing dishes turned around as he heard the sound.

"Good morning Rabbi," Mr. Scarlati said with a grin. "What a pleasure, what a pleasure." as he reached into the display case and removed a cookie. "Try this one, I filled it with prunes and apricot. I think it will be a big hit for your Purim festival. I think it's called hammanschweig."

"Close, you're close, its Hammantashen. A Yiddish word. Not a German one." He replied as he placed the cookie in his mouth. Hmmm, this is really good, but you need to work on the shape, it has to look like a triangle mimicking a hat that people used to wear in Persian times. Give me a second and I'll show you, he murmured as he removed his phone from a pocket and started to search. This is what it needs to look like, can you do it?"

Mr. Scarlati, stroked his chin. "I need to buy some molds, but I can do it.

I've seen those cookies in other bakeries, I just didn't know what they were for." Give me a week and you will have your hammantashen."

"Excellent, excellent," David said as he continued munching on the cookie. "really tasty. I'll take some home for Rachel and Ari. How much are they?"

"For you my friend, they are free. I am catering two of your kiddushes next month. Would you like to see the menu?"

"Yes, yes, of course, can I have some water? He croaked as he attempted to clear his throat.

Mr. Scarlati removed a glass from a shelf and opened the refrigerator door to his left and removed a container of water. "What can I do for you today rabbi?" he asked.

"I want to talk to you about Matzah."

Trouble in Paradise? Late April

The phone was answered by a woman with a soft, slightly accented deep voice. "Good evening, Sandy Talbot's home"

"Adriana? Is that you? It's me Rabbi, no uhm, David Duvin, do you remember me?"

"I'm sorry Mr. Duvin, this is Margolit. Adriana's in class it's my day to cover."

"To cover? Margolit? Are you Israeli?" he asked.

"Well, partially, my mother is Israeli. My father was born in the States and I was raised in both."

"Can't hide an Israeli accent," the voice replied.

"May I speak with Sandy?"

"Just a minute, he's writing. I'll see if he can be interrupted."

"David, it's Sandy. To what do I have the pleasure?"

"Well, something's come up and I need some advice."

"Advice is cheap," Sandy replied, "But first, are your plans in place? Are they operative?"

"Sounds like an undercover operation," David replied. "yes, all is more or less going according to plan. I've initiated a number of items, most of which are bearing fruit. I think in another few months, the situation will be under control, unless he brings in re-enforcement. But that's not why I called. I have a prob… (he hesitated) a situation that requires your advice."

"Margolit, you can hang up now. I've got this."

"Sandy," David said in a low voice. "Can I ask you a question about your… your staff."

"Certainly," he replied. "Oh, you don't understand what's going on and its making you a bit uncomfortable. That's it, he quipped. Isn't it?"

"Yes", he replied with a sigh. "That's it."

"Well, it's really quite simple. Unconventional but simple. You don't know me, but I've always had difficulty with rules and conventions. These two sometimes three beautiful women live with me. Usually for up to two years. They do things for me. Not everything, but they cook, and I get to advise them about theater, and food and culture. It's really fun. And in return, I pay for their graduate school and give them a place to live. Basically, I get to live with gorgeous intelligent women. And they get to take care of me. I'm not so young anymore you know."

Aaah, David said, "I never thought… that's really quite creative. As a matter of fact, it's kind of wonderful."

"Yes, Sandy responded. And sometimes when they feel a bit lonely or perhaps they pity me for being an old man, they get into bed with me. Which is wonderful. I never ask. It's always up to them. Maybe it's kind of a grandfather or great grandfather fixation. I don't let it bother me."

'Thank you, Ra….Sandy. I appreciate your explaining it to me. Don't worry, I'll never…"

"You can do what you want David. I don't care. I never cared. Well, maybe when I was much younger. But now, (he stopped). That's not why you called me. Why did you call?"

"I have a situation and don't know how to respond.""

"I'm listening and don't start the responding to me with a sigh. Just tell me, straight out."

"Okay, okay" David said. "In the Fall I started what developed into a Talmud class. It's not really a Talmud class, though sometimes we study Talmud. The class began with one person and because I wanted to make him comfortable, we drank wine while we studied. Sometimes we didn't exactly study, we just talked about Jewish things."

"Nu?"

And the word got out and his friends started coming and in time they brought their friends. And then someone started supplying the wine and they began to call themselves, "The Kiddush Club."

"Go on, I'm still listening."

"Well, "he said. "I had to split the group into two different nights."

"and…."

"When this began I thought it was because I was able to interest these men in studying. What I found out was that they were attending my classes, and enjoying them, mind you, because they thought that studying Talmud would improve their sex lives."

"Hold on! Hold on boy! That's one hell of a jump. How did they get from studying Talmud to better sex lives?"

"I kind of, jokingly at the beginning mentioned, no I didn't mention but I allowed one of my congregants to think the reason my relationship was so," he paused, "satisfying, was because of the way I studied Talmud."

"Got it"

"And he believed it. After a while he told his friends and they told their friends and so on."

"That's great," Sandy said laughing. "Very creative. I wish I had thought of that year ago when I was in a pulpit. So, what's the problem?"

Barbara Schwartz.

"huh?"

She wants to join the group. If I refuse I'm being sexist. If I permit her to join, the group will fall apart. The fact is nearly forty men have become friends. They talk about their relationships, they share their feelings over good wine and all this occurs while learning something about their religion."

"To top that off," David continued. "I've been monitoring, no watching them and as a result of these session they are emotionally opening up and learning new things about both Judaism and wine and they are becoming better husbands. And," he started to say,

"Their sex lives are improving."

"Exactly, but what do I tell Barbara?"

"Margolit? Excuse me David, Margolit! Could you bring me a glass of white wine? Not sweet. Not like the desert wine we had last night. Sauvignon blanc, French. David wait a minute I want Margolit to hear this conversation. I'm going to put this conversation on speaker phone."

"Speaker phone?" David gasped. "why would you do that?"

"Because dummy, I'm teaching her about men. She needs to listen."

"But what should I say to Mrs. Schwartz?"

"Tell her the truth boy. Tell her that in addition to study these men are sharing their feelings about hair loss, prostate cancer, and job loss. Tell her, a woman's presence in the group would alter the conversation. I can feed you enough information about gender differences that will provide her with food for thought."

"But what if she insists?" he asked.

"Ask her if she knows how difficult it is for these men to open up?"

"Ask her if she would rather have the men watching sports and drinking beer all of the time or coming together once a week to study and learning how to share? How to be better men? And then tell her, if, if she would consider you to be gender neutral, you would be glad to work with her and a few of her friends to develop a similar model for the women in the congregation. See how she responds. If it fails, tell her you need to think about it and will get back to her within a week."

"I'll try it, he said.

"No, do it! Margolit! Thank you for the wine. Now what did you think of the way I responded to David's situation?"

Parry, Repost: THE BIBLE CLASS

"Good morning, Rav Duvin," Yudah said as he entered the rabbi's study. "It's Torah study time."

"Yes, it is," he said as he closed his iPad. "I've been giving a lot of thought to what we've been doing these past few months and I realize that some of the topics we discussed were a little...to challenging," David said as he reached for a book placed on the corner of his desk. " Not because you're not intelligent. On the contrary, Yudah, you are very intelligent. It's just," he hesitated, "maybe my style of teaching might have been too provocative, and I really don't want to upset you, I cherish our friendship."

Yudah sat in the chair in front of his desk. He removed a handkerchief from one of his pockets and wiped his brow. "I'm wiping my head in front of you," he said with a smile, "not because it's too hot, but because what you just said was a great relief and I did not wish to be rude."

David smiled back at him and said, "I overdid it last week, didn't I?"

He nodded and replied, "I spent a lot of time thinking about the Talmudic story of Honi the Circle Drawer after we discussed it. When you suggested that it could have been just a story of a miracle worker, and there might never have been a man whose prayers to God for rain were always answered, I became upset. I had been taught by great teachers God heard Honi's prayers because he was so spiritually elevated. When you suggested it was just a myth, a story... and when you asked me, no," he stopped, "challenged me," he raised his voice, "to consider the possibility that people of great faith couldn't do what he did today what he did two thousand years ago, I, I, didn't know how to respond! It never occurred to me this might not have been a matter of faith but that the story was there for a different reason." He shook his head, "I couldn't let go of it all week."

"I'm sorry," David said as he reached out to grasp his hand. "I'm really sorry. That's why I chose something entirely different for us to study today. Something which shouldn't be upsetting. Something where we might have similar views."

"Really? What are you suggesting?"

"This morning, we are going to study the Shema. "

"The Shema?"

"Aah, I see you've heard of it," David said with a smile.

"Heard of it? I recite twice a day, every morning and every night. But why would you want us to study it? It's a prayer?"

"Why not? It's our most important prayer and it's the closest thing we as a people have to dogma?"

"Dogma? What's dogma?"

"Dogma," he said quietly, "attempts to define what we believe. We, believe in God, and so I thought we should study our most important prayer."

Yudah, shook his head from side to side. "We never studied prayer in Yeshiva. We just did it. We prayed. Three times a day because we are command-ed to pray three times a day."

David smiled, "then I can assume you know the words." Yudah nodded. "Good then we don't need a text. Well you won't need a text, I like to read," he responded as he casually opened the prayer book on his desk to the appropriate page. "Let's look at the first paragraph. What is its message?"

'You shall love Adonai your God with all your heart, with all your soul, and with all that is yours. These words that I command you this day shall be taken to heart. Teach them again and again to your children and speak of them when you sit in your home, when you walk on your way, when you lie down, and when you rise up. Bind them as a sign upon your hand and as a symbol above your eyes. Inscribe them upon the doorposts of your home and on your gates.' Deuteronomy 6:4-9

Yudah, smiled, "this is easy," he said. "The message is we should love God all of the time and teach our children to love God."

"I agree, and it comes from the beginning of the book of Deuteronomy. And the second paragraph was also selected from the same book but from a few chapters later on."

Yudah, smiled again. "I can see where you're going with this Rav. You are going to ask my why the third paragraph comes from an earlier book? You are going to ask me why the shema doesn't start with the third paragraph and continue sequentially, aren't you?"

"That's very perceptive of you, Yudah, but unfortunately, I know you know that the rabbis in Talmudic times organized the prayers and they had their own reasons for arranging the shema. Reasons about which we can only speculate. I'm concerned with the second paragraph what do you think it is trying to tell us?"

'If you will hear and obey the mitzvot and I command you this day, to love and serve Adonai your God with all your heart and all your soul, then I will grant the rain for your land in season, rain in autumn and rain in spring. You shall gather in your grain and wine and oil- I will also provide grass in your fields for cattle-and you shall eat and be satisfied. Take care lest your heart be tempted, and you stray to serve other gods and bow to them. Then Adonai's anger will flare up against you, and God will close up the sky so that there will be no raise and the earth will not yield its produce. You will quickly disappear from the gold land that Adonai is giving you. Therefore, impress these words of mine upon your heart and upon your soul. Bind them as a sign upon your hand and as a symbol above your eyes. Teach them to your children, speaking of them when you sit in your home, when you walk on your way, when you lie down and when you rise up. Inscribe them upon the doorposts of your home and on your gates. Then the length of your days and the days of your children, on the land that Adonai swore to give to your ancestors, will be as the days of the heaven over the earth.' Deuteronomy 11:13-21

Yudah closed his eyes and began to recite the prayer. At first, David could see he did it very quickly. Then, he paused, eyes still closed and recited the second paragraph more slowly. He watched his lips move. He did it again. After what he assumed was the third repetition, he opened his eyes and said.

"This is very interesting Rav. We never were instructed to think about the prayers. We were always told to do them. When a prayer was written with the intent to ask God to heal the sick, we know we are supposed to ask God to heal the sick. The second paragraph tell us to love God and if we do, we will be blessed. And if we don't, we, he paused, the world will be cursed."

"Interesting, you used the word, 'we' because the language in this paragraph changes from the singular to the plural. Who do you think the 'you,' (plural) are?"

"Interesting question," he replied. "On one hand the prayer speaks to me as an individual but later on it speaks to everyone" he said.

"Okay," David said continuing, "Yudah, do you believe, if I believe in God, it will rain when it is needed? That I will prosper while those who don't believe will be punished, or, will everyone be punished and all of the nations of the world will suffer?"

He stopped and smiled, "you're doing it again aren't' you Rav? You're confusing me. You're making me"

"Think," he said interrupting him. "I'm making you think."

"Wait a minute," David said hesitantly, "maybe we should stop." He closed the book and sat book in my chair. "We can come back to this later, if you want. I just realized, while you seem to be enjoying our little back and forth, you look a little out of sorts. A little less than your usual self. Is everything all right? Your wife and child, are they healthy?"

"Yes, yes, they are both fine and in good health. I'm just, well I'm just," he paused and looked at him as a younger man would look to one's senior, "Rav can I, would you mind if I asked you for a little advice?"

"Of course, I don't mind. You can share anything you want with me. Anything you say won't leave this room."

"I'm having a little trouble with my work."

"Every day, I go to the hospital to visit the sick."

"So, do I," David responded.

"I know. And when I visit people, I often invite them to my home for Shabbat dinner."

"go on."

"And most of the time they come to my home but most of them ask if it's all right if they leave early so they can attend Shabbat services at your shul."

"What's wrong with that?" David asked.

"I was taught they would stay. And if I asked them to come to my home Shabbat morning, so I could pray, they would come."

"When we first met, you told me you would not start another synagogue."

"I did what my teachers told me to do," he responded. "I started to deliver Challot to people's homes, only to learn that you and your members were baking challot and delivering challot. So, I stopped."

"I went to your religious school and offered to teach them how to bake matzah and learned that your members were baking matzah for the all the Jews and giving some of it away to the poor." He scratched his head. "I know people like me who are succeeding. I know you like me, but I'm failing. I was given eighteen thousand dollars and told to go to this community and make people Jews. I'm running out of money and every time I try to do something. It's already being done. You're a very good Rabbi. I'm planning on going to the town council meeting next week and to ask for permission to erect a huge Menorah in the town square next year. Would you come with me? Would you support it?"

David shook his head. "No," he said. "I don't believe in public displays of religion. Next year, the synagogue will host eight nights of olive oil tastings and baking contests. We will have a crafts fair in the synagogue, its already in process."

Yudah, sighed. He raised his head and looked at me. "I have to succeed. It's my calling."

"I know you do," he replied quietly. "I think we should talk about this another time. I'm certain there is a way. Let me tell you a story that might help you work through your dilemma."

"A long time ago, when King Josiah ruled in Jerusalem, he was concerned that either the Babylonian and Egyptians would subjugate his people. In order to prevent this, he reorganized the government. The three major things he did were, He replaced the system where village elders served as governors with Levites. The Levites were his civil service. They were in charge of interpreting the Law.

The second thing he did was to outlaw sacrificing, which in those days meant worshipping God in the local villages. Josiah demanded that sacrifice could only take place in one place, the Temple in Jerusalem." I looked at him, "you know this right?"

He nodded his head glumly.

He continued, "the problem with that was the people who couldn't afford to travel to Jerusalem and offer sacrifice could no longer worship as they had been for generations. Imagine how upset how bereft they were? If they wished to sacrifice to God, like their grandparents might have done, they could be incarcerated or worse. Are you following me?"

"I always thought the paragraph was about faith," he said slowly. I was taught the words were meant to challenge them to behave and believe in God."

"I understand," David replied "but just stop for a second and think about it. How would you feel if the way you had worshipped God for generations was suddenly taken away from you?"

"I never thought of it that way before," he said. "It never occurred to me."

"The second paragraph of the Shema was written for and to the people who couldn't go to Jerusalem and sacrifice whenever they wanted. It was written for the common people who had to stay home and tend the flocks and take care of their fields. That paragraph told them they still could worship locally. They still could offer sacrifice but! They had to do in in our God's name."

"Yudah, do you understand. The text teaches us there are different legitimate ways of worshipping. And then it reminds us in the third paragraph that the mezuzah which we place on our doors and the tefillin with which we wrap ourselves, are tools to remind us that however we pray we need do it to the God who took us out of Egypt and created the world."

'Adonai said to Moses: Speak to the people Israel and instruct them that in every generation they shall put tzitzit on the corners of their garments, placing a thread of blue on the tzitzit, the fringe of each corner. That shall be your tzitzit and you shall look at it, and remember all the mitzvot of Adonai, and fulfill them, and not be seduced by our heart and eyes as they lead you astray. Then you will remember and fulfill all My mitzvot and be holy before your God. I am Adonai your God, who brought you out of the land of Egypt to be your God, I am Adonai you God---' Numbers 15:37-41

"Think about it Yudah. Consider the message of our most important prayer. I think it has the potential to steer you in the right direction." David stood up and reached out and placed his hand on his shoulder. He took a deep breath and exhaled smiling and shaking his head. "I know Yudah, I did it again," he said.

"But this time, I think I've given you more than confusion. Perhaps a way exists which can make you feel more successful. The text teaches us in a very subtle way, we can be sensitive to multiple populations. In this case, those who have the ability to go to Jerusalem and those who because of their circumstances need to stay home. Perhaps there are other paths to success for you if you desire to stay in our community."

David removed his hand and looked at his watch. "It's late," he said. "Maybe next time we can drink some wine and meet in the evening."

Yudah stood up and shook his head once more. "I think I have to thank you Rav, but I have a great deal to consider. Shabbat Shalom."

"Shabbat Shalom," he replied and returned to his work.

Part Three: I'm on my own

An Evening with Barbara

"Good evening Rabbi, please come in. Let me take your coat. You can place the umbrella in the canister to your right," Barbara said as he removed his coat and entered her home.

"Thank you for finding the time to see me," David said as he pushed back his hair and entered the hallway.

"Michael's watching television, and the kids are supposedly doing homework and studying. We can meet in the kitchen if you don't mind," she said as she closed the doors to the den. The sound of the television and what must have been a ballgame ceased.

"I love kitchens," he replied smiling as he followed her into a brightly lit, well organized kitchen filled with pots, pans and all kinds of devices. "Hmm, lots of books on the shelves."

"I was wondering," Barbara said as she walked toward the refrigerator and asked, "coffee or wine? I heard," she said with a chuckle, "you enjoy wine."

"Wine, of course," he replied as he took in the kitchen and its many appliances.

"Who's the handy one in the kitchen?" he asked.

"It's me," she responded as she reached into the refrigerator and removed a bottle of red wine. She raised her right arm and reached to a shelf and removed a corkscrew. She looked at the bottle, shook her head and returned the corkscrew to the shelf. Following that, she grasped the bottle and slowly turned the twist off cap to the right until it opened. She turned slightly and removed two glasses from another shelf and then slowly filled the glasses.

"Cheers," she said as she reached out and clinked his glass.

"Salud," he replied with a smile as he brought the glass to his lips.

David looked at her. A woman in her early forties. Brown straight hair and an athletic build. Maybe five feet four five inches, a nice complexion and a face that looked like it smiled easily.

"I was wondering," she began, "why you wanted to meet in my home instead of your office."

"I've never been to your home before," David answered. "I always find it more comfortable to speak, to meet in one's home than in a cold office, and by coming to visit you it also provides me a better understanding of you and your family. I know Amy, because I see her in religious school, but I really don't know her. After we finish our conversation, assuming you're still talking with me, I want to say hello to both of the kids."

"You're kidding, right" she asked. "Of course, I'll continue to talk to you. I just might not be pleased with you."

David took another sniff of the wine and then placed his glass on the table. "Let me explain."

Barbara smiled weakly and said, "You don't have to explain. Just tell me why I can't join your Talmud class."

He waved a hand, "I said I'd get to that, let me try to explain."

She placed her wine glass on the table and began to tap her foot. "Okay, I'm listening."

"Please," David said. "Don't get angry, at least not yet. In order for me to tell you why you can't join the class I need you to listen to what I have to say. This is not a black and white situation. This is more complicated. Look, I schlepped all the way out here and you offered me a glass of wine. Give me a few minutes to provide you with a little background and then, if you still want we can address your concerns head on."

Barbara caught herself and smiled graciously. "I hate this gender imbalance. I'm smart and I'm successful, more successful than my husband and... and... you're right. You came to see me. You deserve the opportunity to present your case."

"Barbara are you a lawyer?"

"No, but I keep the calendar for a city judge. I've learned a little about the legal process in the last fifteen years."

David took a deep breath and paused. "I want to start again," he said. I'm going to ask you to listen what I have to say about gender development. I don't want to make you angry, but I need to explain what I've learned from people who study gender. If you've heard this before, stop me. I don't want to bore you."

David took a breath and began. "I'm sure you know that boys' brains and girls' brains develop differently." She nodded affirmatively.

Here's an example. You have two children. Do you remember when they were toddlers?"

"Of course," I do she replied tersely.

"Do you remember how yummy they were?"

"Of course, I do," she replied.

David glanced at foot the one that was still tapping. "Do you remember how Michael responded to them when they were that age?"

She looked at him quizzically. "What exactly do you mean?" she asked.

"Well," he continued, "did he pick them up and throw them over his shoulders and smile and they would either scream or laugh with joy?"

"Of course, he did," she responded curtly. "And I told him to stop it because he was going to drop them and break them."

David smiled. "And what did he do when you told him to stop?"

"He stopped. He put them down and I never saw him do it again."

"Barbara," David replied softly. "This is how men are programmed to demonstrate love. This is how men teach their children how to be comfortable with their bodies. This is how they teach their sons and their daughters not to be afraid and to risk. Would you want your children to grow up not being physically comfortable with themselves? Would you want them to grow up being afraid to take risks?"

David reached out and grasped the wine glass and lifted it once again to his nose. He inhaled, "can't drink this slop," he said to himself and returned the glass to the table.

"Barbara, this is just one of many examples I can share with you. I want you to understand sometimes men and women, as equal as they are in every respect, sometimes act or react to situations differently."

Barbara took a sip of the wine, looked at David and said, "Rabbi, I understand what you're saying. But that doesn't explain why I can't join your class."

"Barbara, I'd rather you chose not to join the class, because…" he stopped. "Does Michael have many male friends?"

She paused, "no, not really. As a matter of fact, my friends, my women friends have often spoken about that. Why do you ask?"

"Because the Talmud class is providing the men in the class with the rare opportunity to share and to develop male relationships that aren't competitive. Yes, we study but at times questions arise about aging, or health or difficulties at work, just for a moment," he paused. "The Talmud class is the only opportunity these guys have to let just a little bit of it out. I'm afraid your presence could alter that dynamic. Do you understand?"

The foot tapping stopped. Barbara paused. She looked at David in a very serious way. "Rabbi, she said in a soft voice, I don't like what you said. As a matter of fact, it really bothers me. But you expressed yourself very well and I understand what you're saying."

She shook her head and turned away just a bit. "I'm intellectually starving. I can't stand those book groups. My husband has to be dragged to lectures. I'm bored with teas and sisterhood trips. All my friends who belong to the synagogue have husbands who for some reason are becoming more interesting men. And if they can have that opportunity then I want it too! What can you do for me?"

David picked up the glass of wine and ran it under his nose.

"You really don't like the wine, do you?" She said.

He laughed, "I guess I wasn't very clever about hiding my tastes. No, it's not for me." He paused and smiled and then softly asked, "Barbara, there is something I could do. "I'd be willing to study with you privately. If you wanted to bring a friend, you could. That's how this kiddush club thing began. With one person and then somehow, I guess by word of mouth, it grew. What do you think?"

"Could it be for couples?"

He shook his head. "It could be, but I doubt you would be satisfied."

"Hmmm, I understand," she said. "Let's try it one-on-one and see how if it progresses. Do you think you can have someone call Michael and invite him to the kiddush club?"

Mid May – The Annual Meeting

"I can't believe it," Leonard said. "The Synagogue is packed! Maddie, look at all these people! New people! Young couples! well-dressed couples. This is unbelievable!"

Maddie smiled as they walked toward the podium that had been erected in front of the Ark where the Torahs were housed. "I know Leonard, she said with a smile, it's like Yom Kippur at yizkor time. I knew we were gaining members, I know the numbers and I've seen some of these people at Friday evening services and, she said haltingly," I've seen some of them at the evening minyan which meets just prior to the youth activities and education committee meetings. It seems someone," she paused and rolled her eyes, "has been inviting people to attend committee meetings."

"Not a bad thing," Leonard replied as he began ascending the two steps leading toward the podium. "He apparently changed the way the education and youth committees functioned by introducing…a

"I know Leonard, "an opening prayer and a short study session."

"That's not what I was going to say, Maddie. Stop being a lawyer. I was going to say, has begun to invite local professionals, some from the congregation others from the community at large, to lead discussions about issues surrounding childrearing. It brings out all or most of the parents."

"All of the schools used to do similar things until their budgets were cut," she said slightly nodding her head in agreement. "Well, here we are, the end of my first year of my third two-year term."

"But not consecutive terms," he chirped with a smile.

"No, you're right, not consecutive terms and", she added as she looked around, "It might actually be my last term based upon the increased level of involvement we are experiencing. "

"Are you aware, that the kiddush club is sponsoring the desert and that Mr. Scarlati has prepared all the food in honor of the rabbi, gratis?"

"No," she said, "I was just told the kiddush club agreed to make an exception and serve kosher wine this evening since it is an official synagogue event. By the way, I know we should have discussed this earlier but work too often interferes with synagogue life, you did prepare a financial report, didn't you?"

"Of course," I did, he replied. "If we disregard the cost of the new carpeting and painting thanks to those anonymous donors," he chuckled, we're doing very well. It seems that past members have renewed and are giving more to the Temple. It also seems we have grown by nearly twenty-five new families and the number of students in the religious school has increased significantly. Fifteen families have registered for next year's special post b'nai mitzvah program and attendance on Friday evening and even Saturday morning continues to increase."

"Has the rabbi signed the new contract?"

"No, not yet," Leonard replied, "but he will. It demonstrates our appreciation for him. Oh," he continued, "I just received a text from him," he says as he lowers his eyes to read it. "It says, he's sorry but he will be a little late." Leonard looked up, "apparently he had a private lesson at the pizza shop with a couple of the pre-b'nai mitzvah kids and had to stop off at his house to change."

"The Board still needs to vote on it according to our bylaws," she commented, "and I assume we can afford it."

"Oh, yes," Leonard replied with a smile. "The increase in salary is modest but Mark Eisen, the used car dealer donated a car. They really need a second car and, and, what's her name? Oh, yes, Sarah Kandel's husband assumed the cost of the car insurance. I'm certain he will sign on for the next two years and then, we'll see, hopefully, negotiations will be someone else's problem by then."

"Things certainly have worked out this year, "he continued. "New members, increased funding, and the Hasid seems to have disappeared."

"I heard he was transferred to Atlanta."

"Isn't that where the rabbi used to work?"

"Yes," Maddie replied. "The rabbi told me that the Southern communities in general were more open to his kind of Judaism."

"Could be," Leonard said as he shuffled through his notes. "I have the financials somewhere," he mumbled. "The people in the South tend to have stronger tendency towards fundamentalism. He probably will do very well there. Look! There's the rabbi."

"Wow, look at the way he's dressed. A suit, not just a jacket and tie."

"He takes this very seriously," Maddie commented. "As he should. After all this is his livelihood, his calling, his baby if he plays it right. It's time to call the meeting to order."

"He seems to be becoming more assertive, more confident. Would you agree?

Hold on! What's going on? Isn't that Bari Reisman?"

"Aaah found them," Leonard said as he extracted some papers from his briefcase. "I'm ready when you are," Leonard looked in the direction Maddie had indicated, "yes that's Bari. She doesn't look very well. Her face is red, her eyes are puffy. It looks like she's been crying."

"A death in the family?" Maddie asked.

"Don't know, but she certainly has the rabbi's attention. Hmm, she's showing him something. I wonder what it is?"

"I guess we'll find out shortly. Here he comes, and he looks very serious."

Maddie and Leonard paused as David approached.

"Maddie, Leonard, I can't stay. Something just came up and I have to leave."

"Not until the meeting's over and you've schmoozed with the community," she said as she waved a hand acknowledging the large group of people in sitting in the pews.

"No, I'm sorry. I really can't stay. Please trust me on this one."

"Is it a death in the family?" Maddie asked.

"No," David said slightly shaking his head, "if it were just a death, I know this sounds crass, I wouldn't feel the need to leave immediately. This is different."

"How different?" Leonard interjected. "In my experience, almost everything can wait, Rabbi." Leonard added. "I assume you have a very good reason for bailing."

"Leonard what I just learned is more than a family issue; it is a potential community concern. This is very, very different." David replied as he maintained eye contact with them. "Look, I know you're pleased with my work. I also know that you know, for some reason, which I am just beginning to figure out, that all of this growth, look around you, "he said as he gestured at the growing number of people filling the room, "just kind of happened. Somehow, I did the right thing at the right time. But this situation is different. I understand it. I've studied it. And Bari and her husband need me now."

Leonard and Maddie looked at one another. Leonard shrugged and said, "What will we tell the people?"

"Don't worry, I can handle this," David said with a grin. "Our people will understand. Trust me. Will you trust me?"

It's your wedding or your funeral rabbi," Maddie quipped.

David nodded, and he turned toward the group and raised voice.

"Ladies and Gentlemen, my friends," he said with a smile. "I want to thank you for taking time out of your very busy lives to be with us tonight. I, we," he said acknowledging Maddie and Leonard with a nod, "are honored by your presence. Unfortunately, I just learned I am needed elsewhere. It can't wait. So please forgive me for running out on you. But thank the kiddush club and Mr. Scarlati for doing such a wonderful job. I hope to see each of you soon. But unfortunately, not tonight."

"This better be good rabbi. We like what you're doing but you are still responsible to the Board and," she said in a firm voice, "contractual offers, can be rescinded."

"It's not good," David said. This isn't something I can make disappear in a few days. This about Hebrew-Christians."

"Hebrew-Christians? What's that?"

"Jews for Jesus," David said. "And Bari's thinks her daughter is being brainwashed. Gotta go," he said as he turned around and walked out the door.

The Talmud Trials

Robert moved the window shade aside as he saw the two cars pull into the driveway. He walked to the door, opened it and proceeded to walk towards the driveway.

"Thank you for coming so quickly rabbi," he said. "I thought you would be unavailable, the annual meeting."

"This is more important," David said as he escorted Bari into her home. He gently guided her with his hand supporting her elbow. As she entered the house, David released her and reached out and grasped Robert's hand.

"We can sit in the kitchen," Robert said as he turned and walked toward the kitchen. "I'll pour us something to drink. Bari, you're a mess. Don't cry, this isn't the end of the world. We just have to learn how to deal with it. It could be a lot worse. She could be injured or…he hesitated, or," he took a breath and cleared his throat. "Rabbi, we're in shock. We just learned about this a few hours ago while speaking with our daughter Elana on the phone."

"I don't know Elana," the Rabbi said. "I met her briefly when she last visited during the Winter break. What is she, nineteen? Twenty? And she lives in Boston?"

"No, she had a boyfriend in Boston for a while. She's a sophomore at Shadkhan University about twenty miles from here. It has good film and communications program." Robert said as he topped off three glasses of Scotch. "Almost twenty years old and very bright."

"And very shy," Bari added as she picked up two glasses and handed one to the Rabbi."

David brought the glass to his lips and inhaled. His nose wrinkled, he turned his head to the side and sneezed. "I'm sorry, Robert, I can't really handle hard liquor, but I would appreciate a glass of wine."

"Not a problem rabbi," Robert said as he retrieved the tumbler, placed it on the counter and opened the door to the wine cooler. "Red or white?"

"Aah, white please."

"Burgundy?"

David smiled, "You clearly deserve a good grade from the kiddush club for serving me burgundy."

They sipped and sat.

"Let's begin at the beginning", David said. "How did you learn about this?"

"I think," Bari started,

"You're trembling dear," Robert interjected.

"I know I'm trembling, I'm upset. Just let me say it my way."

"Okay, I'm sorry. You're right. I'm a little on edge as well."

"I think it started a few months ago, when we thought she had someone, a new boyfriend. She told us she was going to lectures and concerts and movies with a friend and she wouldn't tell us the friend's name."

"We figured it was a boy." Robert added.

"And then two weeks ago, I told her," Bari continued, "we had plans the following Sunday and I would have to postpone our Sunday noon call. "

"We have a tradition," Robert interjected, "of speaking every Sunday at noon."

"I see, please continue." David said motioning to Bari with his hand.

"We told her we would call her Sunday evening around seven and she said, that wouldn't work because she had a prayer meeting."

"She tried to cover it up. When we asked her what kind of prayer meeting? She said it was not really a prayer meeting but more of a social group that talks about social issues and feelings. Robert asked her if that's the case then why did she call it a prayer meeting?"

"She said in a dismissive tone meetings always begin with a prayer and we had nothing to worry about."

"And," Robert said as he sipped his drink. "that's when we began to worry."

David raised his glass to his lips and slowly inhaled. "There are all kinds of religious groups

"I'll be right there", David responded. "Where are those notes I took so long ago. They have to be here somewhere?"

"Rabbi we're drinking a Rhone wine called Cornas tonight. Have you heard of it?"

He stopped fumbling through the papers and looked up. "Cornas? We're drinking Cornas?"

Yum! Eddie we are in for a treat. Have you opened it yet?"

"Bobbie's cousin said it needed to be opened for at least an hour, so I left work early and took care of it." He shook his head, "there are a lot of people here tonight, I had to open three more bottles."

"You had three bottles of Cornas in the synagogue?" He asked incredulously.

"Bobbie's cousin sent us a case. Twelve bottles. He likes the fact that Bobbie's studying Talmud and that his family has started to come to Friday night services. What are we going to study tonight?"

"Aaah found it," he said proudly. "I knew it was here somewhere. Study? Hmmm," he stroked his chin, "I think, that we are going to study what the rabbis called "Avodah Zarah."

"Come on Rabbi get up, we're late," he said as he reached out and grabbed David's hand and helped him to stand. What's Avodah Zarah?"

"It means strange seed, or strange worship," David replied. "We're talking idolatry from a Greco-Roman perspective," he said. "But I think, in light of the circumstances, we are going to update it more than a little."

Eddie, opened the door to the Board room. It was filled with close to twenty men ages thirty-five to about sixty. The table was set in its usual Talmud class fashion. Wine glasses, place mats, small cheese snacks highlighted by strategically placed open bottles of wine.

David walked to the head table, still shuffling the papers he found in his study. "Good evening class," he said.

"Good evening Rabbi," the group answered.

David looked at the group and nodded to several of the men. "Welcome back Joe," he said. "We missed you last week. Hello Marvin, I know your wife's surgery went well, I hope she recovers quickly."

He placed his papers on the table, removed one and began to read. "This is from one of the many Haggadot that is used during Passover," he said as he placed his glasses on his nose and began to read.

"How many matzot do we have at the table?"

"Three," someone called out.

David, raised his eyes and said, "I don't want anyone to respond. Just listen. Just listen. I'll begin again."

How many matzot do we have at the table?

Why three, of course.

What do they stand for?

The Father, the Son and the Holy Spirit.

Why do we break the middle matzah?

Because his body was broken on the cross.

Why do we hide the afikomen?

Because his face has been hidden from us.

Why do we eat it at the end of the meal?

Because he will come to us at the end of time.

He lowered the paper and placed it on the table. He stared at the group.

"That's not in our Haggadah," someone said.

"That's bullshit."

"Crap,"

Why would anyone do that to our book?"

"That's the response I was waiting for Sam. Why would anyone or any group pervert one of most sacred traditions?"

"I know a little about this group," a well-dressed gentleman offered.

"Aaah, Bob," David added. "I thought you would. Why don't you tell the group who they are and what they are attempting to do? Afterwards you can provide us a brief update on our High school program."

"I'd be glad to Rabbi," Bob said as he straightened his tie, cleared his throat and squared his shoulders and began to speak. "I'm in lecture mode," he said.

"Well," someone called out, "stop wasting our time and give us the lecture, the wine deserves some attention."

Bob smiled and once again cleared his throat. A number of people in the room giggled.

"All right, all right," he grumbled. "Hebrew-Christianity is often and inappropriately called 'Messianic Judaism.' It is a movement which reflects the combined efforts of fundamentalists and evangelical Christian churches. Nearly 60 years ago, they instituted a proselytizing effort whose major premise was the acceptance of Jesus as the Messiah and that this was consistent with being a Jew.

Today, Hebrew-Christianity is a world-wide effort. They are primarily funded by groups like the Southern Baptists Convention and the Campus Crusade for Christ."

"Okay, Mr. Professah," someone called out, "but why are they doing this?"

"I'm getting there, I'm getting there," Bob responded. "Just give me a minute, I seem to remember that in general each of these groups basically believes the following:

Every human being is inherently sinful and separated from God.

Jesus was the Messiah as promised in the Prophets.

His death was an act of atonement for each individual's sins.

The only way to become accepted by God is through confession of sins and the belief that Jesus died for the individual."

He paused for a moment and cleared his throat again, "I'm not exactly sure about what follows, I seem to remember if you don't believe this way you go to Hell and they believe that if every Christian and Jew believes in Jesus it will bring the final messianic era."

"You mean," Eddie interjected, "these people want to bring us to you know who in order to bring you know who back?"

"Something like that," Bob responded. "That's why they reinterpret our holidays and laws. They believe if enough Jews accept Jesus it will shift the spiritual scale in a way that causes the return of the Messiah."

"Wait a second!" Jimmie called out. "I thought we were still waiting for the coming of the Messiah? That's what it says in the prayer books."

"Correct," Bob said as he nodded affirmatively. "They are referring to a second coming while we are theoretically, because some people don't believe in the Messiah as a person, are waiting for the first time."

"I have a nephew who was involved with them years ago," someone interjected." He said, he had become a fulfilled Jew, a better Jew because he believed in Jesus. He never had much of a Jewish background and one day he wandered into a shul on Shabbat… but it wasn't a shul. It was one of their places. They had a Torah, they were wearing yarmulkas and tallis's. He thought it was a shul. But it wasn't."

"Rabbi," someone added. "What can you tell us about this group and why bring it up today."

"Thanks Joe," David responded, "I needed a segue. Our Talmud lesson today is to learn more about these groups, their goals and their tactics." He paused and covered his eyes thinking, "I seem to remember something I learned long ago. Just a minute," he mumbled, "it was professor Siegel's class. We were studying the volume of the Talmud called Avodah Zarah. He began the class by saying, by saying,"

Almost 2000 years ago, a group of people acknowledged as Jews began to accept the divinity of Jesus. This brief phenomenon lasted approximately one generation before the final schism occurred.

The contemporary Jewish leadership perceived the danger and potential confusion between Judaism of the time and the developing, ancient Hebrew-Christian community.

The Talmud records a series of confrontations between these two diverging communities. They took place in Israel, the home of the Palestinian Talmud and the birth place of Aggadic, the legendary, Midrash. The rabbis in Palestine, unlike Babylon, were more knowledgeable in Bible.

"I think the implications of these confrontations might be significant for us to hear. You see, they were dealing with a religious group, or groups that wanted to convert our people. They responded to this external threat in a number of ways. One way was to insert specific prayers which Hebrew-Christians would not want to say into our daily prayers. A second way was to record or to create literature that would or could counter this potential threat. Aah", he said smiling, "I remember.

There was a rabbi who we call, Rabbi Abbahu. He was known to have said,

If a man says to you. "I am the son of man"—in the end he will regret it. "I will rise up to heaven" He says this but will not do it.

Abbahu, also said, there is a parable of a mortal King, he reigns and has a father and a son or a brother. Said the Holy One Blessed by He: "I am not like that. I am first, (Isaiah 44:6), I have no father. I am the last, I have no son. And beside me there is no God. I have no brother.

Stories like these were written down to provide future generations with a strategy to counter those who wished to convert them to Christianity. Our ancestors created laws and the placed them in the Talmud for future generations. Today, those of us who live in the modern world would consider them guidelines. They were statements and commentaries concerned with how one lives as a member of a minority religion in a larger polytheistic culture.

"Uhh, rabbi", Eddie said quietly interrupting, "you said you would try not to use words like that."

"What? Oh, of course. Polytheistic speaks of a time when many people believed in many gods. They were Greeks and Romans," David continued, "I'm sure you've seen some of the movies or read some of the books about Hercules and Zeus, and Apollo and Hera."

Almost all of the group nodded in agreement. "The rabbis were concerned with repercussions. Our ancestors wouldn't drink wine that had been dedicated to a god or goddess. They didn't want our people to do something inappropriate during one their festivals because they knew if our people, any of our people, offended one of their gods the results could be terrible."

David picked up his glass and sniffed the wine. He shook his head and returned the glass to the table. "This wine is too good to be drinking while discussing a topic of this nature. We should be drinking scotch. It's more apropos, appropriate," he said looking at Eddie. He sighed. "I know you know where it's been hidden. Find it for us, please."

Eddie rose, nodded and disappeared.

David continued. "We've only opened one bottle and believe me it's too good to waste. Let's make a kiddush, drink our wine and wait for the scotch. Gentlemen our lesson today is create a strategy how to save a young adult child and prevent this from happening again." He raised his glass, everyone followed his example.

"You know what to say,"

The group replied in unison. "amen."

Mid-June

"I'm glad you could make it Rabbi," Leonard said with a smile as he rose from his office chair and reached out and shook his hand.

"Me too," Maddie said as she greeted him with a warm peck on the cheek.

"It was nice of you to schedule this on a day when I was already in the city for the "Lunch and Learn"."

"Yes," Leonard said, "How did it go?"

"It was amazing," David replied. "This was the fourth session and twenty-five people attended. Lou Levine was incredible. He approached me after Religious school one Sunday and meekly suggested a monthly study session in the city. I was doubtful because, I didn't think our members who worked in the city could afford to take the time off. He asked me if I would permit non-members to attend the class." David nodded, "I said, "why not? Let's see what will happen."

"These are great chairs Len," he said as he sat in the leather armchair. "I'm a little wired, could I have a glass of wine?"

"Of course, of course Rabbi," Len said as he walked towards the bar. "I have begun to acquire some fine wines hoping you could on occasion stop by. Maddie there is a cheese platter through that door, could you get it? I," he paused, "we,' nodding at Maddie, have come to look forward to our briefings and frankly," he said as he handed David his glass, "it's great respite for both of us. We've become comfortable with you and you I hope, with us."

"You're correct," he said as he raised the glass to his nose and sniffed. "I enjoy thinking with both of you. The ways you approach problems, no, situations, has taught me a great deal as a problem solver and honestly," he paused, "even though we haven't spoken about it directly, I think I'm learning to become a better husband. I didn't exactly have great role models for parents and listening to the two of you has been a real help."

Maddie blushed and smiled. "The Lunch and Learn?" She prodded.

"Yes, right." David swallowed, "hmm, very good. Lou gathered psychiatrists, psychologists, different types of therapists, a few Doctors and even one Dentist. I didn't know he had an office near Union Square. Apparently, he rents office space to small business in a building he inherited from his father. This was our fourth meeting. It's a great group, at the end of the session some of them asked if we could make it once every three weeks. I told them, I had to speak to you about it because I didn't want to say 'no,' right away." He shook his head and then raised his glass for another sip. It would be too much preparation and time away from the community. However, he said. I had an idea."

"Here we go," Leonard said with a smile. "What will it cost us?"

"Not a thing. It will help us," David said. "These men and women live in the city or in more affluent suburbs. They will never move to our little shtetl. But, they will or already do, feel an obligation to pay for their classes."

"Go on," Leonard said with a nod. "I think I'm going to like this."

"I would like the synagogue to establish two scholarships. One for one of our children to attend a Jewish camp and the other in the local High School."

"The High School?" Maddie questioned, "why the High School?"

"For a number of reasons." David replied. "First we live in what is still a working-class neighborhood. I think only half of last year's graduating class went to a four-year college. Many of those who did, are commuting. Their parents just don't have the funds. A partial scholarship to a State College would make a serious statement about our community and it might motivate some of the other religious organizations to do the same."

"Nice," Leonard said clapping his hands. "very nice and the Lunch and Learn would support it."

David just sat there and smiled. Maddie and Leonard looked at one another and nodded. "How do we set this up?" Maddie asked.

"The scholarship to summer camp will be easy. I can work with our education and youth committees and come up with a few suggestions to take the Board. The school scholarship will be much more interesting. A significant number of our members are college educated and a good percentage of them were raised in the area. I want your permission to ask two or three people who grew up locally, to run this committee. Once they agree, they will need to make an appointment with the school principal. Assuming the principal agrees, and I can't figure out why he or she wouldn't, the school will develop and suggest criteria. Once we have agreement, I'll discuss it with Lou and Lou will discuss it with the class. What do you say?"

Maddie looked at him with a smile, "Len, we did such a good job. We chose the right one. Run with it," she said.

The phone rang. Len picked it up. "Thank you, Ron, please send him in?"

"Are we expecting someone else?" David asked.

"Someone new," Len responded. "I don't know if you've met him yet. He's a new member. I just appointed him to the Board. He might actually, be a future president."

The door opened and an immaculately dressed clean shaven man looking about forty years old entered the room. He crisply walked over to Len and shook his hand. He turned and professionally reached out and took Maddie's as well. His light brown hair was precisely cut to a hair. Everything about him was in place.

David cringed.

He turned to David who stood along with the others as a matter of courtesy and extended his hand in a professional manner. "Rabbi, I'm Paul Stern. It's a pleasure to meet you."

David smiled weakly as they all sat down. "I saw you in shul last Shabbat. You were with a toddler," David said. "I looked for you at kiddush so I could introduce myself, but you had already left."

"Yes, well, I was hoping we would sing *anim zimirot* but when you chose to sing the traditional adon olam, I lost interest."

"Sorry," he said. "The congregation doesn't know it, and I like to end the service with full participation," he continued with a smile. "You have a background, that's great, I'd like to…."

"Yeshiva Etz Chaim," he snapped. "All the way through high school."

"Oh", David said thoughtfully. "That's a rather strict school if I remember correctly. We should talk more about this, I bet you have some skills we sorely need."

"Rabbi," Len interrupted, "we asked Paul to serve on the Board of Directors. He has strong management skills and as you can tell, a serious religious background."

"The Board? So quickly? I don't mean to disparage you Paul, but," he looked at Len and Maddie, "Don't you think a committee would be more in order. We could fast track him, but this way, Paul could meet some of our people and learn more about the community. He just moved into town."

"I don't think I would accept a committee position," Paul replied. "I manage more than fifty people, I'm used to making decisions."

David cringed, "I don't want you to misinterpret this, but being a leader in a synagogue, a volunteer organization, is different than managing a large company. I remember in my former congregation there was a young man and the president of the congregation decided to fast track him. He put him in charge of a committee and asked him to call a meeting. The idea was, the president could observe him, while he conducted the meeting in order ascertain his skills. The gentlemen, let's call him Mike, agreed and the meeting was set for the following week. A week passed, and the Shul President and I went to the allotted room. We were a little late because we attended the evening minyan first. Upon arriving at the designated place, we were shocked to find Mike sitting by himself. He had called a meeting, and no one had come.

"What happened? Mike where's your meeting?" the president asked obviously extremely concerned.

"I don't know," Mike responded. "I sent everyone on the list you had given me an email."

David turned to Paul and said. "It never occurred to Mike that people, volunteers, needed to be called and asked to attend. They needed to know why their attendance was important. They needed to feel appreciated. I know you're a leader and have the best intentions for our community but," David said in almost a whisper, "couldn't we ease you into a Board position after you've had a chance to schmooze with some of the people. Get to know them, let them learn to appreciate your sincerity, your," he shrugged his shoulders, "sense of humor, your seriousness of purpose."

Paul stood up and squared his shoulders and was about to speak.

I don't think this bodes well, David said to himself.

"It's too late," Maddie said interjecting herself into the conversation. "Paul has accepted a position on the Board. Rabbi, we have the greatest respect for what you have and are doing for our community. You've turned us around. For the first time in decades we are growing. We're lively. But Board decisions are our decisions. Your job is to work with Paul and help him develop and execute his portfolio."

David stopped. I've been here before, he thought. I've seen this before. It's time to eat crow, to back off.

"You're right Maddie," he turned to Paul. "I'm sorry, I hope I didn't offend you. I've only been here a year and I'm very protective of the culture we are trying to build. I'm sure you and the skills you bring will be a welcome addition."

Paul dropped his shoulders and broke into a grin, "Rabbi," he said. "I'm certain we will get along just fine. Just fine," he repeated as he reached out and offered his hand.

David extended his hand toward Paul, who grabbed it and squeezed and controlled it until he was satisfied that David understood who was going to be in charge. "I'm late for a meeting," he said as he released David from his grip. "I'll see you at the next Board meeting if not sooner," he said as he graciously said goodbye to Leonard and Maddie, turned and exited from the room.

"That was interesting," he said to Maddie and Leonard.

"We think he will be a real asset," Leonard replied.

"Obviously," David said as he exhaled and shook his head.

"You disagree?" Maddie asked.

"Does it matter?" David replied. "You made your decision. I have to live with it, him," he said correcting himself.

"He has a background?" Maddie said.

"He's young," Leonard added, "and he has money."

He's controlling, arrogant and most probably a bully, David thought. I've seen this before.

Leonard reached out and patted David's arm. "Give him time my boy. Give him time."

David smiled back weakly. "I don't have any choice. Do I?"

"No," Maddie said. "You don't. You don't."

Strangers Among us

It was Friday evening and the synagogue was a buzz. Most everyone was smiling as they entered the sanctuary. Eddie and Mikey were standing at the door and serving as "greeters."

They were casually dressed and not being ones who enjoyed group prayer preferred to stand at the entrance shake hands and greet people with a warm "Shabbat Shalom." As people entered they almost immediately became engaged as they heard the musicians softly playing music of welcome and comfort. The room was filled with feelings of joy and camaraderie.

I had just arrived and had entered as I did from time to time from the door which was behind the platform and the Ark which held the Torahs. I looked out at the group and smiled. More and more teens were coming to the Friday evening service. They would sit together and afterwards, congregate around one of the tables and snack and gack. And since most of them had yet to earn their driver's license they schlepped their parents along as well.

The week's Torah portion focused on the children of Israel being asked to choose how they would live. I planned on using this as a segue way for a discussion about choice. I thought it would be important for parents to hear their emerging adults' views about this concern. The one thing I knew about teens is that if you a question they will always have something to say.

Wait a minute! What's this?

A well -groomed, immaculately dressed young man and a similarly attractive young woman had just entered the sanctuary. They appeared to be in their mid to late twenties. And they looked cool. It was not our practice for people to wear a tallis on Friday evenings Yet both of them were wearing Yarmulka's and tallesim. I knew some Reform Congregations encouraged people to wear a tallit on Friday evenings but from the way these two individuals conducted themselves I seriously doubted they could be Reform Jews.

Unlike most people who upon being greeted with a "Shabbat Shalom," usually wish the greeter "Shabbat Shalom" back and then moved on, this couple proceeded to introduce themselves to others with a smile and a Shabbat Shalom. I watched them from afar. The young woman looked around and noticed they were the only ones wearing a tallit and slowly removed hers. She elbowed her companion and he nodded and did the same.

I looked at people beginning to sit in front of me. Martin and his friends were fooling around towards the back of the room. I gestured to him and caught his eye. I waved my hand indicating that I needed him to approach me. He looked at me and placed his waved in a way that indicated did I really need him to approach?

I nodded affirmatively. "Come here quickly," I gestured.

As he approached the lectern, I leaned towards and whispered. "Go tell Mikey and your Father not to let that man and woman talk to any teenagers."

ELANA

"This is Elana speaking, who are you I don't recognize the number?"

"Elana, its Rabbi Duvin calling you on my cell. Do you know who I am?"

"You're the new rabbi," she said. "I only heard you speak on the first day of Rosh Hashana, you seemed to be okay. I know my mother has been going to services more often and my Dad takes a class with you and has developed a taste in wine. Why are you calling me?"

"I'm planning a trip to campus and I'd like to meet with you if you can find the time."

"Did my mother put you up to this?"

"No," he said. "Why would she?"

Pause…

"Never mind, not important. Why are you coming to campus?"

"I heard you would be attending the Summer session and frankly that works for me," he replied. Beginning in the Fall seven members of our congregation's children will be entering as Freshman and I believe you are one of at least five men and women who are already attending school. Your mother told me you had a good memory, so I assumed you know most of them, if not all of them." He paused. "I was hoping that with your help we could plan a meeting on campus in the Fall. It would allow me to further develop my relationships with them."

"Rabbi? Why are you doing this? We're not necessarily shul goers, if you know what I mean."

"Of course, I understand that Elana. But there are times when everyone could use a clear head. I thought with your help we could plan to have a group schmooze at the beginning of the semester. I'd sponsor a dinner, or an evening in a bar. And if it works maybe we could have a follow up during the Thanksgiving break."

"Rabbi, what exactly are you asking me to do?"

"Not much, just get their email addresses and cell phone numbers and tell them not to be surprised when I call them."

"You're going to call all of us?"

"Yes, of course. It's the only way to get to know people and to get something done. If I came to visit a week from Thursday could I take you out to dinner, so I could get the, so called lay of the land?"

"Yes," I think I could possibly make it," she said. "What kind of food would you suggest?"

"What would you suggest?"

"I don't know," she replied. "I'll give it some thought."

"I'll text you my number. Try to answer me by Friday. Okay?"

"Okay," she said as she disconnected from him. She turned to her roommate and said, "That was a bit weird."

"Step one," he said to himself.

Mid-July

"David?" Rachel asked as the three of them walked in the local park. She was carrying a picnic basket and Ari was running up to trees and attempting to climb them.

"I can climb that one?" he said pointing. "Look it has low branches."

"Yes, I believe you can," David said smiling. "Why don't you try it?"

"David! He might fall and break something," Rachel said, as a little bit of tension entered her voice.

"Probably not," David responded. "leave him alone and just get close to the tree so we can catch him if he indeed falls. Rach, we can't stop him from being a boy."

The two of them stood under the tree watching Ari struggle to climb. David walked over to him grabbed him by the waste and boosted him to the first branch.

"David!"

"Thanks Dad," Ari said with a smile as he reached up and grabbed the branches above him. He lifted his legs and started to climb.

Rachel shook her head, pointed to David to stay where he was and watch him. She walked a few feet away and began to unpack the picnic bag. She removed a large blue and white colored blanket from the basket and proceeded to place it strategically on the ground. The blanket was followed by a series of plastic containers, paper cups, plastic ware and bottled water and napkins.

Still watching Ari struggle on a branch as he inched his way outward, having decided he had climbed high enough, David glanced over to Rachel and said. "you do good work kid."

She smiled back and replied, "Tell your son, time for lunch."

David returned the smile and passed the word along. Ari began the long arduous crawl back to the base of the tree. Lunch passed quickly, and Ari picked up his iPad and began to play games. Within a few minutes, his eyes glazed over, and he laid is head on the blanket.

"Sound asleep," David said. "Just like a five year old."

"I'm glad he's sleeping," she said as she leaned into him and placed her head on his chest. "There's something I wanted to ask you."

"Ask!" David replied with a smile.

"I was thinking of our planning a short family trip and so I took a look at your calendar and noticed you're going to visit Shadkan university next week. What's that about?"

David looked her and sighed, "Do you remember I told you that one of our members had a child who was possibly involved in a cult?"

"Yes," she nodded.

"Well, she is a student at Shadken," he replied. There's a good chance they're Jews for Jesus."

"And?"

"And I thought I do a little reconnaissance. I'm going to meet with our student and to do a little research."

"Isn't there someone locally you could call?"

He shook his head, "I don't think so. And if what I think could be going on is going on, she's in trouble. Rach, I have to go there."

"Okay," she said. "I understand. I won't plan our little get-away next week.

"Rach?" he said. "I might need you for this."

"What do you mean? You might need me."

"Did I ever tell you about my old high school friend Donald?"

She shook her head, "I'm not sure," she said. "if you did, it clearly didn't stick."

"Well, my best friend in High school was a boy named Donald. He was smart, a great athlete and a musician. He went to an Ivy League school and performed brilliantly for the first two years.

"And then," he paused and shook his head sadly.

"Something changed. Don loved to argue. He was a great lawyer in the making and one day he got into a discussion with someone who called himself a Hebrew-Christian. That person, let's call him Dean, engaged Donald in a series of long discussions, well, they were more like informal debates about the nature of the Messiah.

He claimed that he was a fulfilled Jew because he understood that Jesus was the Messiah. He showed Donald verses in the Bible and explained, no, he persuaded Donald to believe that he, Dean, understood the text. Donald was at a loss. Hebrew school hadn't prepared him for this kind of, today we would call it bullying. Dean challenged Donald to come to a class and to learn the true meaning of the Bible. Donald acquiesced."

David sighed. "We hadn't see each other for more than a year. I spent a year in Israel my junior year and didn't see him until I had become a senior and was considering applying to rabbinical school. I reached out to him, after all we were close friends. When we finally met. He was a different person. He had dropped out of school and was supporting himself as musician and composer of religious music in one of their churches. He wasn't speaking with his parents and barely had a relationship with his siblings. Rach, these people are dangerous. I don't know what to do about this, but I know I have to do something."

She reached out and placed a hand on his arm. "What do you want me to do?" she asked.

"I don't know. At least, not yet."

Rachel pushed herself away and looked directly into David's eyes. "David," she said, "you're changing."

"What are you talking about Rachel, I'm the same person I've always been."

"No," she replied thoughtfully. "You're more confident, more decisive."

"Would you say I'm mission driven?" he replied with a smile.

"No, you've always been like that. You're just becoming more of you. That's why the synagogue community is growing."

"Rach," he said, "All this stuff is happening all around me and I know I must be doing something right, but I have yet to figure it out."

"You are figuring it out," she replied as she replaced her head on his chest. "It's just that you're doing it your way. You are just beginning to understand and use your strengths. You have no idea how pleased and secure that makes me feel. Now tell me how you plan on handling this situation."

David took a deep breath and stretched. "Years ago, I met a few people who called themselves, "counter missionaries." They used to and probably still attempt to rescue people who have been sucked into a cult. They pride themselves as being "deprogrammers."

"Does it work?"

"Sometimes, not always." What does happen is after a number of years some of these young adults begin to realize this isn't the life they wanted, and they attempt to leave, that is if they haven't been married off and become parents. I want to speak with them and do some thinking and then we can plan together. I, We need to do this."

"I like the 'we' part," she said with a smile.

August – The Ritual Committee Meeting

"The rabbi," Paul said in a firm voice, "is consistently changing the tunes in the service. It's becoming impossible for me and, he continued as he looked around the room, "and for many others to be able to pray. Rabbi, I think you and your musical group should let us sing the old tunes. The tunes we know. The one's we heard as children."

The men and women of the ritual committee with the exception of one young man, nodded their heads in agreement.

"Excuse me, the young man said, Paul? May I speak?"

"Go ahead, John, the floor is yours."

The man named John smiled and said "thanks. I like what the rabbi's doing, the new tunes move me and my family. They have transformed the services of my childhood from something I ran away from to a warm embracing experience. For the first time in my life, I want to go to synagogue on Friday night."

"I don't like the music," someone murmured.

"I can't follow along. I don't read Hebrew and it's difficult for me to follow in the transliteration booklet," someone added.

"There are too many young people and its noisy," a third added.

David winced.

"But," John added. It sounds to me that I'm one of those young people who have become active and you don't want me and my family to attend! Don't you realize you're supposed to want to attract young people. You're supposed to be willing to accept the rabbi's innovations?"

"My son and half of the b'nai mitzvah class has been attending Friday evening services because they like what's taking place. They, no we, attend and then we stay after the Shabbat oneg and help clean up. Are you implying that we should not be interested in bringing future generations of Jews to Judaism?" a woman in her late thirties interjected."

All of a sudden everyone in the room had something to say. And they all said it at once. Voices began to rise and one women clearly in her eighties stood up and began wag her finger at a contemporary who sat across the table. Paul sat at the table's head and smiled. It was his first ritual committee meeting.

Not being able to stand it anymore David rose with the intent of stopping the madness. Paul reached out and firmly grabbed his arm forcing him back into his chair. "Let it go for a minute," he said. "they'll calm down."

David pulled his arm free and glared at Paul. "don't you ever touch me again," he spat.

"Or what Rabbi?" "You'll fire me?"

David caught his breath. "I don't like what you're doing, and we have to stop it right now. Either you do it, or I will."

Paul smiled, "now that's the way I like it." He turned to the people at the table and raised his arms over his head. One at a time, the men and women in the room noticed his gesture and stopped haggling with one another.

"Ladies and Gentlemen," Paul began. "It seems we have a situation. One which might take us a while to resolve. The question before us is what we do with the Friday evening service."

"It's the service that most people attend," someone added.

"I've never seen so many children and young people at one time," another chimed in.

"I miss the old tunes,"

"Me too," another chimed in.

Paul turned to David all smiles. "Rabbi," he said. "What do you think we should do? How can we satisfy both groups?"

David was fuming. This guy could ruin my life, he thought. He could unravel everything I've done, either because he enjoys seeding destruction, or perhaps, because he really wants to relive his childhood. What should I do?

"Rabbi," Paul asked. "what should we do?"

David glared at Paul. I must, I need to take this meeting back what can I do?

Got it.

"Let me tell you a story," David began. "It's a midrash that we can date around the 8th century. We are told, and I'm sure many of you have heard the legends the midrashim that there were worlds before ours."

Many of the men and women at the table nodded in agreement.

"Well this midrash explains that prior to the creation of the world, the Lord held three council meetings. The initial one was comprised of all of the members of the heavenly host. Angels, *seraphim*, *ofanim*, and *chayot hakodesh*. God gathered them in a great assembly and announced that he was going to create the world.

Immediately hundreds of the members of the heavenly host cried out. "God don't do it! You don't need to do that. You have us the heavenly host we can fill you with glory."

And we are told that the Lord disagreed, and he breathed deeply, and his eyes began to glow with fire and there was a puff of smoke and every member of the host that had protested disappeared.

David looked around the room. He had everyone's, even Paul's attention. He smiled.

Sometime later the Lord God called for a second meeting. And once again the entire heavenly host attended. This time the Lord looked at those whom he had created, and he said. "My Gentle friends. I am going to create mankind.

The heavens erupted in anger. "Don't do it?" You will create mankind and they will disobey you. They will anger you. Man is frail and mortal while we are strong and immortal. Please don't do it. You don't need the *tzouris*."

And, we are told that the Lord of all creation, huffed and puffed and his eyes glowed and there was a puff of smoke and all of those who stood up in dissent, vanished.

The midrash concludes shortly after the Lord assembled the remnants of the heavenly host for a third and final meeting. The Lord gazed at them for brief moment and simply announced. "I am going to give mankind Torah."

The host remained silent. Except for one angel who was standing in the back of the room. He stood up strait and tall and cried out. "Don't do it God, Mankind will abuse Torah!"

And God just looked at him. Stared at him. And after a moment, said, "what is your name sir?"

The angel replied, "My name is truth."

David paused and looked at the group sitting before him. "It's interesting he said, how this Midrash ends. He looked at Paul and nodded his head. "The midrash ends on a unique note. We are told that the Lord picked up this angel, grasped him in his hands and cast him out of heaven. The Lord threw him out of heaven and he landed on the earth."

"Truth, my friends, truth cannot be in heaven. It is amongst us on the earth. Our task, and we are not going to solve it tonight. We need to discuss the Friday night services another time. When feelings can be put aside. Another time." David said as he stood up and walked out.

BEING FULFILLED

The wooden plaque on the door said, "Ministers of Peace" It was surrounded by several Stars of David and a series of different types of crosses in different colors creating a warm and happy but somewhat juvenile effect. David lifted the heavy wooden knocker and let it fall twice. As the knocker impacted with its base a deep almost Buddhist bell like sound reverberated through his hand. He reached for the doorknob and attempted to turn it. The Bell rang a third time, this time without assistance. There was a click and the door sprang open. He gave the door a little push and entered a small hall with coat hooks on either side of the room and what appeared to be cubby holes on the floor.

At the end of the hall was a table filled with literature in both Hebrew and English. A mezuzah had been affixed to the appropriate side of the wall.

"Hello? Hello." He said as he entered the room.

"You can hang your coat on the coat hooks, "a voice said coming from somewhere in the room. "I'll be right there, just a minute. No," the voice continued. "Keep walking you'll find me behind the parochet."

"Parochet?" David said as he began walking towards where the voice originated. "What's a parochet?"

"It's the curtain we place in front of the Ark where we keep the Torahs," a young man said in a muffled voice. "Just walk behind it, you'll find me at the table. I need to finish rolling the Torah before I can formally greet you."

Following his voice, David walked into a multipurpose room designed to look like a sanctuary. A piece of rope tied at both ends to large ten-foot poles held a curtain. Behind it was a table upon which a Torah rested. A man was slowly rolling it closed.

"I'm Reb Shlomo," he said as he rolled the Torah closed. "You can help me dress it and put it away. Do you know what to do when I lift it?"

"Actually, not really," David replied. "I remember seeing this in Temple many years ago. But I haven't done it myself. Maybe once at a bar mitzvah."

"Grab the covering on the chair and slide it over the Torah so that the holes at the top fit over the top."

He did as he requested. He watched as Reb Shlomo lifted the newly dressed Torah and placed it in the Ark. He pulled the chord on the side and the curtain closed. This was followed with the shutting of the doors at the outside of the curtain. Reb Schlomo had a pleasant friendly face, straight brown well-groomed hair and a nice smile. A Yarmulka with a cross and a Star of David rested on his head.

About thirty-five, David guessed. Dressed in jeans and a work shirt. Blue eyes and fair skinned. The least Ashkenazic person I have seen in years.

"What's your name?" he asked. "And what brings you here?"

"Oh," I said shyly, "I'm sorry. I'm David. David Eisenstadt. My wife and I recently moved to town. We are sort of considering joining a community and I did a search and found your address and thought I might stop to see what it's like."

"Okay, I get it," he said with a smile. "Pull up a chair and we'll schmooze. But let me ask you a question, why us? Why here? What brought you here?"

David blushed and then smiled. "Well, my wife is Jewish and I'm kinda Jewish. If you know what I mean. I don't do anything Jewish, my father was Jewish. I had a bar mitzvah. When we got married, Rachel, my wife and I decided we wouldn't practice anything until we had children. If we had children, then we would let them decide about religion. We had a child a couple of years ago and we decided maybe it wasn't such a good idea to let the kid make these types of decisions. Maybe we should do something about it first."

"Good, good," he nodded. "Continue please."

Rachel agreed to look at some of the more modern liberal churches and even a Reform and Renewal synagogue. I chose to investigate the smaller, less institutional organizations."

"Hmm," he said, "can I ask you a question?"

"Sure," he responded.

"Do either of you believe in God?"

"No," he said in a scoffing tone. "Or course not."

"Why not?"

"Seven Days? Ten plagues? Can't eat this and can't do that! That's not religion, that isn't going to spiritually stimulate me or help me become a better person."

"Well," Reb Schlomo said softly. "I believe in God. I believe in a God who will bring me to a better place. Who will take care of me after I die and all I have to do is believe he died for our sins."

"That's Jesus," I said. "I can't believe in Jesus. I'm a Jew."

"Didn't you just tell me you didn't believe in God and you didn't practice Judaism?"

David nodded.

"I don't blame you," Reb Shlomo said continuing. "I wouldn't either. But," he paused. "if I really believed in something. I could become a better Jew. A fulfilled Jew. Wouldn't you and Rachel and your, what's your child's name?"

"Ben," he added

"Ben," he said continuing. "Wouldn't you want your family to know they are and will be taken care of, no matter what."

"Maybe," David replied. "I'm not buying what you're selling."

"I wouldn't expect you to David. We just met. Why don't you come to services one Friday evening and check out what we do? Afterwards, if you like it, we, and I mean we, both of you and I can talk about it. We do some wonderful things for the community for emerging adults, for the elderly."

"Excuse me," David said interrupting, "Did you just say, you work with college students?"

He smiled, "emerging adults? Of course, they are so needy. Always questioning, looking for answers as they find their places in the world."

David looked at his watch.

"Don't you want to talk theology?" Shlomo asked.

"No, I studied theology in graduate school among other things. I'm not that kind of seeker."

"Really," Reb Shlomo replied with a smile. "I don't exactly believe you. I think we should spend some more time together. I find you intriguing."

David glanced again at his watch.

"Do you have to leave?"

"Yes, unfortunately I do. But I might take you up on your offer. How long do the Friday evening service last?"

"The service lasts, around an hour and it includes the Torah reading and discussions. Afterwards we meditate and then we tea and cookies, vegan cookies. It's very peaceful," he added. "Tuesdays and Wednesday evenings. We have Bible discussion and group minyan."

"Minyan?"

"Group prayer," he said. "Thanks for coming."

"Oh, just one more thing," Reb Shlomo asked. "Do you have an email address some way I can contact you? Just in case I want to send you a special notice about a lecture or a service schedule?"

"Isn't that the information I would find on the website?" David responded.

"Yes," he replied. "But on occasion we offer special classes for people who we think would really benefit from them."

David stopped looking at him and said, "really?"

Reb Shlomo turned to him offering a winning smile. "It's something that isn't public, at least not in its initial stages and it's a two-step process."

"Huh?"

"Yes, an interview is required to ensure the prospective candidate is intellectually and spiritually open. That's why I need your email address."

"Oh, I see," he responded nodding my head. "That might be somewhat of a problem. You see, Reb Shlomo, I'm a very private person and I work very hard. Because of the unusual nature of what I do for a living, I'm not at liberty to talk about it. Even my wife has come to understand I can rarely even tell her who my clients are."

"Do you work for the government?"

"No, it's a private company. Nothing illegal. But highly personal."

"Perhaps," he said haltingly, "I can arrange the interview for you without an email," he offered.

David hesitated. "How would that work?"

"Well," he continued thoughtfully. "Come to services Friday evening. Bring your wife and child if you'd like. Afterwards, during what we call the Shabbat delight let me know if you're still interested. If you are, are you free during the day?"

"Somedays," he responded. "I have a certain amount of flexibility."

"As I was saying, if you're still interested in the special program. Just thank me during the evening and then plan on being in the school café Wednesday say around 3pm. My assistant who runs the women's program will meet you for coffee."

"I think I can manage that," he said. Thank you, Reb Shlomo." He walked towards the door.

"Step two," he said to himself.

Miami once again:

"Good morning Luiz," David said as he exited the Uber and entered the Miami Beach High Rise.

"Luiz no longer works here," the Concierge replied.

"Oh", David said. "I'm sorry, I thought… it's been quite a while since I was last here."

The Concierge reached up and tweaked his mustache and answered him in a cultured voice.

"My name is George. Not Jorge, just George. My mother named me George. You can call me George or Mr. Rodriguez. It's up to you."

David grasped his hand and exhaled. "Thank you, I was really embarrassed." My name is David Duvin and I'm here to see…"

"Sandy. Yes, I know you are expected thirty-sixth floor."

"Thank you again," David said as he walked to the elevator. "Couldn't have been more awkward," he said to himself. "Gotta do better."

He entered the elevator and pushed the appropriate button. The door closed, and he ascended to the designated floor. He exited the door and proceeded to the appropriate apartment. He reached up and pushed the bell. A tall attractive dark-haired woman answered the door.

"Adriana?" he said.

The women looked at him and smiled. "No, she's in class today. You can call me Tiffany."

"What happened to Margolit?" he asked.

"She's away at a seminar. You must be David, Sandy is looking forward to seeing you. He's at the beach and will be up shortly. Please", she said as she led him into the living room. "Come sit. Make yourself comfortable. I'll bring you a glass of wine and a light snack while you're waiting."

"Two for two," David said to himself. "And these things come in threes." He walked to the window and looked at the ocean. "Gorgeous view, just gorgeous. Maybe someday," he paused and turned as Tiffany, carrying a tray upon which was a bottle of wine centered in an ice bucket, several glasses and a plate of crudité, entered the room. She placed the tray on the glass coffee table and motioned to him to sit down. She was wearing a tank top, short shorts and high heeled shoes. Her long brown almost black hair reached her shoulders. David couldn't prevent himself from staring.

"Rabbi," she said. "You're staring at me."

"That's number three" David said as he raised his eyes to meet hers.

"I'm really sorry," he said. "I'm not used to interacting with young beautiful women dressed in," he paused. "South beach style. Same thing occurred when I first met Adriana. Usually, when I speak to women, it's in my office or in a more public setting and they are dressed either in business attire or more fully covered because they're in a synagogue. Please excuse my naivete."

She grasped the bottle of wine and poured each of them a glass of wine. "Arneis," she said as she raised the glass to her nose and inhaled. "Italian aromatic. Perfect choice, David, for a Sunday in South Florida. "

"Thank you for the wine and thank you for overlooking my staring."

She replied with a smile and said. "It's okay. I'm used to it. I know I'm attractive and I know how most men are wired."

David exhaled and shook his head. "I have to apologize. I'm really out of sorts. That's why I came to speak to Sandy. I need his advice."

"I know," she said as she sipped the wine and smiled. "You're not the only person who requests his help. I thought I could entertain you while you're waiting. Today is my day to," she hesitated, "to assist him. Sometimes he grades me on my behavior."

"He grades you?"

"You don't really understand the situation, she replied with a smile. "my mother named me Tiffany because it was associated with money. She never made it through high school. But I did. The school guidance counselor encouraged me to take the college board exams. I followed his advice and did very well. He pushed me to apply to college assuring me that scholarship funds could be found. The State provided me with half tuition. He found the other half plus."

"Plus?" David asked.

"Plus," she answered. "Apparently a gentleman approached the school several years ago and indicated he would provide a man or a woman with a scholarship which included one free year in a dormitory and half tuition for the Junior year on condition that if the student did very well the following year's tuition, the senior year, would be fully paid, and a part/time job would be guaranteed if the person applied to graduate school."

"Sandy?"

"Yes, Sandy. I went to junior college for two years and then with his help was able to transfer to a four -year school. I did well enough in my junior year, even though it wasn't part of the original scholarship, he paid for my final year of college. I am currently enrolled in a Master of Education program. Upon completion I hope to teach high school science. The part time job is working for Sandy and learning how to manage money, develop an appreciation for Theater, Dance, Art and Food."

"He's your mentor," David stated.

"He's much more than that," she said continuing as she reached out and poured another glass. "He interviewed me intensively. I had to promise not to date anyone seriously without his approval. I had to agree to all sorts of things, she paused, "not sexually. Last month, he took us to London. We went to theater, toured and had wonderful meals. We don't get to choose our clothes. Just the casual ones like what I am wearing. He hired a woman, a personal shopper, who advises us and helps us make appropriate selections. We have elocution lessons, tennis lessons and a list of required books which must be read during the semester. It's demanding work and it's a dream," she added. "A Cinderella or depending, a Cinderfella story."

"Wow," David said. "You're really lucky that's amazing."

"I know," she said as she looked at her phone. "He should be here any minute. Excuse me, He usually needs lotion on his back and neck after he swims. And Oh, she said with a smile, "you'll notice he has a slight limp. Please don't mention it to him. We're hoping it improves."

"Don't worry", David replied. "I won't and Tiffany, thank you for your time."

And then something completely unexpected occurred. Tiffany reach out and grasped his shoulder. He felt an invisible physical connection between their bodies. "David, "she said. "I mean Rabbi," she corrected herself. "He's not the man he was a year ago. His mind is still sharp, but he often needs to reconstruct what he wishes to say before he says anything. The words aren't always his anymore. Do you understand what I'm saying?"

David paused wanting to respond by saying, "yes of course, I understand." His training instinct automatically kicked in and instead he asked, "how does that make you feel?"

She pushed him away and looked him in the eyes, "I don't know if you can truly understand the impact he has had on me and on several others. He literally pulled us out of the gutter and gave us new lives. And now he's beginning to fail. We are losing our father and we don't know how to take care of him."

David, was stunned. His body was beginning to experience all the wrong signals. He was drawing on her warmth. His instincts commanded him to hold her and offer her comfort. His eyes couldn't leave her neck and at the same time his head was warring with his body. He stepped back as she pushed away from him. It was clear to him she needed physical support. It was equally clear to him that he should not be the one to provide it.

"He's still capable and functional," David replied. "I understand your fears, but we have time to prepare for the worst. You and your friends just need to adjust to the changes. As long as he remains lucid, you're all right. If it changes," he said instantly regretting it, "you can call me."

Bam! The door slammed and in he walked. "The house rule is no one, no one dates the staff, especially a married man." Sandy said as he strode towards David a smile on his face his arms open wide to embrace. David turned toward him and opened his arms for the hug.

"It's so good to see you again, Sir," he said warmly.

"Sit down, sit down!" He motioned with his hand. "I see Tiffany has provided you with," he paused, glancing at the wine and the food on the table, "with everything you needed. I'm so glad you've chosen to visit. Face to face, person to person is so much more satisfying than phone calls. I've always said, there is no substitution for personal contact."

David lowered himself into the leather arm chair which faced the ocean. He watched as Sandy hesitantly lowered himself as well, using his hands to control his descent into the chair. Sandy turned his head and caught David staring.

"It's the leg," he said. "Perhaps it's the hip or the knee. I'm not certain they both hurt. This aging is really a bitch."

"Have you seen a doctor?"

"No, and the women are beginning to insist that I do." He grimaced slightly as his body slid into the seat. "You know how it is with Men and Doctors and I know if I start at my age, it will never end. Have you ever been to a gathering when bowel movements and doctors' appointments were the only topics being discussed?"

David chuckled, "This sounds like an emerging or a previously existing comedy routine."

"Yes, I know." Sandy said smiling. "Tell me David, how have you been? Are you and your wife making friends? Let me hear about you before we begin to discuss what really brought you here"

David raised his glass and closed his eyes as he sniffed the wine. "My family is doing well. My wife and son have made some friends. The shul is growing by leaps and bounds. I'm about to embark on a quest to rescue, well, I'm, as of yet not certain, it will be a rescue attempt, but it appears that I have a child who is being drawn into a cult."

"Hebrew-Christians?"

"Exactly, "David said with a sigh. "I think I can handle this one. I had a similar experience while serving in Atlanta. I would like to say I came to see you because I missed you and that would be true but; the truth is I have an emerging leader who's going to cause trouble. I think he doesn't have the slightest idea how out of place he is. I have the feeling he is positively motivated to help the shul, but I firmly believe the way he will do it will create tensions amongst our volunteers and potential membership that shouldn't occur. He is part of the for-profit world and doesn't have a clue how to guide a volunteer organization."

"They never do," he interrupted.

"He is being promoted by my current leadership as the next President. Every time we meet it's a contest of wills. I don't work for him I work for the community but he's like a bulldog. He's a finance guy and manages lots of people. He doesn't understand working with volunteers requires different techniques. I'm afraid he's going to undermine the culture I have begun to create."

Sandy smiled and began to speak. "Let me tell you a story son. Years ago, I started a schul. I saw it as a challenge. I chose an area outside of Manhattan that was growing and lacked a neighborhood synagogue. Once I found the place, I rented a room in a local hotel, purchased an ad in the local newspaper which stated, "Anyone interested in creating a Jewish community should come to a meeting the following week." Fifty people showed up. We began a series of discussions which eventually lead to monthly services in a local church, a religious school in someone's home and week by week, month by month we grew.

Over time, we developed committees. There was delightful young man, a vice president in bank I believe, who became the head of the ritual committee. I asked him to call a meeting and he agreed. Have I told you this story before?"

"Yes," David replied smiling, "and I've actually used it recently."

Sandy smiled and continued. "Then I won't bother to tell it to you again. Does your nemesis have a name?"

"Let's call him "so and so," David added.

"Well," Sandy continued, "your Mr. So and So, clearly doesn't and most probably will never understand the difference between the corporate and volunteer worlds. You might have to cultivate someone behind him who will call and empower your volunteers. Someone whom you can teach how to engage people and make them believe their actions are important and will make a difference." He paused, "where was I?"

"You were about to…"

"Oh yes, I remember." Sandy continued. "I think I could be more help to you with the Hebrew-Christians than with what you currently have to deal with, but, but" he paused and just stared blankly at the ceiling, "My point is, (pause) that people in the for-profit world don't always understand how to make the transition. Sometimes they need to be lead. Sometimes an end run around them is required. And sometimes they have negative charisma." He stopped, picked up his glass and sipped. "where was I? Where was I? Oh yes! No, hmmm."

David caught Tiffany's eye. She nodded affirmatively. "You were commenting on my existing dilemma." David replied.

Sandy looked up at him and smiled. "Exactly, there are times when they can be guided and there are times when you just have to confront them. Years ago, I had a young modern Orthodox woman in my employ. She was a product of an intermarriage and was raised as a Reform Jew. At some point in her life, I suspect it was in her college years, she decided, I think she met a guy, to become more observant. The Orthodox rabbi insisted she undergo conversion which she willingly did."

"And?" David asked.

"Don't worry I didn't lose this one." He answered with a smile. "And some years later she ended up in my employ. In addition to her work, I often helped her with her studies. It wasn't what you and I would call 'study', it was a lot of stories that reinforced a fundamentalist attitude. I know you know what I mean."

"Tiffany is there any more wine?" David asked. "Something red and perhaps a little cheese. I think Sandy and I might be here for a while."

"But of course," she said in a demure voice as she exited the room.

"She's really lovely," David said as he watched her leave the room.

"One of my best," Sandy replied. She has a flair for languages. I think I will take her and Adriena to Paris with me next month. "

"Please Sandy, continue. I suspect this is going to be a fascinating story."

"Actually," he said thoughtfully, "it is. I remember it was just few weeks prior to Purim. She was all excited about her costume for a Purim ball and that is was permissible for everyone to get really drunk. At least that's what her so called teachers told her. I don't recall exactly how it occurred but at some point, I intervened, in her best interests," he said in an excited tone.

"I told her the message of Purim wasn't to get soused but was intended to teach the fight for freedom was a continuous effort, especially for a minority culture. And I told her that the Purim story was a myth."

"Aah, thank you my young friend," Sandy said. "It's no longer appropriate for me to say, "my dear," he said with a smile as Tiffany placed the tray filled with wine and cheese on the table. "Back to the gym for me, first thing tomorrow," he whispered. "Gotta straighten out this knee."

"Fabulous," he continued. "A Burgundy, from the Cote de Nuits. Excellent selection and oh David look at the cheese. Two selections one of goat and one of Lamb. Thank you again," he said with an appreciative smile.

"Where was I? David did I ever tell you the story of ....no, no... that's not where I was." He looked at David and said. "I tire easily after a swim and when I tire, I forget. Do me a favor, our conversation is important, where were we?"

"Purim, you told her Purim never took place. That it was made up by someone or someone's."

"Shouldn't have done that," he said shaking his head. "Shouldn't have done that. Two weeks later I received a registered letter from a lawyer claiming spiritual harassment."

"What? There's no such thing."

"Well, I knew that," he replied with a smile. "It was obvious that one evening she was sitting with a lawyer friend, an Orthodox lawyer friend, and they thought they could extort money from the organization where I was working. The letter was so poorly written."

He shook his head," the language was poor, the grammar atrocious. Do you know what I think would be spiritual harassment? Planning on hurting someone or stealing something and being hounded by a host of angels! What do you think of that?" He snapped pounding the arm chair.

"I, I don't know what to say," David replied. "Frankly, I've never heard of such a thing. What did you do?"

"Well," he added. "it had to be addressed. I took it to my leadership and we discussed capitulation or a hardline response. Finally, one of my Board members said. "Confront the ......, I'd rather not say the word," he replied. "After all I'm Tiffany's role model.

And that's what I did. Eventually the threat went away as did she. Sometimes, when you are confronted with a situation you can't negotiate around it. You must deal with it head on. The only problem I envision is that this gentleman, in light of what he does for a living, might not respond well to confrontation."

"Then what should I do?" David asked.

"What?" he asked as he glanced around the room, his eyes resting on his watch. He touched it gently and paused, "David, I'd like you to spend the night. Could you find Tiffany and ask her to make sure the guest room has been prepared? It's not that often that I receive visitors and you know I care for you." He paused and dropped his voice to a whisper.

"I know you can tell I'm not the person I was when you were last here. There are some things I'd like to share I don't know when another opportunity like this might arise. I always made a point of visiting friends because one never knows," he shook his head. "I never wanted to be one of those people who said to themselves, 'I should have visited him, or I should have... you'll stay, won't you?"

David, nodded and replied. "Of course, I'll stay. But what about my situation, what should I do?"

"Wait it out my boy. Wait him out. And pray that you succeed."

Get me to the Church on time

"My father told me I should never enter a church," Rachel said.

"He also told you not to marry me and that I would never be successful." David replied.

"I know, I know," she said with a smile. "And I have visited churches and gone to church in my time. I've been to church weddings and christenings and even midnight Mass."

"I didn't know that," David replied. "Why did you go and where was it?"

"Paris, after college. Very moving, I almost became a Catholic," she said as she playfully pushed him. "If our religious services created similar moods on a regular basis I might really enjoy going to shul. If it wasn't that I wanted to learn from the rabbi and enjoyed sleeping with him, I'd probably never go."

"Stop it Rachel, we need to be serious. "

"Don't worry," she said placing a hand over his mouth. "I've got this."

"Remember we are the Eisenstads not the Duvins," he said. "And remember…."

"I said I've got this, dummy. Don't you remember who the drama queen in your life is?"

"Okay, sorry," he said as he opened the door and entered the hall walking towards the large well-lit room.

"Nice music," she quipped. "Mood music, soft and ethereal. Who knows I might like this place. Ouch!" she said as he pinched her arm.

Upon entering the sanctuary, they were greeted by a man and a woman casually but elegantly dressed. "Shabbat Shalom, Good Sabbath," they said with a smile. "Welcome to our home. You don't look familiar is this your first time?" the woman asked.

"Yes," David replied. "We recently moved into town and we've been researching religious communities for our son. I spoke to Reb, Reb," he hesitated.

"Reb Shlomo," she stated in an affirmative tone. "You must be the Eisenstads. Reb Shlomo told me he had met you and you might be trying us out. I'm Crystal and this is my husband Ryan. We," she said turning to the man with a smile, "we are the unofficial greeters." She said as she grasped David's arm as Ryan similarly reached out to Rachel.

Rachel took a step back, "It's okay Ryan said. I'm just going to escort you to your seats. Don't be afraid. This is our way."

"The service will begin in a few minutes, this is our," she hesitated as if looking for a word. "Schmooze time. Coffee and Tea and light snacks are over there," she said pointing to a series of tables across the room. "And you can see that we attract the young and the old."

David glanced around the room.

"Their faces are too clean," Rachel whispered. "Why do I feel like I'm in Kansas?"

"Can it Dorothy", David whispered. About twenty-five-thirty people were either sitting, sipping coffee or standing around conversing in soft tones. A young man who appeared to be of college age, noticed them and stopped talking to the young woman with whom he was holding hands and.

"You must be new. First timers?" he said as he extended a hand to Rachel.

"I'm Fred, welcome."

"Rachel," Rachel responded with a smile.

"Great child-sitting pool," Crystal whispered into David's ear. "Clean cut, responsible and hard working."

Still holding Fred's hand, Rachel turned around slowly taking in the room. She took a deep breath "I might like this place," she said smiling.

"Let's take our seats," Ryan said. "It it's okay, we'll sit next to you. That way if you have any questions you can just ask either one of us," he said as he sat down next to where Rachel was standing and gently tugged her arm.

"I've been worshipping here longer than Ryan and will be able to answer any questions you might have with a little more depth," Crystal said with a smile as she similarly sat and tugged on David's hand. "Reb Shlomo told me you were some kind of academic. Ryan likes to talk about sports and cooking, I'm more of an academic type."

"Uhm, okay," David replied as he sat. "If I have any questions I'll ask," he said as he glanced at Rachel who seemed to be heavily involved in conversation with Ryan.

The lights dimmed, and Reb Shlomo entered the room. He was casually dressed, jeans and sport shirt. He waived to the group and approached the platform in front of the Ark. A table rested on the platform. Reb Shlomo stepped onto the platform and approached the table upon which rested a large blue and white prayer shawl. He picked it up wrapped it around his head and dropped on his knees to the floor in a humble but dramatic gesture.

"Great shtick," Rachel murmured under her breathe as she leaned toward David.

"Ouch!" she quipped as David's elbow smacked her ribs.

Miami continued

"Thank you, Sandy. It was a lovely evening," David said smiling as he admired the two beautiful women sitting on either side of the table. I can't tell you how long it's been since I was able to just sit and enjoy a dinner and relax.

"David," Adriana said, "but you have a family. Aren't family dinners relaxing?"

"I raised two younger siblings, while going to High School, Tiffany interrupted. "Trust me, quiet time is special."

"I guess you have yet to have children," he said with a grin. "It's extremely difficult for both of us. I've made a practice of turning off my phone when we sit down to eat. And I," he raised his glass and sipped the wine, "do my best not to talk about work. Every so often, Rachel and I are able to slip away for an evening. We usually pick a town at least ten miles away from ours and then look for a restaurant. Most of the time, well, some of the time, I'm not recognized."

"But you take vacations, don't you?"

"I admit it's been a while since we were able to really take a vacation and frankly to afford to go away. I think that will change in the next year or two because the congregation is turning a corner and I have more support. But," he looked at her and smiled, "it doesn't mean its without stress."

"Which is why," Sandy interrupted as he rose from the table and walked towards the living room, "David, it's time we had that chat. Come along."

David quietly excused himself and followed Sandy into the living room. "Not the living room," he said. "The terrace. Bring your glass and the bottle." Sandy said as he walked through the living room toward the terrace. He pushed open the sliding door and motioned to the two chairs separated by a small end table which looked out over the Ocean. They sat listening to the crashing of the waves. After a few minutes, Sandy broke the silence.

"Pity we don't smoke," he said. "This is a cigar moment." David smiled, and Sandy continued.

"I'm fading boy. I'm fading," he said wistfully.

"It seems to me," David responded. "That you're doing pretty well. How old are you?"

"A little over ninety."

"You?"

"Don't' interrupt I know I look younger. I've always looked younger." He paused and sipped. "Nothing like a little Sauterne to end the night. I never understood how people could drink whisky as a nightcap." He paused and slowly nodded to himself. "You know I'm fond of you, don't you?"

David nodded.

"I've outlived my children and they never had children. The girls, those who came before, and you in a sense, well, I consider you to be my children."

"Why are you telling me this."

He sighed, "It's not about taking responsibility for my death. I've already taken care of that. It's because I think I've learned a few things in my life, and I would like to share them with you."

"Does this mean I can ask you questions."

"You've always asked me questions," he said.

"Yes, but never the one's I really wished to ask. Like why you disappeared twenty years ago?"

He smiled and sipped his wine. "I suppose there's something to be said for that. Let me share with you two of the lessons I've learned. Maybe," he said softly, "if you remember them, maybe they will be helpful and maybe they will provide you with the answers you seek."

"Will they answer my questions?" he asked.

"Depends my boy. Depends on how much wine you drink and if I can intuit your questions. If I can't," he said quietly, "then you can ask."

"One thing I always thought was important was how one models themselves. Fathers serve as models as soon as they become fathers. Most don't realize that everything one does with a child in some ways imprints. If they read to their children, they are teaching their children that a father reads to his children. If they aren't active as volunteers or let's say they only attend synagogue on the High Holy days, they are modeling. Whether it be one's faults or one's strengths, parents are always modeling. And we all make mistakes.

Most people don't even remember the extra effort one makes to help them but it's important that you do. I remember there once was a rabbi who learned of his congregants' children was marrying a woman in England and they were to be married in the Church of England. The parents were extremely upset and did not know what to expect. The rabbi looked up the marriage service, went to their home and explained it to them. If that wasn't enough, he drove them to the airport as a gesture of support. That impressed me. It taught me. I tried to act similarly in my rabbinate.

Many years later, I began to realize I enjoyed what I was doing less and less. I found it increasingly more and more difficult to interact with the men and women who represented other organizations. I became increasingly more frustrated trying to work with Seminary leadership even though I liked them as people. My desire to succeed hadn't diminished, it was just," he hesitated," it was…no, I. I realized I could no longer function in a way that provided me with satisfaction and was successful in the current culture. And…"

"And?"

"And that's when I knew it was time to leave."

"I get that," David replied. "But why did you leave the way you did? Why did you disappear? Why did you become Sandy?"

Sandy smiled, "aaah, that's your real question isn't it?"

David nodded as he sipped his wine.

"Because, my boy, I didn't want to be one of those people who lingered on the sidelines. They all asked me, what I would be doing when I retired, and I told them I was going to be like Bilbo Baggins. You remember him, don't you?"

"Bilbo from the Hobbit?" David asked.

He smiled, "most of them didn't get it. I had to ask them if they ever read Tolkien? Most of them said, No, but they saw the movies. That was already part of the problem which heightened our differences. They were so…never mind.

And so, I would explain who Bilbo was and then I would ask them if they remembered what he did on his one hundredth birthday? Of course, they didn't remember. And so, I told them he made party for the community and then he stood on the platform and placed the ring on his finger and disappeared. And was never again seen in the Shire."

David began to laugh. "You were ready for a new life and to do that the way you wanted, you needed to disappear."

"No regrets, my boy. When your time comes. Give it some thought."

On Campus

"Who", Elana said to her friend Debbie, 'Isn't that Rabbi Duvin sitting in Library café?"

"Yeah, it certainly is," Debbie added quizzically, "But look how he's dressed. Jeans, a sloppy sweatshirt. Why he looks like a graduate student. Do you think we should go over and say hello?"

"I don't know," Elana said thoughtfully. "He was kinda okay a few weeks ago when we had that dinner. Everyone liked him, but he didn't look like that."

"Maybe he's waiting to meet with a student and is trying to blend in?" Debbie said.

"No," Elana replied. "That's not his style. I think he could fit in anywhere. He doesn't need to masquerade as someone else. If he's dressed that way, there must be a reason."

"Look!" Debbie said pointing at a young woman approaching his table. She's, she's beautiful. Do you think he's you know, trying to get a little on the side?"

"Let's sit down and watch," Elana whispered. "Why am I whispering? We're in a crowded university café." She nodded to Debbie, "quick grab that table in the corner, we can watch from there."

The two young women entered the café and proceeded to claim a table. They unloaded their backpacks, removing their laptops and their coffee thermoses and placed them on the table. They opened their laptops and began to observe what was occurring just a few tables away.

A woman in her late twenties or early thirties was approaching the rabbi's table. She stood about five feet seven and sported long blond hair which surrounded a pale angular face. She wore a V-neck sweater which highlighted her curves in a manner that would cause most men to become momentarily distracted. She carried a brief case in a lawyer like fashion and could have been a faculty member. A mug which most likely contained some type of ice tea was held in one hand.

"That's Samantha from the meeting house," Elana said. "Wonder what's she's doing with the rabbi?"

"Ssssh," Debbie whispered. "Wait! How do you know her?"

"I know her because we attend the same meditation meetings. "

The two young women buried their faces in their laptops allowing their eyes to observe what was occurring a few tables away.

"David?" Samantha said with a welcoming smile as she extended her hand. "I'm Samantha."

He couldn't help but return the smile as he rose, taking her figure in and extended his hand to meet hers.

"Thank you for coming," he said as he returned to his seat.

"No, thank you. Reb Shlomo said you were extremely special and it would be worth my time to meet with you."

"I'm flattered," he replied. "I just didn't want to give him or anyone my email. I'm an extremely private person and my work is usually confidential. It's important that I keep my life and my work separate."

"Like milk and meat," she replied with a smile.

"What?"

"We don't mix milk products with meat products. It's part of our spiritual system."

"Spiritual system?"

She smiled and reached out to grasp my hand. "I'm getting ahead of myself, yes, we promote a spiritual system. It's a development which originated in the Bible and is way that re-enforces our faith, but that's not why I'm here."

"Then why are you here? Besides the fact that Reb Shlomo asked you to meet with me, which I assume is a follow up to our having attended your prayer gathering last Friday."

"You mean our Shabbat service? They're fun. We have them practically every week." She paused to straighten her sweater.

"I'm here to tell you a little about us and about what I do. I mostly work with women and emerging adults. I bring them together in groups and we talk about life situations. The usual situations," she said as raised her mug to her lips and sipped.

"The usual situations," she repeated, "stress, relationships, awkwardness in social situations, feeling attractive. At times, I hold private sessions as well. I'm a faculty member and often mentor young men and women."

"Do you do this as a volunteer?" he asked.

"I volunteer a great deal of my time," she answered.

"That's extremely interesting," he commented. "So many emerging adults need guidance. Life isn't easy for them, even," he gestured, "on campuses like these."

"Exactly," she responded.

"But that's not all you do,"

"Of course not. After our groups session concludes, I usually lead them in a meditation session followed by a little learning."

"I'm always learning," he said thoughtfully. "What do you teach?"

"You first," she said with a smile and another sip of her tea. "What do you like to study?"

"Well, "he said, "I study language and music and have a tendency to research medieval texts."

"For work?"

"No, for fun. They're hobbies."

"You really are interesting," she flashed another smile.

"And what do you teach?" he asked

"Well, right now, we are discussing certain aspect of the Gospel of John," she replied.

"Are you a Biblical scholar?"

"No, actually I work in the Department of psychology. There is so much in that book, hymns, poems, the concept of 'mission.' Every session is filled with stimulating conversations as my groups challenge and wrestle with the words of a spiritual leader who lived thousands of years ago. It's keeps their minds active and stimulates their souls."

"Souls? Souls? You believe and encouraging people to believe that they have souls. Don't' you?"

"Of course," she replied. "Every living thing has a soul. What we do is to attempt to help people find and develop their souls."

"Through worship?" he asked.

"Yes, through worship and song, and study and hopefully that helps people believe. Everyone should believe in something, don't you agree?"

He shook his head in a thoughtful manner. "I suppose so. It's not exactly my field. I mean the reason we are doing this is for Ben. And, I suppose for Rachel. She has more social needs than I do." He looked at her in an earnest way, "can I ask you a question?"

"That's what I'm here for," she replied. She looked at her watch, "please ask. I'll do my best to answer but if it takes more than five minutes we will have to meet again, assuming you want to. I'm sorry, but I have a staff meeting in ten minutes."

"Well, actually its two questions. The first one is why do you want people to believe? And the second one is why am I here? What do you want of me."

"You don't miss a thing, do you?"

"Excuse me?" he said raising his eyes.

"I, we want people to believe because we want them to live in the world to come. We don't want them to suffer in this life and most importantly afterwards."

She stood up forcing him to look up in order to see and hear her completely. "The answer to your second question, is" she paused. "I want to challenge you theologically. You're sharp and have some interesting hobbies which I think could support your spiritual growth. Frankly after observing you at the Shabbat service, I wasn't certain if I should meet with you at all. You clearly were not engaged, and I didn't want to waste my time.

"But," she continued. "Reb Shlomo saw something in you. He asked me to verify his assumptions. He suggested you could be capable to enter into the mysteries. That's why I agreed to meet with you. To see if you were worthy."

She nodded and smiled. "Reb Shlomo was right. If you're interested, I want you to find the time, say one hour a week to be my student. To think with me, to," she hesitated, "to meditate with me, maybe to challenge me, and if we're successful maybe, just maybe the truth will be revealed to you. Will you give that some thought?"

He shook his head still looking up at this extremely attractive woman who was attempting to woo him," and nodded. "I'll take your offer under consideration. If I want to pursue," I paused, "this…"

"relationship," she added.

"I'll call you."

"Sounds like a plan," she said flashing a smile as she gathered her briefcase and walked towards the hall.

He scratched his head and thought, "The gospel of John, the gospel that preaches that Jesus was the incarnated Word of God replacing the Law of Moses. She's good. They're really good. I've a lot of work to do," He said to himself as he gathered his things and walked toward the door. "A lot of work and Marty and I have a class together in less than two hours. Was she flirting with me?"

The girls, lowered their laptops and looked at one another. "What was that about?" Debbie asked.

"Beats me," Elana replied. "But I promised the rabbi I would have coffee with him, the next time I went home, and my mother's birthday is in two weeks. Maybe I'll ask him then?"

The next skirmish

"Shirley," I'm late for the interfaith seminar at St Claude's," he said as he grabbed his coat from the office closet. My keys? Where did I leave my keys? he mumbled to himself as he quickly ran his hands through his pockets. Maybe in my coat, as he searched for the pockets. No, it will be easier if I'm wearing the coat, as he threw it around his shoulders and stuffed his arms into the sleeves. Ahh, yes! Here they are, "Shirley I will be back at…."

"Rabbi?"

"Yes," David said as he turned toward the voice. "Oh, hello Paul," he replied as he automatically extended his hand. "Nice to see you, and during the day-time, that's a surprise?"

"We had parent conferences at school, so I decided to take a personal day," he said as he withdrew his hand. "I was wondering if we could spend some time together, I have a few items I would like to discuss with you."

"It would be my pleasure," David replied. "But I'm late for a meeting at the interfaith council. We've arranged a meeting with the Mayor to discuss after school programs."

"I see," Paul said. "That's important, but I was wondering if you could spare a few minutes. I don't think it will take more than ten or fifteen minutes."

"I'd love to Paul, but I'm already late. When people want to see me they usually call and make an appointment. I'm sure you understand."

"Of course, I do, but this will only take a few minutes."

"Paul, I'm really sorry. Look its ten-o clock. I can be back by twelve. Could we reschedule until then? Is this an emergency? Has there been accident?"

He shook his head, "no, I don't think so."

"Then it will have to wait."

"I don't think that would be wise," Paul responded.

David stopped. "Look, it's the best I can do. I really can't make the time right now. How about I call your secretary and make an appointment to see you at your convenience. And if you send me a list of your questions or concerns, it will give me time to think about how we can address them in the best possible way".

"Rabbi?" Paul asked in a quiet demure tone. "Do you keep regular office hours?"

David sighed. "yes and no, I'm usually in the office on specific mornings and I make every effort to be in the building to greet parents when they drop off their children for religious school. But sometimes I get called away and have to make choices. I'm sure you understand."

"Yes, of course I do," Paul murmured. "It always difficult making those choices. Like not be able to meet with a member of the Board and a future congregational president."

"Paul, that's not fair and you know it. I'm really sorry, but this will have to wait. Shirley, I'll return calls after twelve." He turned to Paul and said. "I'll call your office this afternoon," he called out over his shoulder as he ran towards his car. "Well, he said to himself, "that really didn't go well."

Two weeks Later at Scarlati's Bakery

"Mr. Scarlati? I didn't know how good your expresso was until I tried it. This," David said as he held the cup to his lips, "is fantastic. It's smooth and strong."

"I make it the old way. The way my grandmother taught me. Hand ground beans, cold water," he said expansively.

"Well its really good," David replied, "and I love the way these few tables have been strategically placed so people can be seen but not heard. Just brilliant."

"Maybe you're expecting someone?" he said with a smile. "Rabbi business?"

"Yes, David replied, "rabbi business and look! Here she is right on time," he said as he stood up and extended his hand to the young woman who had just entered the store.

"Thanks for coming Elana, I appreciate it. Come sit down," he said as he helpfully pulled out the chair.

It was early Summer and Elana was still wearing a light jacket. "It's warm and comfy in here," she said as she shrugged off the jacket and sat down.

"Cute girl," David thought. "Nice smile."

"Rabbi? Can I ask I few questions?"

"Of course," he replied. "I'm going to like this girl," he thought.

She removed a pen and small pad from her backpack looked at him and said, "I want to take notes."

David frowned but recovered quickly, "fine with me. Go for it?"

"First I want you to know that my friend and I saw you on campus a few weeks ago. That was you speaking with Dr. Rizzo wasn't it?"

"Yes, that was me."

"Are you," she hesitated, "or will you be teaching or doing something at the College in the future?"

"No," he replied. "I was doing some research."

"About what?"

"About Ministers of Peace."

She sucked in a deep breathe. "That's my place," she said.

"Yes, I know. Your parents were freaked out about it and so I did a little snooping. They're frightened and concerned that you've been sucked into a cult."

"Is that what you think?"

"I'm not certain," he said. "When I was your age, I went to all kinds of religious gatherings. Once I went to a Santamoro service. It was extremely secretive, and I had to dress in a certain way to blend in."

"What's a Santamoro service?" she asked.

It's a Caribbean religion. Very secretive because they sacrifice goats and chickens. It was pretty bloody."

She snickered. "So, you were just checking them out."

David nodded. "yes, I needed to learn and wanted to see what they actually did, and no, I wasn't interested in dating a woman who occasionally worshipped a goat."

She giggled, "and why did you have to go incognito to observe this?" she asked.

"Probably, because it was there," he said. "It was an adventure. I like adventures."

"I don't know if I should be angry at you or at my parents," she said.

"Why?" he asked. "Don't be angry at them, they love you. I haven't been hiding anything from you. You're my congregant, even if you don't come to shul," he said with a smile. "I need to know you. We could have met at Friday night services a few weeks ago, when Rachel and I were there."

Her eyes opened wide and her jaw dropped. "Get out! You and your wife went to Friday night services in a place that's just "jew-ish"!

"Yup," he said nodding.

"What did you think?"

David, paused. "You knew it was jew-ish. Not Jewish?"

She nodded, "so why were you there?" he paused as Mr. Scarlati approached with two expressos in his hands. "For the rabbi," he said smiling. "and his guest."

She lifted the expresso to her lips and inhaled. "smells good," she said. "And now I'm even more confused. Whose side are you on?"

"Probably both of yours," David said as he brought the cup to his lips. "Great expresso."

"You might be my advocate?"

"Possibly, you clearly understand that Ministers of Peace is not really Jewish. Since you get that, you most likely understand their motives."

She nodded affirmatively.

"And yet," he paused. "What are they doing that attracts you? That doesn't offend you?"

She swallowed. Placed the cup on the table and said, "I like the warmth. The sharing, the fact that people care for one another."

"Even though their goals are to bring you to, you know who."

"I'm not doing well with the belief part," she answered with a grin. "The community feeling is great. The belief stuff doesn't exactly hold together. It's not easy to separate one from the other because some of my friends are really into it and I like being with them."

David stroked his chin. "I always stroke my chin when I'm thinking," he said with a smile. "So how long do you think this will continue? Let me say it another way, where do you see yourself in this process?"

"I'm not exactly certain," she said. "Reb Shlomo just hopes I'll get the spirit and somehow be transformed into a believer. I guess," she paused while thinking and sipping the expresso, "that it depends if my friends decide to go deeper, you know, get more into it, or get outa it."

"How about I provide you with some information. Just a few things and all you need to do, is think about it, or you might want to discuss it with your friends and see how they respond. Depending upon how you and your friends respond might help you make a decision. In the meantime, I might join this special study group that Samantha runs. I think her goal is to lure me in by appealing to me intellectually and somewhat sexually."

"Trust me," she added with a smile. "She gets a lot of mileage that way. There are stories."

"Don't need to hear them," he replied abruptly. He dropped his hand and shook his head. "Rachel's much more perceptive than me. She picked up on the warmth, of the place and almost picked up the handsome young man who attempted to flirt with her. It took me a bit longer to realize that the woman engaging me was flirting, though if I had responded, I suspect she would have denied it. They make it very appealing."

"I remember," he continued. "When I was in the Seminary, every summer huge numbers of attractive, no, hot, young men and women descended into New York. They were in the subways and on the street corners, Hey? Maybe that's how Lubavitch learned how to do it. Anyway, these very attractive young men and women would stop people on the street, mostly the Jewish looking ones. They thought the Sephardim were Muslims, and ask them if they believed in you know who? They did it so warmly and invitingly that you just wanted to flirt them, or more than that if you know what I mean."

"Rabbi," she said smiling. "I had no idea you were so much fun."

"Got it!" he said with a snap. "Elana, I'm so glad you're so solid. Your parents, like most parents, are a bit," he hesitated, "over protective. But even though you seem to understand the playing field, please read the information I will send you. Think of it as some additional ammunition."

"Sure, Rabbi. It seems like we're in this together. "

"If you want to do a little preliminary research think about the concept of Redemption. Redemption in Jewish liturgy refers to the redemption of a people not a person. The concept began to refer to personal salvation after the Gospels were written. When you're in study groups of what they call worship groups on Friday evening and Saturday mornings if you go, listen to how they use that word."

"I can do that," Elana said shaking her head. "And I'll even read what you send me. But no research for me. I've already got a full plate."

"The second item I want to share with you, no, I want to teach you because it will apply to everything you do and learn in your life, is context."

She shrugged her head, "context?"

"Context," he said. "It's something I learned from my teachers. It provides me with a basis of understanding what is happening and helps me understand how I should act. Before I react to any situation, whether it be political, or historical, or social, I ask myself, what is the context in which this is occurring? In the past and even within my family, my marriage, when something occurs, and believe something always will occur, before I act or react, I ask myself in what context did this occur? Think about it. A person who doesn't understand the context of what is occurring, risks living a soap opera type existence. Trust me, no one really wants to live like that."

"Wow," she replied thoughtfully. "that was really cool. No one ever spoke to me like that. Is that what they teach you in rabbi school?"

"No," he replied. "It's one of the most important lessons one can learn in life. And in your case, it just might help you make better choices."

"Wow, rabbi. I don't know what to say."

"Me either," he responded. "that wasn't a rehearsed speech. You might find me in some awkward situations with Reb Shlomo in the future. Please don't judge me. Just think, "context."

His phone began to sing, and he sighed. I have to leave. Apparently, Mrs. Margolis's eighteen-dollar donation wasn't listed in this week's bulletin. Trouble in paradise," he said as he stood up and caught Mr. Scarlati's eye. "Check!"

"No, "was the reply.

"Let's do this again," he said as he was leaving. "I had a good time."

Eating Fowl

"Good Afternoon, Michaels, Bertonoli, Smith and Stern, how can I help you?" the receptionist blaahed.

"Good afternoon," David said, "this is Rabbi Duvin. I would like to speak with Paul Stern please."

"This is the third time you've called today, Mr. Duvin," the receptionist replied. "Mr. Stern is aware you have called. He is an extremely busy man, I mean person, and always, yes," she repeated, "he always returns his calls. Didn't the other receptionist inform you that he usually returns all of his calls after 4 o'clock?"

"No, he didn't," David replied. "But I'm teaching between four and six and won't be able to pick up if and when he calls back. Isn't there something you could do to push this along?

"Well," she said hesitating. "I don't know. What would you suggest?"

"Could you place a note on his desk or just pop in and ask him if he could call me just a touch earlier because I will be teaching between four and six and will miss his call. I'd hate to have him take a moment out of his extremely busy life and not be there to answer. And, "David added, I'm certain you would agree we wouldn't want to frustrate him."

"Just a moment!" she said. "he just walked out of his office. I think he is running out for a meeting. Let me see if I can catch him. Mr. Stern! Mr. Stern!"

"Yes Laura, what is it?"

"There's a Rabbi Du…something on the phone. He's called three times today trying to make an appointment to see you. I told him when you return your calls and he said he cannot be available during those times because he's teaching. Could you call him a bit earlier or later?"

David pressed the phone closer trying to hear more clearly.

"Rabbi Duvin?" Yes, yes, of course. I am very much looking forward to speaking with him. Tell him," he paused. "Tell him I will reserve a seat next to me on tomorrow's train. Tell him, I always try to take the 5:30 out of Grand Central. Third car. Tell him I am looking forward to speaking with him."

"Thank you, sir, I will be sure to tell him," she replied.

"Rabbi Du?"

"Duvin," he replied. "Yes, I heard him. Thank you very much," he said as he ended the call. "Jeez, he wants me to take a train into the city, so I can sit next to him and take a train home. I'm not a dog. But I think this time I'm going to have to learn to heal."

From the Mouths of Babes

"Rabbi," Shirley said as she knocked on his office door. "Rabbi, you have a visitor."

David stood from his desk and opened the door of his office "You really need to learn how to use the phone system," he said, "Oh Marty? What a pleasant "surprise. Come on in."

"I'm not interrupting?" he asked. "I was more or less in the neighborhood and, I misplaced my phone and couldn't call for an appointment. Do you have some time?

David opened his arms smiling. "For you, I always have time. But why aren't you in summer camp? It July and most of the kids are away."

"I didn't want to go away this summer," Marty replied. "I can do sports anywhere, but the summer camps don't have a library as good as what we have locally. And I'm too young to do a summer program at some college. We," he blushed, "Danielle and I are auditing a class at the community college."

"David, raised his eyes questioning, "We? That's interesting," as he watched Marty's face turn red and quickly changed the subject. "What about the bar mitzvah it's in early September do you need some help?"

"Naah," Marty responded with a smile as he walked into David's office and plunked down onto a chair. "I'm done with that. I got the Torah and haftorah portions down cold. I've written my speech. Yeah, I'm a little nervous, but I know I can slam dunk it. That's not why I'm here."

"Do you want to take a walk?" David asked. "Its nice outside and we can talk."

Marty shook his head. "No, I'm comfortable here. It's about the way we've been studying these past few months. I have some questions and I didn't want to ask them in front of Danielle."

"She's in camp, isn't she?" David asked.

"Music camp, mostly daytime," he responded. "I don't want to admit it and my friends, ya know those who didn't want to study with you will really tease me, but I enjoy having her in class with me." He paused and ran a hand through his hair. "I didn't what to talk about this when she was with us."

"Do you have a crush on her?"

Marty blushed, "yeah kind of. But that's not why I wanted to see you alone. When we're together I need to act confident. But lately, I've been reading some stuff that is confusing me, and I think if I spoke about it in front of her, she would think, well," he hesitated. "Less of me."

"Marty," David said softly and with a smile. "It demonstrates great strength to show one's weakness. It's more than okay that you say, in her company, you are having difficulty or didn't understand something."

Marty nodded but didn't respond.

David waited and watched him for what felt like a long time but was probably thirty seconds. "What's bothering you Marty?"

"I'm stuck," he said.

"Stuck on what and why?" David replied.

Marty dropped his leg and leaned forward. He shook his head. 'I've really enjoyed the way we've been studying," he said slowly. "Dissecting the Bible, has made it both more understandable and more confusing."

David smiled, "please explain."

"Well, I like that you taught me not to take the book at face value. It has challenged me to ask questions and to sometimes look for what's not there as well. Danielle likes it too."

David nodded encouraging him to continue.

"We've begun to meet and study together trying to figure out questions that will stump you. A couple of days ago, we were studying the story," he hesitated and corrected himself, "stories surrounding Moses's early years.

Danielle asked me to read the incident of his being found by Pharaoh's daughter out loud. I read it and I read it again and then she asked me, how was it that Moses' sister understood Pharaoh's daughter? Either his sister spoke Egyptian or Pharaoh's daughter spoke Hebrew."

"Great question and excellent reasoning," David replied. "I wish I had thought of that."

Marty nodded silently and then continued. "We started to think what that could mean. Moses's sister knowing Egyptian was more likely than Pharaoh's daughter learning the language of slaves. On the other hand, the Hebrews must have been living in Egypt for some time if a woman was able to learn to speak Egyptian. Maybe they, excuse me, our ancestors were slaves in Egypt. But what confused me was, if that was true, why does the story of the plagues seem so ridiculous? How can you have one and not the other?"

"From the mouths of babes," he muttered. "God, you're going to be some scholar," David said with a smile. "Both of you. You've stumbled, no," he said correcting himself, "the two of you have begun to figure out one of the challenges of Bible study. Texts, most texts have a kernel of truth, some more than others, but everything you read doesn't have to be true."

"It's very similar when you study history," he continued. History is usually written by the winners. Not the losers. And those who write history, let's call them the chroniclers, are never totally objective."

"Yeah," he muttered, "I kinda got that. But two weeks ago, I was sitting in history class, the course is called "Art and Music in the Ancient world." We're taking it because we think it will help us get into a better college, and I don't know a thing about art and Danielle likes to go to museums, well," he paused, "the teacher made a reference to Michelangelo's 'David.' He said it was a great sculpture that extolled one of the great Biblical Kings of Israel. And I raised my hand and said, "he wasn't such a great king and Danielle added David had a bunch of wives and was a thug."

"The two of you are, must be quite a number," David commented.

Marty blushed, "I don't want to talk about that," he said. The teacher, Mr. Jones told us what we had just said was interesting and he would like to discuss it further after class. We both knew what he really wanted to do was to tell us not to interrupt him and if we did he wouldn't allow us to continue."

David nodded and motioned for him to continue.

Marty sighed. "We couldn't understand why he was upset and then after class he accused us of debunking religious figures. We tried to explain we weren't criticizing David and we were truly in awe of the Art; but we felt it was important for him to explain the real David was not the idealized person that Michelangelo imagined."

He used the word, "idealized," who is this kid?" he said to himself.

"Anyway," Marty continued. "He wouldn't buy it and we shut up. Why couldn't he accept the truth?"

"I think the two of you handled the situation extremely well," David said.

"Yeah but that was two weeks ago. Yesterday, we were listening to music. The instructor began the class by playing excerpts written by a man named Handel." He shook his head, "I suppose he had a first name, but the teacher just kept calling him Handel."

Here it comes, David thought.

"He played a piece from a work called "The Messiah" I guess it is pretty famous. I really don't like that type of music, but Danielle does, so," he shrugged. "We listened. After a few minutes the instructor told us what we had just heard was a proof of the Lord's divinity and it foretold the coming of God."

The two of us looked at one another. "It was Isaiah. We studied it with you. Danielle raised her hand. The Instructor said "yes, Danielle what is it?"

She said, 'that's not a proof foretelling the birth of Jesus. That's not what the text says. It's a proof the church used to justify their belief. The instructor became very angry and asked us to leave. Why? We were just telling him the truth."

"Oy!" David said as he paused and looked at Marty. "Marty? He whispered. "Are you upset?"

Marty placed a hand over his eyes and nodded. "I don't understand. We were right. We weren't being rude. We just wanted to help. To explain and he was angry. He doesn't want us to return to class. Imagine that, expelled from auditing a summer class."

David rose and walked over to him, placing a firm hand on his shoulder. "I can fix some of this," he said. "I will write a letter which can be added to both of your transcripts explaining what just occurred. Universities will eat it up. "

Marty nodded, his hand still covering his eyes.

David reached down and slowly pried the hand away from his face. He reached over and pulled a chair to him placing himself directly in front of the boy. "Sometimes," he began. "Sometimes we are placed in a situation where we know we are correct but the person on the other side believes differently." He nodded thinking to himself. "When that occurs, you can either hope to convince that person, though it rarely works, or to agree the two of you disagree. Sometimes, if you're lucky, you will know you won't agree before you have the disagreement. Are you getting this Marty?"

Marty stared at him and nodded affirmatively.

"When that occurs, you need to change the pattern. You need to think about what you should do and can do differently. If you can't achieve your desire consider," he said thoughtfully, "what would be the best alternative."

David stood up wandering around the room. "the next best alternative," he said. "Marty? Do you feel a little better?"

The boy nodded.

"Good, now get out of here and go tell Danielle the two of you really are going to need to stump me when we meet again next week. Right now, I have to work out the next best alternative."

The Worst Train Ride Ever

"Well," David said to himself, "Now I know the 4:15 train to Grand Central is not the 5:30 from Grand Central. Let's see the third car. Is it the third car from the back or from the front? Must be the front because the third car from the back is the quiet car and that would really be an unbelievably harsh form of punishment." He laughed and continued musing, "Imagine that, forcing me to travel to Manhattan so we could speak, and so I could apologize, and then having to sit next to him for almost an hour and not being permitted to speak. Now that would be truly satanic."

"Third car from the front," he murmured as he walked towards the entrance. "Now I guess I am supposed to wait for him like the good pet he desires. Oh! There he is. Here he comes!"

"Good afternoon Paul," he said as he extended his hand toward him.

"Thank you for coming rabbi," Paul answered as he grasped his hand and squeezed until David winced. He released David's hand and gestured for him to enter the train. "Third bench on the right, you sit next to the window." David complied.

They waited in silence as the car filled. Paul placed his briefcase on his lap and busied himself arranging or rearranging materials within as the train slowly pulled away from the station. David waited in silence.

After a few minutes Paul turned to him and said, "Rabbi do we understand one another?"

"I'm beginning to," David replied. "This really wasn't necessary."

"Yes, unfortunately it was." Paul answered with a sigh. "I don't enjoy conflict. I like things the way I want them to be."

"Paul," David said, "I'm really not a thing. I'm trying to rebuild this community and it appears that it's working. Why are you giving me such a hard time?"

"Glad you asked," he replied with a smile. "You see I also have a vision for my family, and for this community. I would like your help, no! I need your help if this vision is going to be achieved."

"Well," David said. "I guess this is a good time to share it with me because I am developing a vision. It's taken me a number of years, but I think I'm on the right track. What's your vision Paul and how would you like me to help?"

"Now," he slapped his thigh. "Now we're beginning to work together. I like that. I want to attract people of means to this community. The houses are modest, the prices are extremely reasonable. Plenty of opportunity exists for some first-class restaurants, and people my age would like it to seem that they lived modestly even if they really don't." He raised his hand to his lips and whispered, "I want to create a community that appears to be downward mobile."

"Downward mobile?"

"Yes," he explained. "The people can dress shabbily, anyway they want, as long as it doesn't appear they are sporting really expensive clothes. They'll drive Priuses, purchase food at Wholefoods. That reminds me we will need a WholeFoods. But, in a very quiet way they will increase the school budgets, and help this tiny little community become more energy efficient."

"And what about the synagogue Paul? How does your vision impact upon the Jewish community and the existing community?"

"Well, that's why I need you rabbi. We need a new building. Not too big but equipped with the best of resources. And we need the best teachers. And we need a great Hazzan and I'm going to need you to help me solicit those funds. Oh, and we are going to need to change the way we pray. I have a traditional background and I think a Cantor with a great voice and a great building maybe with a gym and a health club more people would come to services and we could teach them the old tunes."

"But our young people won't resonate to those tunes. You heard what they said at the ritual meeting. Didn't you?"

"Don't you understand?" he said shaking his head. "They don't really know the old tunes. So, we tell them they are the new tunes; they'll like it and learn them. What do you think?"

"Hmm," David said to himself as he turned to face Paul. "I think you certainly have a vision. It's impressive."

Paul preened.

"And I think I can help you in some ways. I'm not certain we both want the same thing when we discuss the nature of how we pray. You see, I don't think it's about the tunes. I think it's about feeling connected and learning and being comfortable. I'd be glad to work with you, after all you're going to be the next President. I'm willing to work with you on the services rather than have conflict if you're willing to listen to what I have learned."

"Sure, that's a good business practice. Know what exists, its strengths and weaknesses and then, once you've determined your plan of action. Go narrow and deep."

"Okay, no more fights in the ritual committee meetings agreed?"

"Agreed," Paul said as he extended his hand to David.

"Not too hard," David said. "It hurts."

Paul smiled.

"We can meet a day or so before each service if you'll take my calls. And I will share with you what I am planning to do and what I'm hoping to achieve. That way you won't be surprised. Okay?"

"Okay," Paul said smiling and feeling victorious. "My secretary will schedule the calls with you in advance."

"I appreciate that," David said. "Oh, one more thing."

"What is it?' Paul asked.

"I have next Friday night off. I'd like you to drive me to Shadkan college."

"Drive you on Shabbas?" he asked.

"It's important. I'd rather you drive because I, well, I don't feel comfortable driving on Shabbat and there is something I'd like you to see. Will you do it?"

Paul shrugged. "You won't tell me why or what I'm going to see correct?"

"Correct."

What time should I pick you up?"

"Around six, and Paul, dress downward mobile."

LAST CALL

A warm and engaging voice answered the phone. "Sandy Talbot's residence. To whom am I speaking?"

"Tiffany, its David Duvin can I speak with Sandy?"

"No David its Adriana, Tiffany's at the hospital with Sandy. How may I help you?"

"Sandy's in the hospital! What happened?"

There was a brief pause, David could hear her taking a breath. "He fell. No, I think his leg just gave out and he fell. He was just getting out of the bath. I was at school and Tiffany was waiting for him in the bedroom. We recently began to help him dress," she said. "She heard him stand and then there was a thud and he was screaming. I'm told his leg was more or less hanging from his hip. She called an ambulance and they took him away."

"When did this happen? Why wasn't I called?"

"It happened yesterday, we've been up all night with him and I don't know," she sputtered, "we were, so preoccupied with him we didn't call anyone. He's our father our grandfather our dearest….." she stopped as her voice choked.

"He is heavily medicated, and they are going to replace his hip tomorrow. I've been on the phone finding specialists, Tiffany's doing the home care research. They say, he'll be walking the same day. But I don't know, he was in such pain."

"If there's one thing the Doctors do well in Florida its replace hips. I wouldn't worry about that," David replied. "Was his mind clear before he fell?"

"Yes," she replied tearfully. "He's losing words more often and doesn't always remember what he just said. But he's still Sandy."

"Are there any family members or old friends you should call?" he asked.

"Not many, outside of the locals whom he knew and often supported in a number of ways. There are a few of his younger colleagues like you with whom he has had regular but limited contact."

"Maybe you should call them or send them an email and let the know what happened. No matter what he says about visitors, even if he says I don't want people to visit me, ignore it. Believe me visits are appreciated."

"When will you be here?" she asked.

"I'm not sure," he replied in a serious tone. "There's something I have to do this weekend and I can't put it off. Hopefully early next week. After the operation. Both of you will probably need a break at the time anyway. I have to cancel some family plans. But that's what friends do," he said quietly.

"No," she said. "That's what rabbis do, good rabbis."

The Next Best Alternative

"I see a spot over there, on the right, "David indicated while pointing straight ahead.

"Put your hand down Rabbi," Paul said. "I see the spot."

"We can walk from here, it's only a few blocks."

"Why can't we park in front of wherever we're going?" Paul asked.

"Because you're driving a Mercedes, that's why." David replied. This is a college campus and," he said staring at Paul, "even your dressing down, is over the top."

"I still don't understand why your schlepping me all the way out here," Paul said as he opened the car door.

"Okay," David said. "It's preparation time. I'm going to take you into a place you're not going to like. I need you not to react but to sit and to listen and to watch everything that goes on. Do you understand?"

"Yes," Paul said. "I promise."

"After the service has concluded, we are going to linger for a bit. People are probably going to come up to you and introduce themselves. Some of them already know me I want you to remember your role, your job is to be polite and say wonderful pleasant things. Got it?"

"Yes Rabbi. I've got it."

"Okay," David said. "Let's walk. It's only a few blocks."

The two men walked in silence. As they rounded a corner, Paul saw the sign on the door that read, "Ministers of Peace."

"Are we going…?"

"Shhh," David said. "Remember, no questions."

They walked down the long hall. I hear "Shabbas music," Paul said.

"Shhh" was the reply.

They entered the main room. It was filled with young men and women standing around a table filled with cakes and cookies. At the far end of the table an attractive woman in her thirties was pouring beer. "David!" she called out. David! Over here," she said as she waved her hand.

"Come on," David said. "Follow me. Samantha! It's great to see you. This is," he said as he turned and indicated Paul, "my friend Paul. We work together."

"It's a pleasure to meet you," she said extending her hand and flashing him a smile. "Paul, or should I call you Saul?"

"Actually, if you want to call me by my Hebrew name, I suggest Pincus," Paul replied with a smile.

Samantha grinned. "You brought me someone with a background," she said. "Perhaps he should join our study group?"

"Study group?" Paul asked.

"Yes," David replied. "We meet on occasion and learn scripture together."

'Hmmph," Paul harrumphed.

"Oh, time for the service," Samantha said as she grabbed their hands. "Come sit with me."

Paul, glanced at David. David nodded and the two of them joined her. Chairs were arranged in a semi-circle creating a sense of intimacy. They sat in the middle. The music stopped, the lights flickered and....

"Oh! Its Reb Shlomo," she said in an excited voice, as she turned to David. "He's wearing a rainbow tallis."

Reb Shlomo walked to the Ark and reverently kissed the curtain. He stood in front of the Ark for fifteen or twenty seconds, he took a deep breath and turned to face the crowd.

"Welcome," he said with a smile. "Shabbat Shalom."

"The Jewish New Year, Rosh HaShana will take place in just a few weeks," he said. "And it's time for us to begin to prepare. A new year brings new life. It provides each of us," he said as he began to walk towards the center of the room, "with the opportunity to be reborn. Just like our Savior was reborn. It provides us with the opportunity to see things more clearly. Everyone!" he said raising his voice and gesturing with his hands, "Take a deep breath! Hold it and count to eighteen, the number which signifies life and then slowly exhale."

The group followed suit.

"Feels good? Doesn't it," he said. "So good that it makes you want to pray. Stand up and let's sing the shema, first in English and then, then," he paused. In the *lashon hakodesh*, the holy tongue."

Paul grimaced, his facing taking on a shade of red. David pushed him with his leg. Samantha glowed and leaned in to Paul so that her shoulder rubbed his. "He's so in touch with himself," she whispered.

The service continued for approximately thirty minutes. Samantha's leg was intrusively touching David's leg. As a result, David's leg was in constant motion. Paul's aspect seemingly froze. His eyes were glazed his body remained stiff only interrupted on occasion when Samantha leaned into him and whispered. After the mourner's kaddish was recited, Reb Shlomo walked to the Ark raised his hand to his lips and then placed it on the curtain.

"It's time for the closing prayer, the *Alenu*, Reb Shlomo's enraptured voice breathed. "Everyone rise up and face the holy Ark. The *Alenu* prayer means "it's up to us", he breathed. "It's up to us to live a certain way. To be kind and gracious. To give to others, to take care of others and to believe he, through us, will unite the four corners of the earth in harmony. He believes in us and so we need to believe in him. Its glorious. It fills us up! Sing with me!", and he broke into song.

Most of the group joined in. A few minutes later someone called out, "Oneg Shabbat" and a majority of the people left their seats and strolled, some faster than others, to the table at the other end of the room. The table was filled with pastries, donuts, and assorted junk foods.

"Don't forget, someone else called out. Say the blessings!" Reb Shlomo was surrounded by a group of twenty somethings, "Menachem!" he called out. "Say the blessings!"

"Can we go now?" Paul asked.

David looked around. Samantha was engaged in conversation with two young men.

"I want us to mingle with people and learn what they have to say," David replied.

"I can't stand this," Paul said in a tense voice. "I need to leave, now!"

"Okay, Okay," David replied. "We can go." Paul quickly turned and began to move.

"Walk, don't run." David murmured.

Paul slowed down and the two of them exited the building.

"Why did you take me to that place!" Paul said in tense tone as they began to walk towards the car.

"I said, you wouldn't like it." David replied.

"It was horrible," he said shaking his head. Suddenly, Paul stopped and spat on the street. "Ycch!" Yccch!"

"I'll explain once we're in the car," David said as reached out and grabbed Paul's arm in an attempt to slow him down.

Paul jerked away from him and continued walking down the street. David followed at his own pace. They reached the car, entered and Paul began to back out of his spot. "Damn it!" he said as he backed up and realized he was nearly boxed in. "Damn it."

"It's okay Paul, "David said in a soothing tone. "It's really okay."

Paul pulled the car into the street. "Slow down, Paul, you're upset and the last thing we need is getting a ticket. Slow down."

Paul acquiesced, and David began. "Did you see how many young people were there tonight?"

"Of course, I did. It was packed, and it was a, a, a travesty. That's not Judaism and he's no rabbi. He's a charlatan and everything he did was a fake. An act, all designed to bring those young people closer to you know who."

David nodded in agreement. "I do know it's designed to bring people closer to you know who. Did you know there were at least six young men and women in attendance whose parents belong to our synagogue?"

"No," Paul said thoughtfully, "I didn't know that."

"And did you know the evening I ran out of the annual meeting was because the parents, one of our parents, had just learned their daughter was part of this group?"

"No rabbi," he responded. "I didn't know that."

"These groups are a threat and there's very little we can do to resist them."

"Someone should shut them down," Paul angrily replied.

"Yes," David said quietly, "if it were only so simple." He shook his head. "That's why I brought you here. I wanted you to witness it firsthand."

"Why?"

"Because while we can't make them go away, we can do something to protect our children."

"Yeah, what's that?" he answered as he swerved out of the way of a passing car.

"Well, a few of them were trolling for kids in the synagogue a few weeks ago. But thanks to some of our members, they will never have the opportunity to engage our teens in conversation in our synagogue or our religious school ever again. But there is more we can do. Paul," David said, "As a concerned person and a future president. I need you to do something."

"Do what rabbi?"

"First, I want you to slow down and drive more carefully. Second, I need you to find a professor at one of the city colleges, Columbia or NYU, a place with status. And then I want you to fund an annual class for our Juniors in High school."

"Huh?" Paul responded.

"Yes," David continued. "We can protect our own children by providing them with needed ammunition. I want to teach them enough, so they will be able to recognize places like the Ministers of Truth and not step into them. I want it to be important. I want it to be something so prestigious our kids are going to want to attend. We will make it a required class for all High School Juniors. They will have the opportunity to go Manhattan and visit an important campus and have a meaningful lunch and dialogue with a distinguished professor. And yes," he continued, "I want you to pay for the lunch. This is important, and their parents will appreciate it. It will be another example of how the shul gives back to its members."

Paul nodded. "Good marketing strategy. Great idea. When my colleagues hear about it," he smiled, "it will encourage them to consider moving to our little community. Great idea rabbi. I think we are going to work well together."

"I hope so," David replied with a smile.

"We still need to discuss the prayers and tunes for Shabbat morning," Paul added.

"I know," David replied glumly. "I know."

They continued the rest of the way home in silence. The car pulled up to David's home. He exited the car, waived to Paul and walked towards the house. Rachel opened the door to greet him.

"How did it go?" she asked. "Mission accomplished?"

"Mission accomplished," he grinned.

"And are you friends?" she asked.

David shook his head. "No, we will never be friends. But we will work together. He'll give a little and I'll give a little. It will always be a struggle," he said with a smile.

"Are we still going on vacation next week?" Rachel asked.

He shook his head, "I don't think so, I think I have to go to Florida. Sandy is in the hospital. Rach did I ever tell you what Sandy told me about his experience with Dr. Kadushin?"

"No," she said shaking her head.

"Sandy told me that one day, when he was Samuel Talbot, and a struggling rabbinical student, he met Dr. Kadushin in the seminary cafeteria. It was very early in the morning. He was exhausted. He had been teaching in two different states and had just broken up with a girl. He had a Talmud exam in little more than an hour and was furiously cramming and hoping to pass. Apparently, Dr. Kadushin was way into his eighties and stood about five feet tall. He approached Sandy and placed his hand on his shoulder."

"How are you this morning Mr. Talbot?" he said.

Sandy, er, Samuel, replied with a sigh, "Oh Dr. Kadushin life is hard."

"No," Dr. Kadushin replied firmly. "Life is good. Living his hard."

Rachel looked up at David and said, "why are you telling me this rabbinic crap?"

David looked at her and laughed. "Welcome to the rest of our lives."